NIGHT of the STORM

K.N. LEE

INTERNATIONAL BESTSELLING AUTHOR
BOOK TWO OF THE EURA CHRONICLES

Captive Quill Press
Fort Mill, SC 2016

www.knlee.com

Night of the Storm/ K.N. Lee. – 1st Ed.

Dedicated to Simi and Sohana

Table of Contents

ELLOWEN WORLD INFO

Realm: Eura

Human, mermaid, and Mithrani territory

Human Traits

Focus—prominent trait: increased focus

Evasion—the ability to confuse an opponent by making one's image flicker and shift to another spot

Split—the ability to split into two identical beings

Reach

Accuracy—increased precision when using a weapon

Mermaid Traits

Breath—prominent trait: the ability to breathe underwater and bestow the power to do so to others temporarily

Hypnosis—the ability to hypnotize others with their eyes

Mithrani Traits

Mock—the ability to manipulate the prominent trait of every race

Realm: Kyril

Tryan, fairy, and mermaid territory

Tryan Traits

Enchant—prominent trait: the ability to make weapons or items stronger and more powerful

Creation—the ability to create objects from ordinary materials or invent new ones

Blessed shield—a shield of energy that protects its user

Vex—the ability to confuse an opponent temporarily

Mind Telling—the ability to read the thoughts of others

Fairy Traits

Heal—prominent trait: the ability to heal wounds with energy power

Enchant—the ability to make weapons or items stronger and more powerful

Flight—the ability to fly

Soothe—the ability to calm others, including animals

Realm: Alfheim

Silver Elf and mermaid territory

Silver Elves

Agility—prominent trait: the ability to climb and increased balance

Focus—increased focus

Accuracy—increased precision when using a weapon

Stealth—the ability to go invisible

Shift—the ability to change into an animal

Realm: Nostfar

Shadow Elf and mermaid territory

Shadow Elves

Dart—prominent trait: lightning-fast speed

Rage—the ability to become more powerful when angry

Camouflage—the ability to blend into their surroundings

BARRIER
BARRIER
BARRIER
GOLLUSH
GOBLIN CITY
AURORIA
FROZEN PLAINS
CHIMERIA
SILVER RIVER
CAIR OCEAN
MERMAID TERRITORY
TOLRIN
RAEDEN
OREN
GARDENS OF FLORN
JORDAN
INDU
PREKAR
TERINTON

PROLOGUE

"SHE'S GONE."

The one Dragnor had hunted for almost eighteen years.

Lilae. The Flame.

Master was not pleased.

Dragnor looked up at the night sky, still frozen in awe by the amount of power his prisoner had displayed in that very courtyard just seconds ago.

"I knew this would happen," he whispered as she vanished from his sight like a shooting star.

His sharp glare stared at the disturbed clouds. He just let his only bargaining tool escape.

"You disappoint me."

The eerie voice made Dragnor's body stiffen with dread. As if he were all around him, Wexcyn came to him like a monster in a dream.

The world went dark. Nearly a hundred palace guards surrounded Dragnor, and yet he was the only one to notice the strange darkness that smothered him like a blanket.

A god, even a forgotten one imprisoned by the other gods—could do remarkable things.

"I brought you back from the dead. I gave you power," Wexcyn said. Far away in his prison, the forgotten god could still reach his agents.

And there were many.

There was nowhere to hide.

"The Cursed is still yours to command," Dragnor said, his eyes searching for a way out of the darkness that threatened to force him to his knees.

Escape. If only he could fly away, the way Lilae had just done. Too late for second thoughts. Dragnor's life—his soul—belonged to Wexcyn.

"I have weakened the emperor with a potion that will leave him vulnerable to The Horrors and bend him to our will once more."

"You have done nothing but prove that Emperor Kavien cannot be controlled."

"But he can, Master. The Flame's influence over Emperor Kavien was only a temporary setback. I can fix this."

"Dragnor," Wexcyn hissed. His voice made the fine hairs on Dragnor's arm stand on end.

"Yes, Master?"

"Find the Storm, Flame, Inquisitor, Seer, and Steel and any other person that dares to defy me, and kill them. I swear this is your last chance. Do you understand?"

"I will. I swear it."

"Fail me again and I will let Vaugner have you. Do you know what he does to those that escape the Underworld?"

The thought of being sent back to the Underworld, into enemy hands, frightened Dragnor into silence. He'd just escaped the clutches of Vaugner, the Elder that wanted him ripped from the living world. He would have gotten on his knees and begged if he wasn't standing in the presence the Avia'Torenan soldiers and guards.

Until Emperor Kavien was awakened, Dragnor would rule in his stead.

"I will find them and kill them all."

There was no further reply. As Dragnor stood in fear, awaiting Wexcyn's voice, the darkness was lifted, and the world was bright with torches and moonlight once again.

"Clear out. Search the entire city for the slave," Dragnor ordered.

The soldiers and guards cleared the courtyard, going in sectioned troupes to search for the missing slave. Lilae would be halfway across the realm by now, but he had to at least try.

If he had to mount his wyvern, Tari and fly to every kingdom in Eura, Dragnor would do so. He'd done it before. He'd do it again to keep his place in Wexcyn's new world order.

PART ONE

Chapter 1

THE HAIRS ON LIAM'S neck stood on end at the ghastly sight between him and The Barrier.

The head of a Tryan man was set on a pike in the middle of the jungle.

"Stay back," a female voice boomed from the trees as Liam, Nani and Rowe approached The Barrier. "You are not welcome in Nostfar."

Liam's bright blue eyes glowed in the dark as they shot from the pike to The Guardians that awaited. They stood before the open doorway that stretched hundreds of feet into the black sky. The glow from The Barrier's ancient power illuminated the giants before him, swords ready in their massive hands.

They were silent, and whoever did speak was unseen.

His blue eyes narrowed as he looked up to the tops of the trees. The dark leaves rustled with the wind, yet revealed not even a trace of who spoke.

Shadow Elves. They could blend in anywhere.

"Who speaks?"

"Turn around and leave."

Liam's brows furrowed. "This, coming from an elf in the *Tryan* realm."

"Last warning."

His sword. If only he had it on his hip at that moment.

Pain seared into Liam's leg as a thorny black vine wrapped itself around his thigh and yanked him to the slick black ground of the volcano.

Liam hit his head on the hard packed dirt.

No.

He was so close to The Barrier and finally meeting The Flame. Her face came to him as darkness threatened to take over.

Liam cradled his head with a hand. For a moment, he was disoriented. In a haze, he watched Rowe grab a skinny male Shadow Elf by the neck and slam it into the ground with such strength that the sound of crunching bones filled the dark jungle that surrounded them.

"Kill them. They must not enter Nostfar," the same female voice yelled from the trees as several Shadow Elves jumped to the ground with such agility that they were barely seen.

Liam's eyes widened as they prepared to attack his greatest friends in the world. He sat up and reached for the vine wrapped around his thigh. The instant his fingertips touched it, the vine lifted him from the ground.

Cool air whipped past Liam's face as he was slung through the air at such a speed that he saw nothing but blackness. His mind raced as he searched for a way to free himself. Before he could react, more vines reached Liam and snapped themselves around him body, pinning his arms to his side. Like a cocoon, they ensnared him and slammed his wrapped body into the base of a tree that appeared to be dead, yet rumbled like a hungry stomach.

A quick glance at the ground revealed the source of the vines.

The tree branches shot through the clearing, attacking his friends and forcing them into a tight space before The Barrier.

"Liam," Nani shouted, as she tried to fly to him. With a broken wing, he could tell that she struggled. The branches blocked her path, ascending as she fought to fly over their blockade.

"I can't get free," Liam said.

Liam looked at the sky. He could summon a storm.

How would that help? He needed the use of his hands to direct the lightning without harming Nani and Rowe. He used all of his strength to try to break through the vines, and yet they only held on tighter, so tight that he found breathing laborious.

A lithe female Shadow Elf jumped down from her spot in the tree top and landed beside Liam. She looked strong, and tall, with leather over chainmail covering her chest and stomach. Her arms were bare, revealing white tattoos and scars. The points of her ears stuck through her auburn hair that looked to be slicked back by mud.

Ferocity filled her brown eyes as she straddled his chest and held her dagger to his throat.

Not now. Not like this.

Not after Liam had already escaped death once. The Ancients might not give him another chance.

He met the eyes of the Shadow Elf. Lilae awaited him. He had to see her in person at least one time before he died.

Almost as if the Shadow Elf woman read his thoughts, she paused, her brow raising as she searched his eyes with her own dark purple gaze.

Nani shot to the ground, faster than Liam had ever seen her fly. She landed in the center of it all. The mayhem that ensued as Rowe fought dozens of Shadow Elves armed with glowing daggers.

She held her hands out before her and closed her eyes.

Liam raised a brow. He'd never seen Nani so calm in the face of danger.

Before his eyes, she started to change.

Smoke began to rise from the ground and up her body as if she'd recently been engulfed in flames. Liam's eyes widened as the trees began to die all around them. Nani's hair went from purple to white. When she opened her eyes, gold light filled them as she held out her small hands.

White power shot from her fingertips. Screams of terror and pain filled the air as her power shot into every Shadow Elf within the clearing and hiding in the trees.

Rowe held up his hands and froze, but Nani's power seemed to be selective, leaving Rowe and Liam free from its terror.

The Shadow Elves were reduced to nothing more than bone and guts.

Liam held his breath as even that turned to ash and floated away with the breeze, leaving the three in silence as the intensity in Nani's eyes faded.

He hadn't even realized that the vines had let him free. Glancing back at the tree revealed that whatever Nani had done had killed it, leaving its vines lifeless and shriveled on the ground.

"Liam," Nani called in a small, timid voice.

Liam stood and turned to her. Her white hair gave her an eerie beauty as it was lifted by the breeze. Whatever power Nani had hidden from them all, made her hover off the ground despite her broken wings.

"Nani," Liam whispered.

She smiled and slowly returned to her normal appearance.

She walked over to him, Rowe close behind. "Are you okay?"

"I'm fine," Liam said, running his hands through his thick black hair. "But what was that?"

Rowe cleared his throat. "We didn't get a chance to tell you."

"Tell me what?"

Nani wrapped her arms around his waist. He looked down at her small face.

"I didn't know until today, Liam," she said.

"Know what? Tell me. I'll understand."

She bit her bottom lip and let go of him. Twirling the ends of her purple hair, she flickered a sheepish look at him.

"I am the Inquisitor," Nani whispered. "Please, don't be cross with me, Liam." She lowered her eyes to the ground as she wrung her small hands. "This is all still very new to me."

Liam took a deep breath.

Inquisitor?

Could his dear fairy friend be one of the keys to saving all of Ellowen?

He picked Nani up and hugged her. "I could never be cross with you, Nani. You and Rowe are my best friends, and together we will rid this world of evil."

Liam nodded to The Barrier as the giants started to move from their frozen positions.

"Are you ready for this?"

She smiled at him. "I am."

Chapter 2

SLAVE.

Lilae squeezed her bright green eyes shut against the memories of being called that vile word. Scars and intricate black tattoos covered her body, serving as ugly reminders of the suffering she'd experienced in captivity.

No one would take her freedom from her again. The blood of the men she'd killed started to dry on her skin and stained her clothes.

"Just a moment longer," Delia said. She held onto her staff made of willow and bone to steady herself on the top of the black mountain. "The Storm is just beyond those doors.

Rocks and stone surrounded them, and dark woods that stretched for as fas as the eye could see awaited below, but Lilae's eyes were fixed on the door of The Barrier.

Red hair, wild and glowing in the light of the moon, whipped around Lilae's face as she glanced back at Delia and the skeleton warrior, Garion.

Lilae's lips pursed as she waited with anticipation of finally meeting one of the other heirs of the Ancients.

Adrenaline kept Lilae from shivering. In only the sheer nightgown she'd escaped the palace in, Lilae stood taller than the majority of women she'd encountered during her travels.

Lilae's eyes narrowed at the figure of The Storm as he emerged from the distance. Finally, she would meet this elusive creature.

Clad in gold armor from the Overworld, where the Ancients dwelled, The Guardians turned to Lilae and knelt before her. Their faces and fingers were shielded with metal plates fused to their gray skin.

Each realm had a single entryway that only The Guardians could open. It was wide and under a stone archway that had a film of light stretching from top to bottom.

For years, Lilae and her surrogate family had followed The Barrier along Eura during their travels. Every time she'd imagined what the races on the other side were like. Having met a Shadow Elf and suffered at his hand, she was wary about what creature would step through those doors.

"Lilae," the Guardians said in unison. "The Storm is in position. A new era is upon us. It is time to destroy The Barriers."

Lilae's throat was dry. She swallowed and looked at Delia whose dark blue eyes watched her.

"I don't know how to do this," she whispered.

Delia gave her hand a reassuring squeeze. "Use the power that the Ancients gave to you. I've watched you grow from a tiny baby to a strong, beautiful woman. The Ancients chose you because of your courage and heart, Lilae. Make me proud. Make your father proud."

Breathless, Lilae nodded, her heart thumping.

The Guardians stood from their kneeling positions and motioned together toward the doors.

"Your power will link with the Storm. Only such power can destroy The Barrier," Delia said, and patted the top of her hand.

Power.

The Ancients had given her a wondrous gift.

Lilae looked down at her bloodstained hands. The Shadow Elf, Dragnor had stolen her divine power, leaving her defenseless for nearly a year. Now, it begged to be free, urging her to destroy everything in her path.

"You can do it. Remember all that I taught you."

"I remember," Lilae said.

"Good," Delia said. "Let that power flow now,"

Lilae smiled at having Delia grant such permission.

Delia stepped away as threads of light encircled Lilae's body.

This is new.

The sound of sparks along the stone columns caught Lilae's attention.

Her hair flew back as the storm raged on above. Lightning flickered across the sky, screaming and crashing down onto the stone structure. The wind ripped around them, smacking her in the face. The feel of the Storm's power nearly overwhelmed her.

Lilae clenched her jaw and stood upright in the vicious wind.

Warmth encircled her like a warm blanket as her hands were set ablaze. She sucked in a breath and focused on creating two large orbs of fire that settled above her palms.

While the Storm's raging wind and lightning fought the magic of The Barriers, Lilae's flames sparked within the air causing vibrant colors to cut through the darkness. With great concentration, the orbs grew larger and larger until it seemed that the balls that contained them would explode.

Lilae grinned as the light illuminated her face.

The power had raged inside of her for so long.

Finally, it relished in its release as the flames around her body intensified.

Slamming the orbs together created a bubble that she could step inside. Surrounded by red flames, Lilae leaped into the air. She rode the wind, exhilarated by the smooth feel of the air gliding past her as she ascended. Higher and higher she went, releasing the flames like a flood of fire.

The Barriers began to crumble and crack. Stone and debris fell to the ground. Lilae's flames and the Storm's lightning stretched across the entire structure, traveling farther than her eyes could follow.

The ground shook beneath them.

The dark sky grew brighter, and the air grew colder. There was the sound of crackling and sizzling as their power fought with that of The Barriers. The glow of The Barriers dimmed as the stone turned to black dust and faded away.

"Thank you," The Guardians said. They opened their massive black wings that stretched the span of at least six feet and flew into the darkened sky.

Delia stepped forward, her face pale in the moonlight. “You did it, Lilae. Now, we begin.”

They heard footsteps crunching on the debris of the destroyed structures.

The Storm had arrived.

Chapter 3

AS THE STORM STEPPED closer, Lilae clamped her hands over her mouth.

It's him.

Lilae had met this man before, numerous times, in what she had thought was her secret world, tucked deep into her dreams and imagination.

The Storm was more rugged than his dreamlike perfection. Her heart quickened when their eyes met. They were strikingly blue, unnatural but beautiful. Messy black hair fell onto his face as he beamed at her.

The distance between them closed as he approached Lilae. He bowed before her, took her hand, and kissed it with his soft lips.

"Prince Liam Marx of Oren."

"I can't believe it's you," Lilae whispered. She wanted to throw herself at him, wrap her arms around his neck, and hug him tighter than she'd ever held a man.

"I know," he said, reaching for her. "Finally, we meet. I'm sorry if I'm too forward. But, you are even more stunning than in our dreams."

Heat came to Lilae's cheeks, reddening them. She was still unsure of how to respond to compliments. Two men in her entire life had remarked on her beauty.

Liam was now the third.

His skin glowed as if a light shone from within his body.

A Tryan.

Lilae's eyes lingered on his hands, not hesitating to place her own within them.

The touch sent delicious warmth along her skin. His grasp was tender as he stroked the back of her hand with his thumb and pulled her closer to him.

Every dream and moment of suffering had led to this moment, to the day when she would meet the man that seemed to be the missing link to make her whole.

"Thank you," Lilae said, her lips trembling as she looked at Liam.

He cupped her face in his hands. "For what?"

Lilae sucked in a breath and closed her eyes. How was it possible that she felt so safe and secure in his hands?

She held onto his hands as he stroked her cheeks. "For being there for me when no one else was. For giving me strength when all I wanted to do was cry and give up. To die."

She opened her eyes.

Ash fell, covering the black ground like a white blanket.

"You saved me," Lilae whispered, her eyes welling as she looked into Liam's.

When he pulled her into a tight embrace, she clutched to his body, not caring that he was technically a stranger from a faraway land. To them, they were more than that. They'd helped each other heal, and persevere, for longer than either even realized.

"You're bleeding," Liam said, holding her at arm's length to get a look at the blood that stained her clothes and skin.

"It's not my blood."

Liam looked into her eyes and pursed his lips. Concern filled his eyes, but he breathed in relief. "Good."

He hugged her tight to his hard chest.

Liam smelled of the sea and the jungle. Lilae didn't want him to let go.

"Welcome, Prince Liam," Delia said, breaking them from their intimate moment.

When Lilae pulled away, she noticed a hint of a smile on the Elder's lips as she watched them.

"I am Elder Delia. It seems you've already met Lilae."

"Lilae," Liam repeated. He held onto her hand. It was clear that neither of them wanted to let go. "I knew your name had to be beautiful."

Voices came from the wreckage.

"Nani and Rowe are my dear friends from Oren," Liam said, motioning to the odd pair. "Rowe is a soldier, and Nani is a healer."

Lilae rubbed her hands together, her eyes taking in the fairy and a tall Tryan man as they stood beside Liam before a scene of fire and wreckage.

Lilae tensed when Rowe looked at her. His brown hair was short, and a beard had started to grow on his chiseled cheeks and chin. He was as tall as Emperor Kavien and similarly built with large muscles and a broad naked chest that glistened with sweat.

"Hello," Rowe said.

A faint smile came to Lilae's lips. There was something kind and gentle about the giant before her. She didn't fear him, despite the scars that covered his chest.

"Hello."

"We are an army of five," Delia began, looking at each of them. "Against a formidable force."

"They are my most loyal friends. They wouldn't have stayed behind if I'd told them to. And they are more than capable to aid us in any way necessary," Liam said.

"You're stuck with us," Nani said. She smiled at Lilae and flew over to her. Her wings glowed and shimmered in the dark. The bright purple of her hair was a beautiful contrast against her olive skin.

"You're The Flame?" Nani's gray eyes looked Lilae over, judging her.

Lilae straightened her shoulders. "I am."

Nani moved her face close to Lilae's and scrunched up her little nose. "Pretty…*but* too tall for a girl."

"Nani," Liam said. He looked embarrassed, his eyes darting to Lilae's as he raked his hand through his hair with a nervous chuckle.

"Don't mind the fairy, my lady," Rowe said in a deep voice that was surprisingly soothing. "She's like a child. She'll say whatever's on her mind."

With rapidly flapping wings, Nani glanced back at Rowe. "I'm not like a child. I'm just honest. I've never seen a *woman* that tall before."

Lilae didn't mind Nani's comment. Seeing a real fairy intrigued her. Lhana, the woman who had helped raise her, could tell amazing stories.

When Lilae was a young girl, sitting around the fire on those frigid nights in the woods with the twins, Jaiza and Risa, and her father, Pirin they would listen eagerly, imagining the beautiful fairies Lhana told them about. Never had she anticipated seeing one in person.

Nani was everything she had envisioned. She had purple pigtails and gray eyes. She wore brown leather pants tucked into her knee-high boots and a ragged cream-colored shirt tucked into her pants. It appeared that she'd been through hardship, but that didn't affect her beauty.

"What are you staring at?" Nani paused to turn around on Lilae.

Lilae blushed. "Sorry. I can't help it. You're just very pretty."

Nani smiled as she flew closer to Lilae, a broken wing catching Lilae's attention. She touched Lilae's hair with a giggle.

"I've never seen someone as pretty as you, Lilae. Not a human anyway."

Lilae tilted her head. "But I'm the first human you've ever seen."

"Exactly," Nani laughed.

Lilae smiled. She didn't mind Nani's jokes. She reminded her of Risa, always speaking her mind.

"What about compared to Tryan women, or fairies?"

Nani shook her head. Her smile lingered. "Maybe prettier than a Tryan, but you can't compete with a fairy."

"You are honest."

Liam looked at the sky. "We stand in the middle of Eura and Nostfar?"

"Yes," Delia said.

"Not what I expected," Liam said.

Lilae spoke in a soft voice. "What did you expect?"

Liam smiled at her. "I'm not sure. Eura's sky looks quite similar to Kyril's."

"So," Rowe said as he looked into the horizon. "We are the first Tryans to walk the human realm in centuries."

"And I am the first fairy," Nani added.

"I'm sure you're more than that," Delia said, meeting Nani's gaze.

"What do you mean?" Nani batted her eyelashes, giving Liam a glance.

"I am an Elder. I know who and what you are. I see your aura, and you are not merely a fairy. Not anymore, that is."

Everyone looked at Nani as Delia motioned for her to come closer. "We are fortunate to have another chosen one amongst us."

Nani smiled, pride in her eyes. "I am honored to be a part of the team."

Lilae's brows rose. She never expected to meet another of the Chosen Class so soon. Meeting The Storm was exciting enough, but she knew what evil and danger awaited them all.

"But Nani is more than even that now. The god of the fairies has long since sacrificed herself for her people. As heir, Nani is now the god of the fairies."

Nani's jaw dropped. "They didn't tell me that!"

Delia's eyes narrowed. "Who?"

Shrugging, Nani flopped to the ground and crossed her legs. She shook her head. "It sounded as if the wind spoke to me."

"The Winds," Lilae and Liam said in unison.

Stunned, they looked at each other.

"The Winds speak to you too?"

Liam nodded. "They do. For as long as I can remember."

"So," Nani's eyes widened with hope. "I can repair my wings?"

Delia motioned for her to come. "Of course. You can do much more than that, dear. Stand."

Nani rose to her feet.

"Spread your wings."

Nani spread her beautiful wings. The broken wing was jagged and ripped, like a butterfly that had caught its wing on a thorn. Still, it glittered in the moonlight.

"Call forth your Inquisitor's power, and this time, you must focus the energy on repairing yourself."

Black smoke emerged from Nani's feet, rising up her body until she was shrouded by it. Her hair went from purple to white. Her skin glowed white as she closed her eyes to focus.

A bright light shot through the clearing. Everyone winced as Nani burst into a million sparks that stretched into the air around them. A cold gust of wind swept through, and the sparks sizzled as they returned to Nani's spot, recomposing her body into a stunning young woman.

Lilae's heart raced as she beheld Nani in her new form.

"Oh my," she whispered.

Stunned, everyone stared at Nani. This new Nani. No longer a small fairy with ragged clothing. She was born anew, her short purple hair now long enough to brush the small of her back. Still short, she looked regal, in silver robes that clung to her body.

Liam stepped forward when Nani's eyes opened.

"What happened?"

Nani twirled in her robes, looking down at herself in awe. "Telryd and Ulsia spoke to me about my new home in the Overworld. Pyrii helped me choose my crown. I saw things." She looked at Lilae. "So many things."

"The Storm, The Flame, and The Inquisitor—a god amongst us," Delia said. "Let's prepare for war, shall we?"

Lilae never would have guessed that the small fairy was just like her and Liam, descendants of the Ancients, let alone an Ancient herself.

Liam rubbed his chin, still looking at Nani in bewilderment. "Do you think it will come to war?"

"Yes, Liam," Delia said with a nod. "Emperor Kavien will do whatever Wexcyn orders. You will lead our army."

"I'm ready," Liam said.

"So am I," Lilae said. She looked away from Liam when he glanced back at her. "But, Emperor Kavien is more than what he seems. I saw his *true* self. He's more of a slave than I ever was."

Delia nodded. "I know. I witnessed what you did. You changed his heart in ways we could never imagine."

Lilae swallowed. Emperor Kavien's kiss would never be forgotten. Having him hold her in his bed while they slept would haunt her. A yearning filled her entire being.

She missed him.

The man that made her his slave.

A sigh escaped Lilae's lips.

"But I fear that even if Kavien has a change of heart, Dragnor and all of Wexcyn's other agents will execute his plan."

"Yes. He has many traitorous agents," Liam said.

The sadness in his voice caught Lilae off guard. His jaw clenched for a moment as if his memories put him in a foul mood. She wanted nothing more than to console him and find out the cause of such pain.

The moment passed quickly, and his face relaxed. "Where are we to find an army?"

"We go to a land of warriors," Delia said, her eyes brightening. "There is a kingdom that no other army has dared test since the creation of The Barriers. They are the only humans that stood up to the other races during the first war."

"I've seen Kavien's army," Lilae said, crossing her arms across her chest. "He chooses only those with a particular skill. We need warriors if we are going to try and defeat him. Where is this place?"

"Auroria," Delia said. "It is time to take you back to your birth family."

Lilae swallowed. "My birth family?"

Delia nodded. "Yes."

My brother, Ayaden. My real *mother.*

The idea left her feeling unsettled and her stomach churned.

"Now," Delia said before turning to Garion, her skeleton guard. He stood there, slack-jawed, swaying as if the wind pushed him gently from side to side.

"Scout our path down the mountain," Delia told him.

Lilae shivered as she watched him seemingly come to life once again. He straightened his back and stood tall, alert, and fierce. Without hesitation, the skeleton bid its master's command and left

Delia's side to start the descent down the rocky path of the black mountain.

Seeing him kill all of the palace guards for her successful escape had been appalling. Garion was a dead man, just bones covered in black steel. But he was stronger than anyone she'd ever seen.

While Garion looked fearsome, Lilae knew she was safe around him.

Lilae peered into the dark woods that stretched far into the horizon all around them.

"We must leave this place," Delia said. "There is no telling who or what heard what the two of you just did. And we shouldn't wait to find out."

GARION LED THE WAY DOWN the mountain, his eyes glowing as he searched for any signs of danger. It was a treacherous descent. Thick woods of charred black trees that loomed above them, filling every open space, making it difficult to navigate the stone covered ground.

The foot of the mountain gave way to a thick forest alive with creatures.

Lilae peered into the darkness, wary of basilisks. She put her hand to her stomach. Memories of how she'd come to bear the wound from a basilisk's sharp claws came to her. The pain would remain with her, but so would the curiosity and intrigue of the first time she'd seen Liam.

Glancing at him, she admitted to herself that she'd suffer that pain again to have met him in her dreams.

Lilae's bare feet bled from sharp rocks and stones by the time they reached the slightly softer ground below. She stumbled to a nearby boulder with a flat surface and sighed as the pressure was lifted from her wounds.

"We can set up camp here," Delia said, using her staff to light the area around them. "The mountain will keep us safe from at least one side. Rowe, you can take first watch."

Rowe nodded. "I'd be happy to. But, who is going to muster up some supper? Nani and I haven't eaten in days, and who knows what Liam had to eat while he was cheating death."

"Death?" Lilae glanced at Liam, who blushed.

"The Mother Tree in the fairy village of Tolrinia gave me her blessing," Liam explained. "It saved me. So did a very kind mermaid, but that's a story for another time."

"You have been blessed, indeed," Delia smiled. "Lilae can trap forest creatures like none other."

Liam's brows furrowed when he looked down at her as she examined her dirty feet.

"Are you all right?"

"I'm fine," Lilae said.

"Delia," Nani said. "I can call forest creatures with my magic. Let Lilae rest. Her poor feet are bleeding. You don't mind if I heal you, Lilae?"

"That would be nice. Please. Shoes were the last thing on my mind when I escaped the palace."

"Very well," Delia said. "Work your magic, Nani."

Nani grinned. "Gladly."

Lilae rested on her hands as Nani walked over to her. She watched as the fairy rubbed her hands together and white light came from her palms.

"I take some of the life force from nature to fuel my healing powers," Nani said, glancing at Lilae under thick lashes when she noticed Lilae staring that the grass that began to shrivel and go limp. "It will regain its vitality within a few hours. Do not worry."

Lilae nodded, watching as the open wounds began to close.

Such magic was unheard of in Eura. She imagined what good fairies could do for the humans. Destroying The Barrier was looking like a good decision.

Too bad they couldn't keep out the evil that came along with the good.

When she was finished, Nani tucked her hands into the pockets of her leather pants. "Done."

Lilae rubbed her feet in wonder. "You're remarkable. Thank you, Nani."

"You're welcome."

"Splendid," Rowe said, rubbing his hands. "Now, rabbit would be nice. You think you could find some juicy ones?"

"You know better, Rowe. It's really all in the cooking, but I'll summon the fat ones."

A smile came to Lilae's face. "I'd be happy with that as well, Nani."

"Me too," Liam added. He looked down at his shirt where a hole was ripped in the middle.

"Okay then. I'll be back."

Lilae hopped from the boulder. "I'll join you. My feet are all better. I'll not let you go alone."

Nani grinned. "But I'm a god now. I can manage."

"I'm coming," Lilae said. She nodded ahead. "Lead the way."

Nani gave a nod. "Very well."

She flew into the forest, lighting the way with the glow from her wings. "Come out, little rabbits. But only the fat ones," Nani sang.

"Is that how it works?"

"No," Nani said. "I don't have to say anything. I just summon them with my mind. Like this." She paused and hovered above the ground.

Lilae watched as, within only a few moments, brown rabbits hopped from the underbrush of the forest.

"See?"

"Wow. That would have come in handy when my family and I were traveling most of my life."

Nani's eyes darkened as she looked at Lilae. "Lilae," she called.

"Yes? What's wrong?" Lilae searched the surrounding trees for any threat.

"Liam has been betrayed enough by those that we all trusted. I didn't tell the others yet, but I will not be able to join you on your journey. I am an Ancient now, and the rules are clear; that we cannot intervene. It would disrupt the balance."

Tears filled Nani's eyes. "I swear I would rather be a normal fairy again. I love Liam too much to leave his side."

"I'm sorry, Nani. I don't want you to go either."

Nani knelt to the ground and embraced the rabbits as they clamored to get to her. She stroked their fur. "I have to go. But, I won't be able to go with peace of mind if I thought you would hurt him. He's been hurt before, and I refuse to let it happen again."

"What happened?"

"Liam was stabbed by the woman he was supposed to marry. The woman he *thought* he loved."

"Oh my," Lilae said, her heart falling into her stomach. "That's awful."

"She betrayed all of us. I want to find her and kill her for hurting my Liam. But that would be against the rules. Blasted rules!"

Such compassion for a man that she didn't know overwhelmed her. She wanted to go back to camp and hold him. Every time she had been in pain or near death, Liam had been there for her in her dreams.

Could it have been the same for him? Was their time together in their dreams a form of healing?

"I promise," Lilae whispered. "I won't hurt Liam. I wouldn't dream of it.

Nani nodded. "Do you know how long we've heard Liam talk about The Flame? I expected someone more intimidating. I didn't expect a woman. And neither did he. But I can tell he is attracted to you. I don't think he even looked at Sona that way."

Sona? So, that was the name of the woman that betrayed him.

She'd remember that name.

Lilae started collecting fallen branches and sticks for firewood, stacking them into her arms. She was well aware of how Liam looked at her. Within hours, Lilae knew there'd been a shift in her entire world. She was attracted to him as well.

"I expected fairies to be smaller," Lilae said, trying to change the subject.

"Smaller than this?" Nani stood and twirled in the air.

"Yes," Lilae said. "I always heard stories that fairies can talk to animals and use magic spells. There are tales that fairies can even make people fall in love."

Nani brought her face close to Lilae's.

"Of course, we can," she said in a soft, serious tone. "We also steal little babies, and turn little red-haired girls into toads."

Lilae stared in horror at Nani's little face.

Thc fairy god went into a fit of giggles.

"Lilae, I was joking. Don't be so serious." Her giggles continued into the forest as she carried Lilae's pile of branches back to camp.

Lilae stood there for a moment, and her shoulders slumped. She smiled to herself long after the glow of Nani's wings disappeared. She laughed.

Lilae hadn't laughed in ages. She had been trapped in the Avia'Torenan palace for nearly a year, and not once had she truly laughed. With cold fingertips, Lilae felt her face, tracing the outline of her smile—a foreign thing to her.

Tears trailed down her cheeks.

Jaiza and Risa used to make her laugh.

Anic was the first boy to ever show interest in her, to make her feel pretty, to show her what fun was like.

He used to make her laugh. And like her sisters, he was dead.

They were all dead.

Lhana with her fairytales, Pirin with his advice and training. Everyone she had once cared about was gone, forever.

The guilt returned. It was her fault. Lilae thought she had gotten over it, but how could one forget the death of her entire family? How could she keep her promise not to hurt Liam when all that she knew and loved were lost to her?

Their screams flooded her mind like an explosion. She fell to her knees and buried her face in her hands. She had to make up for their deaths. She had to prove that it wasn't all for nothing.

Chapter 5

RETURNING TO CAMP WAS a solemn occasion.

Nani held Liam's face in her small hands, tears streaming down both of their faces. Rowe stood behind them, his face stoic, his arms folded across his broad chest.

Still, she could see the pain in his eyes as he faced the loss of his dear friend.

An ache filled Lilae's stomach. She couldn't look as Nani said her goodbyes to Rowe and Liam. It was too hard. She knew that feeling.

At least, they knew Nani would live.

Lilae focused her power on lighting the fire. Flames rose from the palms of her hands, and she watched them lick the sticks and branches piled high. This was what she knew. She could count on this power. If only everything else in life were as certain.

Once the fire was ablaze, she encircled it with stones, glancing back at Nani as Liam hugged her.

Their eyes met, and Lilae froze.

Do not forget your promise.

Lilae nodded, surprised that Nani's voice invaded her thoughts.

Delia rose from her seat and came to Lilae. "We've lost one of the Chosen Class," she said.

"What does that mean for the rest of us?"

Delis sighed. “Another will take her place. Each race has to have a champion. It’s just unfortunate for us that we will have to find them. Or they will have to find us. Both are a challenge.”

“Elder,” Nani called.

Delia glanced back. “Have you decided?”

Nani nodded.

Lilae followed Delia to Nani, watching Liam turn away from them to step to the edge of their camp. He kept his face from view, and Lilae knew he was taking Nani’s departure hard.

“Decided what?” Lilae sighed as she watched Liam sit down on the ground. If only she could hold Liam, comfort him.

“Just like any Ancient, the choice for an heir is Nani's.”

“I choose my sister, Keyata.”

Liam looked back. “We met back in Tolrinia.” He wiped his face and straightened his shoulders. “Do you think she is ready?”

Nani nodded. “Keyata is stronger than anyone might think. I know she won’t let the fairies down.”

Liam folded his arms across his chest. “I guess there is some comfort in that. Wilem and Jorge have someone to look after them.”

“Who are they?”

Liam looked at Lilae. He looked tired, drained.

“Wilem is a Legacy like Rowe. The last of his clan, they are more powerful than most Tryans because they have power passed down from generations of ancestors. *And*,” Liam added, his eyes lighting up. “He controls the last dragon.”

"COME ON WILEM," Queen Alania said softly, her jeweled bracelets sliding down her pale white arm as she knelt before her youngest son.

The royal family of Raeden stood at the landing of the palace's grand staircase, preparing to leave for the gladiator matches.

Wilem shook his head and folded his arms across his chest in defiance. "No!"

She reached for him, her smile breaking down his defenses. "Come on, sweetheart. You know that you are too young to go to the Festival of Lights. Now, be a good boy and give mama a hug."

Wilem looked around at his older brother, Torian as he snickered.

"Come now, Wilem. Listen to mum and go find one of your friends to play with," Daveed, the next in line for the throne, said.

Wilem glared at him. Why couldn't he be older, like Daveed, and do whatever he wanted?

They were about to leave for the gladiator tournament at the Festival of Lights, and Wilem was too young to go. Wilem knew his mother didn't want him to see such barbarity and blood. But, he was tired of being treated like a child.

"Oh, the little baby has to stay home and play with his toys." Torian teased.

"That's enough," Daveed said. He looked at their mother. "Father is waiting. We must go before we are late."

Queen Alania nodded. Dressed in ivory and gold, she walked over to her youngest son. A golden circlet rested upon her wavy brown hair as she knelt to him.

"Be good, Wilem. I will sing you a song when we return."

"No," Wilem hissed. "I want to go!"

She shook her head. "Maybe next year." She reached out for Wilem with an arm covered in gold bracelets, and he shrugged away. Queen Alania sighed and watched him with disappointment furrowing her blonde eyebrows.

"I love you, Wilem."

Torian mocked Wilem behind their mother's back, pretending to cry like a baby.

"I hate you. All of you!"

Wilem awoke with tears streaming down his face. "Mama! Mama!" he sobbed. It was the same dream every night since the palace had been ambushed and his entire family had been killed.

That was nearly a year ago, and the pain that filled his gut was unbearable. It poisoned him, reminding him of how ungrateful and spoiled he'd once been.

"I love you, Mama," he whispered into the darkness.

There was no reply. The silence that haunted him turned his stomach sour.

"Please come back," Wilem pleaded through tears. "I promise to be good."

That had been the last time he had seen her beautiful face. She had looked so sad at hearing him say those hateful words. The Shadow Elves had come just hours after, and while Wilem played with Jorge in the cellars, his entire family had been massacred. He couldn't stand the guilt.

Wilem missed them dearly. Even Torian.

He sat up in his tiny room in one of the fairy tree houses shook. A shrill creaking sound broke out and the entire room tilted until Wilem rolled off the bed.

Wilem crashed to the bamboo floor with a thud as another loud explosion came from outside. Screams followed, and he scrambled to his feet. He fell over once again as the room tilted to the other side.

Wilem crawled to the door in the floor and opened it. He strained to make out anything below. He shoved his feet into his boots, prepared to take off running into the jungle.

Fog filled the Tolrinian fairy compound. As he stepped down onto the ladder go his room built into the tree of his room, the screams grew. He hopped down the last few steps and turned to see chaos.

Wilem watched the fog thicken over the colony. He heard the commotion all around and felt his pulse start to race.

He stood frozen.

Not again. This cannot be happening again.

Wilem shook as memories of his family's murder flooded over him. His eyes darted to the fairies as they flew past him, nearly knocking him to the dirt with their speed. The stars in the sky seemed to have vanished, and the fog was so thick that soon he felt as if he was alone.

"No,"

Shadow Elves ran through the village. His eyes narrowed at their blood-red armor. They were different from the elves that had swarmed his kingdom. This particular group reminded Wilem of the elves that had searched his palace, seeking out the royal family.

He backed away from the chaos, desperate for a place to hide. Where were the hidden tunnels of his palace when he needed them?

"Wilem!"

As if in a daze, Wilem swayed with the wind and watched a fairy fly past his face.

His eyes followed her. Her glittering wings caught his attention. When an arrow shot through her little body, her shrill scream gave him a start. The splash of her warm blood onto his face ripped Wilem from his daze.

Wilem's mouth fell open as he wiped the blood out of his eyes with trembling fingers.

"Help me, Wilem!"

Jorge?

Wilem turned around to see a Shadow Elf dragging his best friend through the dirt by his hair.

Jorge reached out for Wilem as the elf covered his screams with a gray hand.

Without a second thought, Wilem ran after Jorge like the wind. His legs were young, but they were fast.

The day Liam had found him in the palace cellar and rescued him, Wilem had taken a dagger to defend himself. He reached inside his boot as he ran and clutched that same dagger's hilt into his little palm.

The dagger's blade glowed green with Wilem's Tryan power of Enchantment. Heat radiated from the sharp blade and cut through the fog.

Wilem was the last of his family. The last of the Alden clan. The power of his ancestors had passed down to him the day his line was wiped out.

Such power intoxicated him.

As he jumped into the air, his feet sprung from the ground with such ferocity that he nearly flew into the Shadow Elf.

Wilem was fearless at that moment, driven by the need to protect his friend. The Shadow Elf glanced over his shoulder at the final moment.

Wilem landed on his back, stabbing him in the side of his neck. The three of them crashed to the dirt, almost at the end of the colony, where the dark forest met the beauty of the silver gates of Tolrinia.

Together, Wilem and Jorge came to their feet.

They stared at the body as the sounds of terror surrounded them. The fairies that had shown such love and generosity to them were being killed.

Wilem wasn't prepared for this new life of fear. He'd seen too much death already. From the amount of blood and carnage that surrounded them, it looked as though he and Jorge were in for much more.

Chapter 7

VARS TOOK HOLD OF JORGE, effortlessly flinging him into the air.

"We must hurry to meet the other survivors. Come, Prince Wilem." Ved reached for Wilem's hand.

Wilem was all too eager to grab hold. Ved flew him high into the black sky.

From that height, Wilem strained to see through the thick fog. All he could see was smoke and shadows. He watched the fire that ate away at the fairy compound. Out of the mists came a Shadow Elf, riding what looked like a small black dragon that closely resembled a flying lizard.

A wyvern, Wilem thought as his eyes widened.

Ved looked down to see the threat and cursed under his breath. Wilem's heart started to pound again. What could the fairy do against one of those Shadow Elves, especially since he was carrying Wilem in his arms?

Ved surprised Wilem. He clutched Wilem tightly with one arm and drew his sword.

Wilem shrieked when Ved took off toward the Shadow Elf with such speed that the wind pounded at Wilem's face. He wanted to squeeze his eyes closed, but his intense desire to see what Ved planned to do kept them open.

Wilem looked on curiously. The Shadow Elf didn't have a glowing dagger like the ones he'd seen many times before. He held onto the reins of the wyvern with one hand and reached onto his belt to grab a small, round sphere.

Ved slowed down, intrigued by the object the elf held out before him.

The Shadow Elf grinned at him, leaving Wilem unsettled. Then, he released the sphere, and a bright light was released from within.

Through the fog, the elf disappeared. Ved paused, twirling around as he searched for the elf.

A silver rope wrapped around Ved's neck and yanked him through the sky. Wilem slipped from his grasp and held his breath. Terror filled his eyes as he fell down, into the fog.

He screamed.

"Wilem!" Jorge and Vars shouted in unison.

Wilem cut through the fog and started to scream since he could see the ground coming closer.

"VLETA!" Wilem grabbed the talisman that hung from his neck and squeezed his eyes shut.

The metal heated. A bright light filled the entire sky, and his descent came to a stop. He felt something sleek beneath him. Something massive.

"Master," Vleta, his dragon said. She soared through the air. An ancient power had been summoned: a frightfully large black and gold dragon, the secret weapon of the Tryans.

Wilem sighed with relief and held onto Vleta's thick-scaled neck.

Ved's sword fell past Wilem's face. Wilem gasped and grabbed it. He had an idea, but no time to waste. He held the sword in his hands and called the power of Creation.

He didn't know what he was making exactly. But out of desperation, he turned the sword into light that made their surroundings glow.

Wilem grimaced, feeling something jerk around inside him. Then, his eyes widened, and he shrieked when the bright sword carried him and Vleta higher.

Wilem looked down at the ground as it grew farther and farther away in shock. He cut through clouds and soared upward like a bird.

"What is going on?" he asked Vleta.

Vleta seemed unsurprised as the power of the sword catapulted them higher into the night sky. She spoke clearly, calmly. "You are a Legacy, Master. You now have every ability your clan once had. Every power. Every trait. All is yours."

With a dull clicking sound, the elf reappeared from the sphere. The bright light was so intense that it made Wilem wince.

Wilem covered his eyes and peered through his fingers to see the elf grab Ved by the neck with one arm and reach for his dagger with the other. Wilem swung the glowing sword at the elf and sliced through his arm. Wilem gasped, and the elf shouted out in pain.

Ved slipped free.

The elf's arm bled, hacked completely through with one blow. Ved flew behind and took the chance to stab him in the back with his sword. A loud screech erupted from the elf's mouth before his dying body was carried away by its wyvern, down into the darkness and clouds.

"Are you all right?"

Ved nodded quickly as he stared at Vleta with uncertainty.

"And you, Wilem?"

"I'm cold!"

The fairy turned blue but didn't seem to mind the cold of their high elevation. Wilem, on the other hand, felt so cold that he wanted to simply close his eyes and sleep. He rested his head against Vleta's warm neck.

"Don't worry, you will be warm again soon. Just hold onto the dragon and don't let go."

The air grew warmer when Vleta flew a little lower and Wilem was much more comfortable. His heart still pounded with adrenaline, and he was sure that was why he'd survived the intense cold above the clouds.

Wilem had killed one Shadow Elf, rescued his best friend and saved a fairy warrior. What he had done with Ved's sword still vexed him. Never had he been able to do such things. His father could Create better than anyone, and make things catapult him into the air. Maybe he inherited that skill.

Legacy.

That word finally meant something.

"Where are we going?" What does it matter? Wilem thought. No place is safe. His hands began to thaw, his fingers stiff like ice.

"We need to get you and Jorge to Alfheim. Queen Aria will be there waiting for you."

Wilem's nose scrunched up. "Who is Queen Aria?"

"Prince Liam's mother."

Wilem's face softened. He missed Liam. He'd never felt as safe as he did when Liam was around. Maybe Liam's mother could make him feel the same, but he was afraid to get his hopes up.

"What's happening down there?" Wilem hoped that Lady Evee was safe.

She was always so nice to him all of the time. She always made sure he and Jorge had enough food to eat, and that the fairy boys would include them in games. He would hate to see anything bad happen to the fairy queen.

"Kyril is falling apart. This is no longer our home."

Wilem sighed. His hair blew in his face, and he squeezed his eyes shut to keep the strands out. "Home is a word that means nothing to me anymore."

"Do not worry. We will protect you and Jorge, Prince Wilem."

"I wish everyone would stop calling me that." Wilem scrunched up his face in distaste. "I am not a prince anymore."

"As you wish," Ved said without question.

"Thank you." Wilem flew closer to Ved. "What is Eura like?"

Ved shook his head. "I do not know. But we shall know in a matter of hours."

"Really? It's that close?"

"Yes, The Barrier is just over the sea. We can be there by tomorrow evening. Can you handle flying that long?"

"I can." Wilem closed his eyes and wished that Alfheim would be a better place and that Liam would find him again someday.

Chapter 8

LIAM RUBBED HIS HANDS in front of the fire.

Delia and Rowe had been asleep for a few hours. Both Nani and Rowe had fought to find their way to Liam. Now, Nani was gone. The Overworld was her new home.

Liam missed her. Her laughter and love could cheer his gloomiest moods. He'd never wanted to see the Overworld so much in his life. Just one more time, to see his friend once again.

Dawn wasn't too far away, and yet Lilae was still awake.

From the corner of his eye, he saw Lilae roll over onto her back. She sighed and looked up at the sky.

"Can't sleep?"

Lilae turned onto her side and rested her head in her palm.

Her red hair fell over her shoulders, the tips pooling into the dirt. She pushed the mass of hair behind her and shook her head.

"No," she said. "I can take your watch if you'd like."

It was unfortunate that Garion couldn't watch over them while they slept. Delia's control over the undead skeleton warrior was weakened in her sleeping state. So, while she slept, she reduced him to a single bone.

To recharge.

"I'd be happy if you simply kept me company."

Lilae nodded and stared at him, her big green eyes taking in every inch of his face.

Not even Sona, despite her spell over him, had made him feel unsure of himself the way Lilae did. He cleared his throat.

He would not waste another moment thinking about the woman who betrayed him. Not when the girl from his dreams was right there, beautiful and real.

Liam sat beside her. "What were you thinking about before I came over? Is something troubling you?"

She lifted a thin red brow. "Other than the god trying to kill us?"

"Yes," Liam said with a smirk.

"I was thinking about Auroria. No one told me *anything* about my birth mother." She stared into the fire, her eyebrows furrowing. "Until my father was killed."

"I'm sorry to hear that." He wanted to pull her into his embrace and console her. He barely remembered his own father. Queen Aria had raised him on her own. She'd never taken another husband.

"I never even knew he was my father until seconds before his death. Can you imagine learning that your mother was a queen? After living like a peasant all of your life. After thinking no one cared about you as more than a nuisance or duty."

"That must have been hard."

Lilae shrugged. "Being made a slave forced me to think about other things," she said. "Like staying alive."

The thought of her being in danger turned his stomach.

Liam took her hand. When she didn't pull away, he held it, comforted by the warmth of her palm against his. He couldn't believe how much chemistry there was between them, in just hours of meeting one another.

"When I learned of your capture, I wanted to rescue you."

"Why didn't you?"

He sighed. "Yoska, my mother's advisor told me that you would have to escape on your own. That I had other duties."

He couldn't look her in the eye at that moment. Shame washed over Liam at the thought of Lilae being enslaved by their enemy, and doing nothing about it. He should have trusted his instincts and gone after her. But there she was, safe, and had done just as the Ancients thought she would.

Liam glanced at her. He could tell that although she looked innocent, Lilae was a formidable adversary. Luckily, she was on his side.

"I wish the Ancients would look at us as more than pawns in a game," Lilae said. "I could have been killed by that filthy Shadow Elf. With the same dagger that he used to kill my father."

Tears welled in her eyes. Her fist was clenched.

"But you were strong, Lilae. You did exactly as they knew you would."

"But why?" Her bottom lip trembled. "What was the point of making me suffer? I suffered enough by losing my *entire* family. How am I supposed to go on after so much tragedy?"

Liam didn't know what to say. He'd lost almost the entire Order of soldiers under his command. Each was a friend, and now they were gone.

Lilae rubbed her eyes and then covered her face with her hands. "My father would be so ashamed to see me in tears. I wasn't always this weak."

"You're not weak." Liam stroked the back of her hand. "I know that for a fact."

"How?"

"Because you're sitting here with me right now. You fought your way to me, just as I fought my way to you. Against all odds. Here we are."

Lilae tilted her head. "I dreamt of you. Many times." She rubbed her eyes again and drew her legs into her chest. "I thought you weren't real."

A smile came to Liam's lips. "That's funny. Because I thought I made you up."

"And here we are," Lilae said. "Together at last."

"Get some sleep, you two," Delia called from her place beside the fire. She sat up and stretched her legs. "I'll keep watch. Tomorrow we will stop in a town called Dunn for supplies."

Lilae laid her head on her arm and looked at Liam from across the fire.

"Good night," she whispered.

Liam smiled at her. It was surreal that they were finally in the same place. As she closed her eyes, he felt cheated. He'd give anything to lay beside her and stare into her eyes forever.

What was that feeling?

He'd thought he'd felt it with Sona once before, and it had been real to him.

He refused to believe that everything he and Sona had shared was part of the enemy's plan.

The spark that fluttered in his belly felt too good.

Too real.

Liam's smile faded.

He pushed it away, and rested on his back, his eyes fixed on the stars above.

Sadness washed over him as he told himself to resist her charms.

Charm couldn't be trusted—no matter who they came from.

Chapter 9

LILAE HAD TO REPRESS THE urge to cover her mouth at the horror she saw as they walked into the southern town of Dunn.

Heads cloaked, they entered the newly conquered city, where the people were unlike those Lilae had seen in the palace. These people looked much like the ones she had grown up with. She'd seen so many shades and types of people through her travels but never had she seen the aftermath of one of Emperor Kavien's conquests.

Hanging by their necks from the branches of trees were Shadow Elves. She had only encountered Dragnor in her life, yet these elves were different.

What were their crimes?

She stared up at the Shadow Elf woman and what looked to be her young grandchildren. There were two boys of about seven and eight and a small girl.

All in a row.

"Delia," Lilae whispered, her eyes transfixed on the little girl's face. She nearly burst into tears at seeing her tiny body hanging there, but held it in.

"Yes?"

"What's happened here?" Lilae nodded toward the dead bodies, but tried to avoid looking at them again. The smell was enough to turn anyone's stomach.

Delia didn't glance at the bodies. She looked ahead. "War, Lilae. This is what war looks like. The humans have suffered many raids and attacks from Shadow Elves over the year. So much so that they have lost the ability to separate the innocent from the guilty."

Dunn reminded her of Lowen's Edge, and just like when she and her family had entered the busy town, the suspicious eyes now followed them as they walked the road into the town square.

There were similar two-story cottages with shops on the bottom and winding dirt roads. The people looked about the same—pale, freckle-faced, with brown hair. Still, there was a sense of gloom that lingered in the air. This is what Avia'Torenan armies had left behind when they conquered a city.

Lilae's face paled as she listened to the whispers. She shot a look at the woman and man who stood before a goat chained to a post.

"Liam," she said.

"Yes?"

"They are talking about your glow," she said.

"Let them talk," Delia said. "We are only here to purchase supplies. They will have to deal with the presence of Tryans for a few hours."

Liam and Rowe nodded.

Lilae's heart quickened when she noticed the crest of the Avia'Torenan palace on the shoulder of some of the men's armor. Fear rose as she noticed that there were Avia'Torenan soldiers all around the town.

The only sounds were of their laughter as they harassed the townsfolk.

Delia glanced over her shoulder and saw the soldiers as well.

"Come," Delia said. They veered off the main road and entered the closest building.

Inside, there was an old man wiping the tables with a wet rag. He paused mid-stroke and looked them over. His gray beard was long, yet he only had sparse hairs above his ears.

"You need a room?" His voice was tired.

Delia shook her head. "No. We need food for the road. And clothes. If you can provide this for us, I will give you this bag of coins," she said, lifting her coin purse from her belt.

The man stared at Delia before his eyes went to the other three and down to the coin purse. "Cally!"

"Yes, Pa?"

"Get out here."

A young girl rushed from the back room. Cally couldn't have been older than nine, but she wore her apron proudly. She rubbed her wet hands on her apron and looked at her father. Her hair was braided in two blonde pigtails that reached the tops of her shoulders.

"Get these folks a few packs of food and jugs of water. And pack some of Paddie's old clothes." He looked back at Delia. "Hungry?"

"We don't have time for food," Delia said.

"Well, you're not leaving in the daytime without the soldiers seeing you and entertaining themselves with your deaths," he said. "You might as well eat, and stay inside until nightfall. I can help you out of town."

Delia pursed her lips. She turned her back on the old man and spoke in a hushed tone. "He's right. We don't want any trouble. We will hide inside until this evening."

"I'll take that as a yes," he said. "I'm Morrow. Have a seat back here in my private house."

He led the way from the main dining area to the back, where a dark hallway opened to a small room with a wooden table and chairs. Lilae looked around. A pot of potatoes sat on the table, peelings littered the table and floor beside it.

Morrow said something under his breath and started cleaning the peelings up and putting them into another pot that would probably be used for a stew.

"You Tryans with your glowing skin," Delia said as she looked at Liam and Rowe.

Liam shrugged. "There's not much we can do about it."

"I know," she said. "It's not your fault your Ancient loves pretty, glowing things."

Rowe pulled out a chair and sat down. "I'm not opposed to a meal while we wait."

Morrow nodded. "I have some goat and potatoes I can bring out."

"That is fine," Delia said. "We appreciate your kindness."

"No need to thank me, miss," Morrow said, holding a chair out for Delia.

She accepted it and sat down, her hand on her staff and the other in her lap. "Thank you."

He went on, pouring cups of water for everyone. "We do not agree with what those soldiers are doing to our town. When they attacked, they took all of the young men that had any interesting traits and killed the rest. And our women—slaves back in the empire."

Lilae lowered her eyes, her chin clenching. She knew this story all too well.

"Those Shadow Elves hanging out there did nothing to us. They soldiers will kill you for no reason other than being different."

"I am sorry for your loss," Lilae whispered.

Morrow shrugged. "No need to apologize. It was not your fault." He picked up the pot of potatoes from the table and headed to the archway. "I'll bring the food."

Lilae plopped into a chair beside Liam.

"I wonder how many towns are occupied by soldiers," Lilae said, picking up her cup of water. She took a long drink and felt the cool liquid travel to her empty belly.

"I'm guessing most are. I'd be surprised if any kingdoms or cities this far south are still free from Emperor Kavien's empire," Delia said.

"Holy Elahe," Liam said. "So you think that the North is the only free land in Eura."

"Yes, Liam. I'm afraid so."

They all thought about that in silence. The armies Kavien must have gathered were more than they could ever amass.

Morrow returned and set down a platter of goat in a dark sauce and a plate of potatoes. He set an empty plate before them all and left once more.

Lilae didn't wait. She dug into the goat, tearing off a chunk for herself. She bit into it and groaned with delight.

"It's so good." She wiped her mouth of juice with the back of her hand.

She was pleased when Liam put some potatoes onto her plate. She smiled at him.

"Thank you."

"Anytime," he said, returning the smile.

They ate in silence, happy for the delicious dish before them.

The flavors of goat were familiar. The sauce reminded her of one of the dishes in the Avia'Torenan palace. She stopped eating and looked down into her lap.

Rahki and Faira—the harem girls that had been her friends and helped her when she was beaten by Dragnor.

Lilae had left them behind, and that fact knotted in her stomach.

A great commotion outside made Lilae tense. She strained to hear what was going on outside. A quick glance at Liam and Rowe, and she could tell that they were doing the same.

Why were the people of Dunn shouting?

A loud screech of pain made Lilae's blood run cold.

Morrow returned, a fresh loaf of bread on a plate.

Liam stood. "What's going on outside?"

Morrow set the bread down. No one even glanced at it. The screams outside were too unsettling to think of food.

"A Shadow Elf woman and man were found camped on the outskirts of town," Morrow said, rubbing butter from his fingers onto his apron. "The soldiers are going to kill them."

Lilae shot to her feet. She had no allegiance to Shadow Elves, but she refused to let the soldiers kill innocent women.

"Lilae," Delia called, placing a hand on her hand. "We cannot reveal ourselves."

Lilae clenched her jaw, and looked at Delia. "You all can stand by if you'd like. If it were Risa and Jaiza, I'd want someone to rescue them."

Delia's eyes searched Lilae's, her face softening. She shook her head, waving a dismissive hand. "Fine," she said. "We'll not be staying until night," she told Morrow.

Lilae headed for the back door.

"But," Delia said to the old man. "You might want to stay inside."

Chapter 10

THE VILLAGERS PULLED A young Shadow Elf woman and an older elven man by ropes tied around their necks and hands.

These elves were nothing like the one's Liam had fought back in Kyril.

They weren't ruthless soldiers. Just simple civilians. Their hair was shiny and black with small sticks and leaves entangled as if they'd been sleeping in hay. The last girl cried and screamed for them to stop. Liam's heart immediately went out to them, but he was curious to hear their crime, if any.

"Let's us go," the woman pleaded, her hands bound before her. "I swear we didn't do anything. Please, we will leave your land and never return."

The man hushed her. He was on his knees, but his back was straight, proud, his white hair neatly kept despite the state of his clothing.

"That's enough, Oksana," he said. "The humans do not care. And Ryus do not beg."

Oksana nodded. "Yes, father," she said, her lips trembling.

Liam stood in the doorway, keeping back so that the soldiers didn't notice him. His mind raced with ideas of what to do.

Where was Lilae? She'd slipped out the back and vanished.

A tall soldier, with a long brown beard braided to his chest and a tattoed bald head, backhanded Oksana.

Liam sucked in a breath. His hand reached for where his sword used to be.

"I can't watch this," he said through clinched teeth to Delia.

"The Elder says that we need to remain unseen," Rowe replied.

"Wait, men. The Shadow Elves didn't do anything. Let's just let them go," the soldier said.

"Captain Garthem, let me string them up with the others."

Oksana closed her eyes.

"No," Garthem said, a grin coming to his thin lips. "Take the woman to the camp for now. She can be of use for a few days. Kill the old man."

The other soldier pulled on the rope the old man was yanked onto his back. He freed his dagger from his belt and readied it at the man's throat.

"No," Liam shouted as he stepped from the doorway.

Liam froze as a flash of light flew past him. He gripped the doorframe.

All within a flash of a second, she used the soldier's dagger, stabbed him in the heart, sliced the rope, and vanished away with the old elf.

Stunned silence filled the village as everyone's eyes were fixed on the empty space where the elf had been. His daughter covered her mouth.

Their eyes hadn't caught what had just occurred— but Tryan eyes were so equipped for tracing Shadow Elves, that it was unmistakable to Liam what Lilae had done.

While it was barely a flash of light to the villagers, Liam could clearly see Lilae's determined face.

A grin came to his face—a surprised one, but also pleased by her determination and fearlessness. Lilae inspired him.

Liam should have saved the old man.

Then, it happened again, and the villagers started to run, leaving the soldiers to arm themselves.

Lilae swooped in and saved the woman, vanishing with her, and reappearing alone to stand face-to-face with Garthem.

Garthem's eyes met hers, and the color from his skin faded as she held his gaze.

What had he seen that reduced him from a loud instigator to the shivering mortal that stood there?

"Let's go," she said, appearing beside Liam. "Meet me in the jungle."

He jumped at seeing her move so quickly, and before he could speak, she was gone again.

Liam stood aghast for a moment, his heart thumping as he processed what had just happened.

There was something eerie about Lilae's powers.

Yoska had once said something about The Flame that lingered in his mind.

Even though she was younger and not trained in her power, she was even more powerful than Liam, Yoska had said.

Liam finally let out the breath he'd been holding and looked back at Delia and Rowe.

"We better move quickly," Delia said as she gathered her skirts and emerged from the inn.

"Seems we've lost our elves but have gained two Tryans," a soldier said as he and another soldier blocked Liam's path.

"Where do you think you're going?" The soldier towered over Liam, hate in his eyes.

Liam looked up at the man. "Please step aside."

Rowe stepped forward, between Liam and the soldier. Taller than any man in the village, Rowe looked down at the soldiers. "Is there a problem?"

Liam noticed that Rowe had grabbed an ax from the wall in the back.

The soldiers noticed as well, and eyed the large weapon within Rowe's hands.

He stood ready, with his feet apart and a glower on his face.

"Really? And what are the two of you going to do against all of us?"

"We seem to have lost our captives for today," the soldier said, a bit more hesitant now that Rowe had stepped forward. "Somebody needs to be hung in their stead," he said loudly, summoning more of the soldiers.

Rowe motioned them forward. “Come on. I *beg* you. It’s been a few hours since I’ve crushed some skulls.”

There was silence between the soldiers.

“This isn’t good,” Delia whispered as she returned from her spot on the path.

A soldier shoved her aside, “Move, woman, before you get yourself hurt.”

Delia nodded, and she struck him in the jaw with her staff. He lay in the dirt, unconscious.

Unflustered, Delia sighed and folded her hands, meeting Liam’s eyes as every soldier in the village charged toward them. “Try not to make a mess.”

“I can’t promise you much,” Rowe growled.

There was a clashing of steel against flesh and bone as Rowe tore them both down with one slice.

Liam ducked just in time and rolled away. Rowe sawed right through one soldier and his ax lodged into the rib cage of the other in one fluid move. Blood splashed and Rowe yanked his ax’s blade from the fallen soldier’s chest. Blood dripped onto the dry ground as Rowe turned on the other soldiers.

They looked up at him in horror as guts rolled off the blade like slime.

“Come on then,” Rowe coaxed. His eyes narrowed as he looked down at them. “You were all so energized a moment ago. Who’s next?”

Liam climbed to his feet. “I need a weapon. Do you have something? Anything?”

Delia pulled a small knife from her boot and handed it over to him, hilt first. “Can you Create?”

The instant the knife touched Liam’s palm, his fingers curled around it and the blade started to glow.

“No,” he said as the blade became a bright red. “But, I can Enchant.”

Rowe glanced back. “So, we’re showing off, are we? His ax began to glow green.

There were no introductions, or any words left between the two groups. The battle quickly grew to a roar as trained soldiers attacked from all sides.

Close combat wasn't Liam's preferred fighting method, but he was fast, and he needed every ounce of speed against the soldiers that bombarded them.

The tip of his knife whistled as it came around, and his blade slashed the neck of a soldier with a shirt beard.

He shrieked, his hand clamping over the gushing wound, and fell to his knees.

Liam didn't pause. He sunk his sword into another exposed throat. He pulled it free and frothing, crimson, blood gushed from the man's gaping throat and mouth. Liam saw their weaknesses and punctured jugulars and arteries.

Rowe, however, was less meticulous. He hacked and sawed away violently, making a scene that caused pause in the remaining soldiers. Heads lolled and other appendages were tossed into the air along with squirts of blood and dust. Those men had no idea how dirty Rowe fought. He was like an animal.

Rowe spun ahead and caught a man with his bare hands before slashing him across his belly, his glowing ax burning through his armor, spilling his guts. The man screamed in agony as he looked down to see his own intestines falling out of his body. He passed out, and Rowe dropped him.

Someone kicked Liam behind his knee, dropping him to the dirt. Liam rolled out of the way and jumped to his feet.

Liam ducked and lunged at the man as the blade just missed the top of his head. Liam caught the soldier's tattooed wrist with his left hand and heaved his blade into the soldier's chin.

When Liam removed the knife, the battle had ended. He surveyed the aftermath.

Every soldier in town lay in the dirt, covered in blood.

Delia walked surveyed the carnage. She ignored the gawking stares of the people of Dunn.

"Best leave now," she said as she stepped over bodies. The people of Dunn made a path.

They were free from the soldiers.

For now. Horrified faces watched silence as Rowe, Liam, and Delia left their village.

THE SHADOW ELVES watched Lilae in silence. They'd thanked her repeatedly, but as they waited outside of the town's perimeter for the others to arrive, not much else was said.

Lilae was short with them, unsure of what to say. Yes, she'd saved them, but distrust lingered in her mind as she sat on the plush grass, her back resting against a tree trunk.

The Shadow Elves still looked like Dragnor but with thin green eyes like a cat, and that fact alone made her overly cautious. Still, she couldn't sit there and watch them get murdered—or used like slaves or whores.

Their faces were interesting to her. The white tattoos across their eyes and cheekbones were intricate and beautiful. Her own tattoos disturbed her, and she wished she had more clothing to cover them.

"I am Oksana," the older woman said, breaking the silence. "This is my father, Vadim. What is your name?"

"You can call me Lilae."

Oksana sat back on her heels. "Again, we are grateful for your assistance. If there is any way that we can repay you for your kindness, let us know."

"I'll never let injustice happen before my eyes," Lilae said.

"As my daughter has said," Vadim began, his steady gaze focused on Lilae. "We owe you our lives and will repay you for your aid."

"That's not necessary," Lilae said. She heard rustling behind them and glanced over her shoulder.

Delia led the way, her lips pursed as she lifted the bottom of her gray dress to keep it from dragging in the mud.

The Elder still wore her clothes from Avia'Torena as well. The rich fabric did nothing but remind Lilae of Emperor Kavien.

Lilae climbed to her feet when she heard Rowe, Liam, and Delia approach. Her brows lifted when she saw Rowe and Liam covered in blood.

Traces of human guts still clung to Rowe's ax.

"What happened?"

"What do you think happened, Lilae?" Delia stood before her, her hands on her hips, her brows furrowed. "You started a war in that town, and Liam and Rowe had to finish it."

Lilae pursed her lips, glancing at Liam. "I'm sorry. I didn't mean to leave you all behind with the soldiers. I thought you'd sneak out somehow."

"It's fine. We took care of things," Rowe said, wiping the blade clean with his hands and rubbed his hands onto his pants.

"You killed the soldiers?"

Rowe nodded at Lilae. "Every single one."

Delia shook her head, her eyes landing on the two Shadow Elves. "We need to keep moving."

"Wait," Oksana said, standing. "We are going back home to Gollush. The human world is brutal, but we knew the danger when we signed up to be messengers. Come with us. We are closer to Gollush than any other villages for days of travel. We can help you with supplies, armor, weapons, and whatever you need."

Lilae looked from Delia to Oksana. "Go to Nostfar?"

"Yes," Vadim said. "We were heading to a holy man. An Elder. He has been visiting our village for many months now, convincing Shadow Elves to join the resistance against Wexcyn. My family and I have been passing information along between the goblin city and Gollush."

"This was the first time we've gotten caught," Oksana said.

To Lilae's surprise, Delia nodded. "The resistance does need us. A quick stop to Gollush to organize the Shadow Elf resistance could be a good thing."

Lilae pulled in a breath.

Liam stood beside her. "I wasn't aware that Shadow Elves were divided. How long have you all been organizing?"

"For almost a year now," Oksana said. "Vaugner warned us that The Barrier would be destroyed and that war would begin. But, the people of Gollush do not accept the terms presented. Nostfar will stand strong against tyranny."

"Very well," Delia said. "We will escort you home."

Lilae hadn't heard that name before. "Who is Vaugner, Delia?"

"The first Gatekeeper of the Underworld. I trust him with my life. He was *my* teacher."

Vadim lifted a small translucent cube from his side pouch. "If you do not mind, I will summon a trio to help with the journey over the lava lakes."

"A trio?" Warnings came to Lilae, making her feel ill.

"Yes, just guards from Gollush," Vadim said as the cube glowed in the dim light of the jungle.

Liam looked suspicious. "Why didn't you summon a trio before?"

"They cause too much attention," Vadim replied.

"That is fine," Delia said. "I'd very much like to meet with your leaders."

Vadim nodded and spoke into the cube, the light from the sides intensifying.

"Thank you," Oksana said. "The journey will be much quicker if we fly."

Chapter 12

THE SOUND OF A HORN sent Lilae and Liam to their feet. With the loud sound came dim lights in the night sky. They'd gone deeper into the jungle where the shiny, black trees were less dense. Vadim had said his necklace made it easy for the trio to locate them, and a clearing would make for a better landing.

Delia's eyes went to the sky. "They're here."

Rowe was on his feet within seconds, a scowl on his face.

"What is that?" Rowe's eyes narrowed

Lilae ignored the cold as her ears picked up on whispers from the sky above. Her mouth parted as the swishing of the dark sky caught her attention.

Black wings flapped against the night sky, heading toward them.

"Those are wyverns," Vadim said. "The fastest way to travel in all of Nostfar."

Rowe watched them fly closer. "Only three?"

Lilae looked to Delia. "Are you sure about this?"

"Yes. Making an alliance with the Shadow Elves, even a small division of their race, could only help us," she said, holding out her staff. The glow that erupted from the top brightened their surroundings and the sky above.

"Friends," a female voice called. "Please, accept our humble gratitude for saving our valued messengers. We have come to escort you all back to Gollush."

Delia held the staff higher, trying to get a better look at the stranger's face.

A Shadow Elf woman, with long purple hair braided into two braids and eyes that glowed looked down at them. Two other female riders waited behind her.

"Who are you?"

"I am Pretica, Chief of Gollush. When Vadim told us of your great deed, I wanted to welcome you myself. Please, let us take you to our village. Vaugner has mentioned you a great many times."

Pretica smiled down at them as her eyes went from Lilae to Liam. "And, you have both The Storm and The Flame. Our luck has greatly increased."

Lilae didn't like that this stranger knew who they were.

"In Gollush, we have weapons and supplies to help you on your journey, and the Council meets in just a few days."

"Weapons," Rowe repeated. "I like the sound of that."

Delia nodded at Pretica. "Very well."

"You won't regret this; I assure you." Pretica nodded at companions. "Ely, Caty, summon the wyverns for our new friends."

Lilae hoped that wherever they went that it would be warm. She longed for comfortable clothes.

Ely and Caty tossed six ivory eggs from the leather sacks secured at their waists. Before the eggs floated in the air, the women whispered to them and without delay, wyverns emerged.

They soared to the ground, graceful, agile, and beautiful even with such sharp teeth and long talons that were the size of Lilae's arm.

"I've never seen anything like that before," Lilae said, captivated.

"This is only the beginning," Delia said. "This is Nostfar territory that we are entering."

Liam took Lilae's hand. "I'll help you up," he said, leading her to the black wyvern with the long green tail.

Lilae didn't protest, allowing herself to be led forward. When Liam put his hands around her waist to lift her, she sucked in a breath and avoided looking at him. The strength and warmth of his hands on her sent shivers through her body.

"Thank you," she breathed.

Under black lashes, his bright blue eyes looked up at her. "Anytime."

While he went to help Delia onto her wyvern, Rowe pulled himself onto one with an orange tail.

The moon lit their way as they ascended into the night sky.

"Hold on to the reigns, and let the wyverns do the rest," Oksana said, as she flew beside Lilae on a black wyvern with white talons and white eyes.

"Follow me," Pretica said. "The wyverns know the way."

Lilae held onto the neck of her new ride and looked ahead. Flying was something Lilae never imagined herself doing, but as they soared like birds, she couldn't help but smile.

Stars littered the sky above Nostfar. Such a land with rumors of being a desolate, dangerous place confounded her.

From what she'd seen, Nostfar was dark yet beautiful. She realized that not all Shadow Elves would be like Dragnor, and an entire realm was more than rumor and folklore.

The wings of the wyvern flapped gently as they flew higher and higher. Lights ahead caught Lilae's attention. She sat up a little taller, holding tight to the neck of the wyvern.

"Do not worry," the wyvern said. "I will not let you fall."

Lilae's eyes widened in surprise at hearing the wyvern's soft male voice.

"Thank you. I am Lilae. What are you called?"

"Triste."

"I like that name, Triste."

"Thank you. My first master named me Boris. I like Triste much better. Please, don't change it again."

"You don't have to worry about that."

"Good. I thank you, Lilae." She smiled. What a peculiar creature. She'd never spoken to an animal before. The thought had never crossed her mind, and to find such an intelligent creature speak to her was oddly enchanting.

"Are we going to a safe place?" She kept her voice low, glancing at Ely, who flew close beside her.

Ely had black hair that was cut short and long legs that led Lilae to believe that the Shadow Elf woman was, at least, seven feet tall. She looked away.

“Yes,” Triste said. “Pretica is a good chief. She won't harm you. And neither will the village-folk.”

“Why do they need us?”

“Pretica’s youngest sister and cousin were stolen.”

“Oh my,” Lilae said. “That’s horrible.”

“Almost there,” Triste said.

Lilae nodded. His voice reminded her of an old man's, deep and wise.

She braced herself as they flew to a clearing just before a white path that led to a black mountain much like the one Lilae and Liam had met on. She rubbed her cold ears as they landed. She paused, watching Liam jump off his wyvern and come to assist her.

“Thank you, Liam. I can get down by myself.”

He ran his hands through his hair. “Of course, you can,” he said, looking away. “My mistake.”

When she jumped to the ground, her bare feet sank into the black mud. She groaned. Maybe she should have accepted his help. Now her feet were a few inches deep in the thick, cold substance.

Lilae left Triste to join Pretica and the other Shadow Elves onto the white path that was lit by tall torches stuck into the dirt. White dust that made up the path stuck to her mud-covered feet.

“This way, friends,” Pretica said, leading the way to the mouth of a massive cavern that jutted out from the base of a gray mountain.

Keeping close to Delia, Lilae followed Pretica, who stood almost taller than she with a body that was slim and toned.

On either side of the torch lit path awaited a thick, dark forest. The buzz of insect life filled the silence as they headed to Gollush

Lilae paused at seeing the four Shadow Elves guarding the black door that protected Gollush. The elves wore the same green armor that seemed to mimic tree moss. Lilae imagined it would help them blend into the surrounding woods.

“We are honored by your presence,” Pretica said as she approached the guards.

"I am pleased to hear it," Liam said. "Just hours ago, my companions and I were attacked by Shadow Elves just within The Barrier to Kyril."

Pretica glanced back at Lilae and Liam. A frown creased her forehead. "I apologize. Not all Shadow Elves share the same beliefs. I assure you, we are friends. You'd be surprised by all that I know about the two of you."

Each guard bowed their heads and made way for her. A latch was released, and the door lowered into the ground by a mechanical device.

It was intriguing to see a door open that way.

Lilae looked down at the top of the door, now secure between two plates of iron. She stepped over it and noticed the inside of the cavern gave way to a ceiling that stretched hundreds, maybe thousands of feet high.

"What made you study us?" She eyed the Shadow Elves that emerged from the adjoining hallways, eager for a glimpse of the human, Tryan, and fairy.

Lilae doubted they knew Delia to be anything but what she appeared to be. If they expected her to be the Elder she was, they'd all hide and pray her blue eyes never rested on them.

"You become enthralled in legend, prophecy, and history when it affects you personally."

Liam entered and stood beside Lilae. He folded his arms, a stern look on his handsome face. "How is that?"

Sadness filled Pretica's brown eyes as she froze before them. She sighed and clenched her jaw. "Because my sister is the Seer. She was stolen by Bellens."

THE INSIDE OF THE CAVERN OF GOLLUSH was remarkably pristine.

Once they made their way from the sliding door, and through the main hall, Lilae and the others were led to an opening that made her take pause and behold its beauty.

The floors were a smooth dark stone that covered the entire dome-shaped citadel. Gollush's citadel was bigger than Lowen's Edge, the last town Lilae had lived in before her capture. The stairs were wide, stretching across the entire dome, with halls and towers leading to the center.

Lilae's eyes followed the towers upward to the dark ceiling that was too far away to clearly make out.

A bustling place, thousands of Shadow Elves went about their daily business.

"Don't you all sleep?" Lilae watched them go on as if the sun had just arisen.

"We do. During what you consider daytime. Shadow Elves like the dark," Pretica said.

Caty and Ely nodded. "This is our waking mid-day. When the sun sets, we awaken," Caty said.

Caty and Ely both had short black hair that barely brushed the tips of their pointed ears. But, Caty's smile was kind, and she had even kinder chestnut brown eyes that were thin as slits. The two gruesome scars that trailed from the bottom of her eyes to her chin, however, were distracting.

Ely had a stern look about her as if a smile was foreign and abhorred. She looked down her nose at Lilae, her muscular arms folded across her small chest.

"Interesting," Lilae replied, looking away. Weariness started to take over, and she yawned.

Maybe she'd actually be able to sleep after being up for what felt like days. Just yesterday, she had locked in a box in the Emperor's bedchamber, fearing that Dragnor or the leader of the Bellen's, Sister Eloni, would finally come to kill her.

"Thank you again," Oksana said, her father standing beside her. "We must report to our leader and prepare for our next mission."

Lilae smiled at her. "Of course. Be safe on your next mission."

"Yeah," Rowe grunted. "Try not to get caught."

Oksana looked up at him. "Once out of sixty-two isn't so bad."

"Maybe. But getting killed won't make your record any prettier."

With that, Oksana kept her mouth closed, a pert smile on her lips as she bowed to Rowe. "Well said. Be well, Rowe."

Lilae and the others watched Oksana and Vadim leave the group to head into the city.

Pretica stopped at the edge of the stairs. "You all must be exhausted. Come, you can meet the council members tomorrow. I think rest is what you all need right now. Your weapons will be prepared when you awaken."

"We can't thank you enough," Liam said.

"I can imagine how you must feel to be without your weapons," Pretica said. "As a warrior, I know I'd feel quite naked without my spear and daggers."

Delia stood beside Lilae, looking just as tired as Lilae felt. Dark circles were forming under her eyes, and she leaned on her staff for support.

"What is this council you speak of?"

"Vaugner has organized it. The council makes up the Shadow Elves that resist Wexcyn and Inora. It's unfortunate that our god has chosen the side of treachery. But, not all of us are in agreement about the fate of Nostfar," Pretica said.

She put her hands in the pockets of her black pants and stared at a crack in the stone floor. "The elves here do not want to be a part of the extermination of the other races. I hope you can believe that. Though we've been separated for so long, a world without the other races seems unnatural," Pretica said. She pursed her lips. "We may be creatures of the night, but we are not monsters.

"No race is completely evil."

"Thank you, Elder." Pretica folded her hands and led the way from the platform down the stairs.

They stepped down to the main level.

The Shadow Elves started to take notice, pausing at merchant stands stacked high with exotic materials, fabrics, scrolls, and vases stuffed with long twigs that burned and emitted various scents into the air. Vendors sold delicious looking meats that turned on spits over open fires, and brightly colored fruits and vegetables that Lilae had never seen.

"Are any of you hungry? My cook makes the best soup dumplings in all of Gollush. I could get her to steam a few baskets for you all."

"I'm exhausted," Rowe said. "But I'd never turn down a meal."

Liam chuckled. "I'm with you. The rabbit Nani cooked for supper was good, but I'm starting to feel a bit hungry myself. What about you, Lilae?"

Lilae smiled with a nod. "I'd like to try the dumplings as well. Then, I'm afraid I need rest."

"Of course," Pretica said. "Caty, run along and tell Eiko to make enough dumplings for our guests."

Caty nodded and darted into the crowd like the wind. She vanished just as quickly as she'd taken off.

More glances from the elves were cast their way. Lilae was used to being stared at. She just wished she had her cloak to cover her hair and hide her face.

The presence of apparent social classes intrigued Lilae. The wealthy wore jewels and long, elaborate dresses that seemed to glide across the floor. They differed from humans in dress, with more skin revealed than Lilae was used to. The people of Lowen's Edge would have blushed at seeing such exposed flesh.

Their bosoms were partially exposed by plunging necklines and slits that came as high as their hips.

So much smooth and dark skin surrounded them. That wasn't what surprised Lilae though. After only having Dragnor as her representation of what Shadow Elves looked like, the beauty of the men and women before her mystified Lilae.

Such delicate features made her stare at the women, who seemed to glide across the floor with each fluid step. It was like a dance, with elves bowing to each other when they came together, touching shoulders in greeting and stepping back on a pivot when saying goodbye.

Even the men were much better looking than Lilae remembered Dragnor being. To her, Dragnor was the epitome of evil, with his long black hair and a scowl on his slender face. But these men were tall, fit, and nice to look at.

"Tell us about your sister," Liam said. "When did the Bellens take her?"

"Nasty women," Rowe added. "They've been taking our girls for centuries."

"Nothing more than witches," Liam said with a nod.

Lilae kept her thoughts to herself. She'd felt the power of a Bellen before: once to heal her, and another time in an attempt to kill her. Eyeing Delia's staff gave her comfort. Sister Eloni's soul lingered in that staff, waiting for Delia to return her to the Underworld.

Before Delia had rescued her, Kavien had stood up to Sister Eloni, knowing the consequences of defying her.

She sighed memories of Kavien's dead body on his bed. Was it wrong that she missed him so dearly?

"She's been missing for two weeks now. It wasn't common knowledge that Ayoki was the Seer. She's mute and so many denied any claims of her being one of the Chosen Class. So, we trained her in secret. But, someone must have shared the truth of her abilities."

"Have you looked for her?"

Pretica turned on Rowe, her brows furrowing, her lips tight. "Of course. She is my only blood relative since our parents died when we were children. I searched for days without food or sleep."

"I didn't mean to offend you," Rowe apologized, bowing his head. "Trust me. I know the feeling of loss. My brother was killed in a raid when I was a young man. My wife and child may be dead for all I know."

Pretica put a hand on his arm. "I'm sorry to hear that."

Lilae was sorry as well. Wife and child? She'd never have guessed that Rowe was a married man.

"But I am not worried," Pretica said, leading them through an alleyway between two slate gray towers full of light and conversation as voices wafted from the open archways of dozens of levels. "Ayoki can protect herself. And Vaugner has sent one of his greatest assassins to help her escape."

"I look forward to meeting Vaugner," Lilae said.

"You will," Delia said. "We are to meet him in the Goblin City before we go to Auroria."

Goblin City?

Lilae stepped closer to Liam so that their arms almost touched.

When he took her hand into his, she couldn't suppress the smile that followed.

She felt good. Safe. Having Liam take her hand only assured her even more.

Something was going to go wrong.

Lilae just knew it.

Chapter 14

THE SHADOW ELF GIRL skipped across the stones that floated on the surface of the green water. Her white tattoos glowed under the light of the blood-sucking fireflies that nested in the hanging leaves of the trees.

The underwater temple was the quietest place to be before dawn, and she could relax without the constant scrutiny of the Bellens that had captured her.

Ayoki knew exactly what she was to them.

A war prisoner.

An experiment.

Yet Ayoki did nothing to stop them.

She sighed, letting out a long breath. Just the thought of using her power—even to save herself and her friend was enough to make her shudder.

"Ayoki!"

Ayoki jumped to another white stone and paused on one foot as she looked back.

Mai's voice startled Ayoki, but she kept her balance above the still lake. She frowned as the fine hairs on her body stood on end.

The amount of freedom given to her was minimal. The Bellens had her watched at all times as she explored the small plot of land that was encircled by a stone wall.

She was lucky to have any shred of freedom, but even the Bellens were afraid of her, even if they tried to hide it. They gave her space. For now. Until their new master arrived.

The name—Sister Eloni—kept coming up, but apparently there was a new leader, one that made the Bellens speak her name in only hushed tones.

They didn't call her sister like everyone else.

Mother.

Ayoki never thought that simple word would cause such fear in women who tortured young girls and used their blood and souls to fuel their own beauty and ability to live longer than the typical mortal.

The sound of the screaming erupted from just beyond the path that led back to the village the Bellens had built in the middle of Jiran.

A loud explosion knocked Ayoki from her place on the stone. Her long white hair blew as a gust of wind pushed her down. She hit her chin on the rock, sinking into the dark water. The taste of blood filled her mouth as Ayoki fought the desire to close her eyes.

Mai jumped in after her.

Ayoki glanced up and saw that she had just missed the fire that extended over the lake.

They dove deep into the water as the fire consumed everything surrounding the lake.

Ayoki's eyes opened to the darkness beneath. An eerie feeling crept into her as she spun around in the clear water, lit by the fire on the surface. A white mist curled up from the bottom of the lake, as if reaching out to her.

Mai glanced back at her and waved.

Hesitant, Ayoki followed Mai as she swam toward the temple. It sat deep at the floor of the lake, surrounded by the white mist and trees that stretched from the bottom to the surface.

The stone temple stood there almost as if it weren't submerged in water.

Quiet.

Abandoned.

They swam at speeds that rivaled the fastest fish in the sea. The fire hovered above the water's surface, keeping them from the air their lungs needed. Something told Ayoki that the temple would provide solace. It called to them, promising safety, and the young women rushed toward it.

Mai fought the water to reach the large silver doors. She pushed with all of her might, and finally crashed into the inner corridor of the temple. The water would not enter. It remained formed to the entryway, unable to spill inside.

Mai stood tall, her gray dress soaked and clinging to her strong frame as they stepped farther inside. The door slammed shut behind them, making both young women jump.

A burning in Ayoki's throat sent her into a coughing fit. She settled onto the stone floor, choking on water that had once been enchanted. It was stale and tasted salty and warm. Her choking ceased when she saw a light emerge from the dark depths of the corridor.

Ayoki would have screamed if she had been born with a voice. So many things in her life would have been different.

If only she had a voice.

Ayoki scrambled to her feet and slipped backward until her back was against the doorway. The light became brighter and filled the room.

Mai stood and shielded her eyes.

"Ayoki, stay there," Mai whispered.

Ayoki watched the light. It shrunk into a small ball that hovered in the air and began to trail down the hallway. The women looked at each other and then back at the ball of light.

"Come on. Let's see where it goes."

Ayoki took Mai's hand and peered at the light. She was unsure if it would take them to salvation or certain death.

"Maybe it's a sign?"

Ayoki clutched her hand. They dripped water along the slippery polished floors as they crept down the halls. Mirrored ceilings looked down at them. Ayoki avoided glancing back up at them.

She didn't like seeing her reflection.

"Hurry now. No time to waste," a voice called from far down the hallway.

They both stopped.

Ayoki wanted to turn and run back the other way.

"Calm down, Ayoki," Mai said as her eyes strained to see past the light.

Their cat-like eyes were better accustomed to darkness than such bright light.

"I see a figure moving down there," Mai whispered. "Who's there?"

"Are you hard of hearing?" A male voice echoed through the corridor as he slid toward them.

Ayoki's eyes widened, stunned by the sudden appearance of a goblin. He was as short as a child, with the face of an elderly man, beady black eyes, and gray skin.

The goblin's bushy eyebrows rose as he examined them. He threw his hands up. "Fine. You want to die? I'll leave you alone." He turned to go back the other way. "I was going to show you a path to Eura. Vaugner told me you were worth rescuing, but if you'd rather stay here, it makes me no difference."

Mai and Ayoki looked at each other then back to the goblin.

"Come on, Gilly," he said to the light as it followed him.

It began to dim, and they saw that it was a small pixie. She was too tiny to make out her features, but they could tell that she was watching them.

"I said come on. They want to be left alone."

The pixie buzzed off like a bubblebee, barely any bigger than one and without a second thought, Ayoki and Mai ran after them.

"Wait!"

He paused and looked over his shoulder.

"Wait for us. We want to come too," Mai said.

He snorted. "Of course, you do." He peered at them with those black eyes as they made their way beside him. "So, you're a bit slow but not completely daft. That's a relief."

Gilly giggled, and they finally got a good look at her. She sounded like a bell when she laughed. Though her blue eyes were too big for her face, she was pretty with short bright blonde hair and pointy ears and chin.

"Let's get a move on then. The fire will spread. We don't want to wait and see if any of those Bellens survived my bombs."

Ayoki's brow lifted. He was rescuing them.

Impressive.

He turned a corner at the end of the hall and began to run. He paused. "I'm Hartwig."

"Mai. This is Ayoki."

He nodded, his eyes lingering on Ayoki's face. Without warning, he turned and ran. Ayoki didn't know why, but she almost felt safe. Mai took her hand, and they followed behind as quickly as they could, surprised at how fast the goblin was.

"Come on, slowpokes!"

Mai glanced at Ayoki. "We are Shadow Elves."

"And as slow as my grandmother," Hartwig replied.

Gilly giggled again, her small voice carrying down the empty hallways.

"We could outrun you," Mai said. "If we knew where we were going."

"Sure. That's what they all say."

Ayoki smiled. The fear and tension dissipated. She liked Hartwig. Perhaps there was hope they would survive after all.

Ayoki needed to.

Despite her fear and doubts, the *world* needed her.

After all these years, maybe she'd finally gotten some good luck.

Chapter 15

THE AIR FELT SCARCE AS AYOKI and the others went deeper underground into smothering darkness.

Used to living underground, her eyes adjusted, dimly lighting the area around her. They came to a dead end where a stone wall stood before them.

She touched the walls, feeling for any signs of life other than Ayoki and her companions.

A breath of relief escaped her lips. They were safe.

For now.

Ayoki hoped Hartwig would take them somewhere safe from the Bellens and their dark magic.

Ayoki rested her hand on belly. She bit her lip at the flutter beneath her hand. For once in her life, she had more than herself to think of.

Pretica still didn't know. Maybe she was better off being as far from home as possible. Ayoki had already let her down. She'd let the world down.

But then, she'd never see Kenichi again.

Tears stung her eyes. She wiped them away before anyone noticed.

Hartwig tapped on the stone wall, and clicking sounds were heard. Ayoki's eyes examined the stone wall curiously, but the goblin pushed the adjacent wall instead, revealing a secret door.

The stones shifted and twisted until the pattern changed and the stones separated.

Gilly entered the small room, filling it with light. A ladder that stretched high above was nailed to the wall.

Hartwig began climbing up the ladder with Gilly lighting the way. Gilly's light made the slick walls shine, and Ayoki realized the entryway led to a cavern much smaller than her home in Gollush. She missed her home, even if there were a few dark memories she wished she could forget.

Mai looked around. "We must have gone quite deep underground."

"Seventy-five feet," Hartwig replied as he lurched himself up the final steps of the ladder.

He reached for Mai. She shook her head and darted up the ladder. She had a self-satisfied smile on her face when she saw Hartwig flinch when she appeared beside him.

Ayoki didn't like drawing attention to herself, so she climbed up and accepted Hartwig's hand. He helped her up and sealed the door to the temple closed.

Crystals clung to the ceilings of the cavern and red orbs the size of Ayoki's fist protruded from the stone floor like flowers. They held light inside that flickered and moved slowly from side to side.

Ayoki bent down and watched the light inside. Something small writhed and spun.

"Better not stare," Hartwig said and waved his hands before her eyes, breaking her gaze. Ayoki frowned up at him, but he simply began down the left path.

"How much farther?"

They had been walking for hours, and their clothing was still damp and clinging to them.

Hartwig's brows rose. "In a hurry, are we?"

"Why, yes. You do know she is the Seer. She has to help the other chosen to save the world."

"Oh, yes. That." Hartwig didn't continue then, and both of the girls looked at each other. His mind seemed to be elsewhere. Ayoki's ears perked up; it sounded as if he was counting to himself.

"You are taking us home, right?"

Hartwig glanced over his shoulder. "Home? No miss. We are heading to the Goblin City."

Mai skidded to a stop. "What?"

Hartwig shook his head. "Why are you stopping? We have no time to waste. You speak of the other chosen. Vaugner knows of all of this. You will meet in the Goblin City."

Vaugner? Ayoki knew that name. He was the one to organize the rebellion against Wexcyn and Inora.

"Well," Mai said with disappointment. "I wanted to go home."

Hartwig nodded back the other way. "You know the way back."

Mai wrung her hands. "I'm not going back alone."

"It's settled then. You're coming with us to the Goblin City," he clapped his hands. "Now, show me some of that speed you keep gloating about. Hustle!"

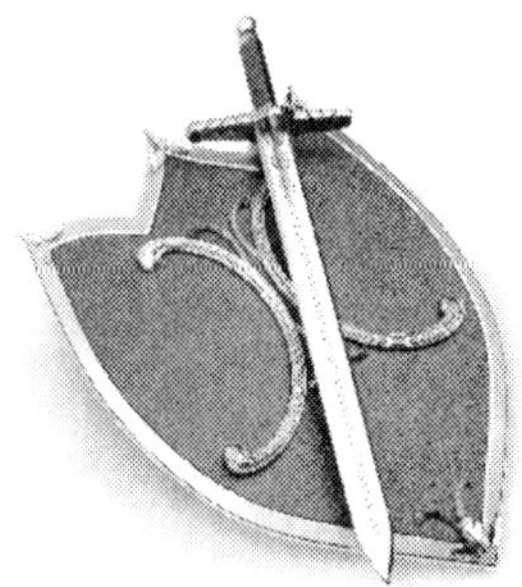

THEY WALKED FOR MILES until Hartwig began to slow as the ceiling went from low to much higher above them.

Gilly lit the way to a fork in the cavern. The walls were full of jewels and precious stones. One could travel three ways. Either they could go straight, to the left, which was too dark to navigate, or right, which looked like it dropped into another lower cavern.

The young women waited for Hartwig to direct them.

"Luc?"

Ayoki felt the hairs stand on the back of her neck as they looked into the darkness. Their eyes had adjusted, but still she saw nothing. A man emerged from the mouth of the path that led to the left.

"Aye," Luc answered. He walked ahead, and the girls saw that he was a Shadow Elf like them. "This is the Seer?"

Hartwig hooked his thumbs in his belt loops and stood straight like he always did. "Aye."

Luc's bright blue eyes examined Ayoki from top to bottom. He looked as if he could be both of their fathers, with thin wrinkles set into his forehead like he worried too much. His hair was braided long and neat. He wore simple travel attire, leather pants, boots, and a belted green tunic.

"Vaugner has patrols set up all along the path from the fallen barrier to the Goblin City."

"Goblin City?" Mai's eyes widened. She glanced back at Ayoki. "I don't know about this."

Ayoki took her hand and gave it a squeeze. She nodded, meeting Mai's eyes.

"You *want* to go to the Goblin City?"

Ayoki smiled and nodded. Vaugner would know what's best. If Pretica trusted him, then she would as well.

Hartwig handed Luc a few of the jewels he had mined from the caverns. The Shadow Elf examined them, closed his fingers over them, and dropped them in his side purse. Luc finally looked satisfied.

"Nothing to worry yourselves with. Just don't be seen by the people native to Eura. The humans don't like the other races, and they really don't like Shadow Elves. But Luc will take care of you."

"But where are you going?" Mai asked, disappointed; they had already gotten used to him.

"Going to see a man about a dog," he replied with a straight face.

Mai stared at him, her face twisted. "What?"

"Most of what he says is nonsense." Luc scowled. "Isn't that right little Wig?"

Hartwig chuckled to himself. "More people to save. Very little time. We will meet again, my friends."

Mai and Ayoki nodded. They'd just met him. He'd saved their lives and would now be leaving them with another stranger.

"Do not worry. You are going to my home. The Goblin City is not a place to fear, I assure you. You just be ready. I will show you a real race," he winked at Mai.

"We are always ready," Mai smiled, exchanging a grin with Ayoki.

Chapter 16

DARK THOUGHTS FILLED DRAGNOR'S mind.

He had searched the human realm for eighteen years for The Flame. Each year the Lilae had alluded him. After finally catching her, she'd managed to slip through his fingers once again.

In his pocket was a single strand of her ruby-red hair. He kept it with him at all times. Now, he pulled it from his pocket and stroked the iridescent red strand. The colors changed in waves from gold to red. He smelled it, his eyes closing as her scent sent shivers along his ash-colored skin.

How she'd managed to cloud Emperor Kavien's judgment was a mystery. All he knew was that he wanted her back.

Her death would buy him more time.

The sound of boots plodding hurriedly down the dungeon stairs ripped him from his thoughts.

"Master Dragnor," the guard called. The smell coming from the torture chamber kept him back, as did Dragnor's dark glare.

"What is it?"

Even over the stench of blood and rotting guts, Dragnor could smell sweat and dirt on the guard and realized that it was daytime.

The guard bowed. "The men you summoned, sir. They have arrived."

A pleased smile came to Dragnor's thin lips.

Dragnor turned and disappeared up the stairs faster than the man's eyes could see.

It took only seconds to reach the top. Straightening his clothing, Dragnor made his way to the entrance at the back of the castle that led to the main courtyard.

Weeks of waiting had finally come to an end.

The castle was dark, just as he had ordered. The palace finally felt like home. All torches and candles had been left unlit.

The dark soothed Dragnor. It reminded him of his prior life in Nostfar and even more of his afterlife in the Underworld.

Darkness was his friend and ally. It allowed him to walk unseen, yet he could see anyone in his path with perfect vision. Servants stumbled to complete their duties, using only the occasional flicker of natural light that spilled through open windows and drapes. He would very much like this darker new world.

Once he stepped into the light that flooded the room from a sky light at the very top of the palace he folded his hands before him. His eyes shone with pride at what he saw.

Standing in the wide entryway was the Maloji Tribe. They were in three sets of twelve and all bowed when Dragnor stood before them. Each man had his hair pulled straight back. Their faces were all tattooed with the intricate white symbols of their clan.

"Brothers," Dragnor said, and they all nodded in respect.

No one spoke, but they all stood to their full height. The palace staff all scrambled around, staring at the Shadow Elves, but trying not to be seen. They were even more intimidating than Dragnor. The Maloji were a specialized sect of Nostfar warriors.

Taken as boys to the underground temples, they were trained to fight with every weapon conceivable and forced to live in the most extreme conditions so that they would learn how to truly survive any situation.

These were the men responsible for the infiltration of the other realms. They led the Shadow Elf armies and trained the soldiers. These men were the reason the Avia'Torenan army would be made nearly indestructible.

Back in the ancient days before The Barriers, the fraud Garion had tried to teach a system of fighting to the other races to prepare them for the devastation a Maloji warrior could cause.

Dragnor grimaced at the memory of seeing Garion in the palace weeks ago. His reputation truly preceded him, and he was made even more frightening after being risen from the dead. He knew how to stop him, though. Kill Elder Delia, and you kill the puppet Garion.

"The work has begun, Master Dragnor," Parvos spoke for his troop. They all wore crimson light armor. It fit sleek onto their slim, toned, bodies.

"We will destroy Kyril."

"And Alfheim," Hitari added. His troop wore black. They simply had to aid what Wexcyn had already started. Plagues, widespread fires, floods, and creatures of the Underworld had been set loose.

The Maloji entered palaces where no one else could penetrate, and killed entire families, making sure no heir survived. To leave a lone heir of any clan would be a terrible mistake. The power passed down to a Legacy would be almost as strong as that of an Ancient.

Dragnor's eyes scanned the assembled warriors.

"What of Nostfar?"

This would be the test to see if they truly were loyal. He didn't doubt any of them. None had families that they remembered. But still, there could be a shred of loyalty to one's race.

Dragnor had given that loyalty up long ago. Wexcyn promised them immortality, the chance to be rulers in this new world while all other Shadow Elves would be totally wiped out.

Nomavi gave a single nod. His troops were all garbed in green.

"There was one problem," Parvos admitted. "We entered the Raeden palace. We killed everyone, however, the Alden heir lives. Our brothers found him in Tolrinia, and he escaped."

Dragnor's grin faded as he watched Parvo's expressionless face. None of those men feared him. They were bred without fear. If it came down to a fight, Dragnor would lose, but his power made him stronger then all of those men.

His jaw clenched. He tried to keep his composure, but Dragnor hated bad news.

"Which one? Was it Daveed, the eldest?" Dragnor could only imagine how powerful that Tryan would be with all of his ancestor's power passed down.

"No, the youngest," Parvos said.

"Wilem?"

"Yes. He lives. The Storm, Prince Liam, rescued him."

Dragnor stared at Parvos then he looked over the other Maloji.

Dragnor laughed. "But the boy cannot be a day over ten years old."

Parvos nodded. "And yet we should never underestimate a Legacy, even one that is a child. Children grow into men. Men that seek revenge for the deaths of loved ones."

Dragnor's laughter was extinguished. "Very well, Parvos. If he is still alive in Kyril, the beasts should kill most of the Tryans as they try and reach Eura."

"He has a dragon."

Dragnor's eyes widened. It took a lot to surprise him. Dragons were rare. They were the most powerful creatures in the world. The vision of a Legacy, commanding a dragon changed things.

"Nomavi," Dragnor turned to the elf.

Nomavi stood still and ready to be commanded.

"Dragnor."

"Find the Alden Legacy. Kill him."

Nomavi nodded, and he turned to his men. They didn't need orders; their duty was understood. They filed behind their leader and exited the palace.

"All right, brothers," Dragnor clasped his hands before him. His gaze darkened as he thought of the many tasks that needed to be carried out. "Now let's get a move on before the emperor is awakened."

"What about The Flame? Are you still searching for her?"

A grin appeared on Dragnor's face. "Don't worry. I've already found her."

IT WAS A LONG WAY DOWN from where Lilae stood on the balcony of her room in the Citadel guest house.

Lilae looked down at the stone beneath her. She clutched the railing, afraid that somehow she would fall to her death.

Lilae was never fond of heights.

Still, she couldn't help standing there, taking in the magnificent view of Gollush and its thousands of citizens.

The cavern was tall enough to house buildings that rivaled any that Lilae had ever seen in her many travels through Eura. The narrow stone towers were sure to house hundreds of elves at a time, with ten to twenty rows of windows that looked out of the circular structures.

Clearly, this civilization had spent thousands of years building, growing, and advancing.

This, Nostfar, was nothing like she'd imagined it to be.

Footsteps drew Lilae's attention. She glanced back at Pretica as she walked from Lilae's room to the small balcony.

"I bet you never expected such an achievement from Shadow Elves," Pretica said with a tight smile on her lips. She stood beside Lilae and shrugged. "I know of your folktales and scary bedtime stories."

Lilae's cheeks reddened. "You're right. I did not."

"That's fine. We have stories about you too," she said with a chuckle. "We thought your teeth would be pointier. Sharp enough to bite our throats like the stories my mother used to tell Ayoki and I."

Lilae's eyes widened, having never seen a sharp-toothed humans in all of her life. "Really?"

"Yes."

Pretica wrapped her long fingers around the railing and used it to stretch her arms. "I much prefer reality to the pictures I made in my head about you humans and Tryans."

"As do I," Lilae said. She stepped away from the balcony and sat on the bench against the wall of the tower. "Your sister. The Seer. How long ago did the Bellens take her?"

Pretica tensed at the mention of her sister and the Bellens.

Lilae was curious. Her experience with Sister Eloni hadn't been pleasant. The woman had tried to kill her after pretending to be a friend and ally. Lilae hoped that the Seer wasn't in any trouble.

They needed her.

"I worry about her," Pretica said, her face becoming serious as she looked out at the city below. "She is fragile."

"How so?"

"Ayoki is not very…stable," Pretica said, her voice lowering. "Her power is not like yours and Liam's. It consumes her."

Lilae sat up straighter, intrigued. "What can she do?"

Pretica turned on her heels, so abruptly that Lilae tensed, expecting to get hit for asking the question.

"Come, you're clean, in new clothes; let's get you some weapons, shall we?"

Lilae nodded, her eyes narrowing when Pretica didn't wait for a reply and simply stalked back into Lilae's room and to the door that led to the stairs.

Now, she wanted to know even more about what exactly the Seer could do.

Whatever it was, it had caused absolute terror to fill Pretica's eyes despite her attempt to change the subject and fix a fake smile to her lips.

Lilae stood and followed Pretica.

Secrets.

She never liked those.

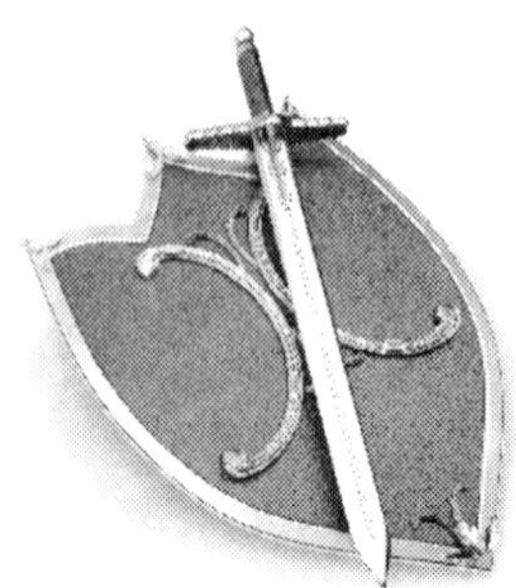

“WEAPONS,” PRETICA SAID, motioning to a long table at the back of the armory on one of the locked lower levels of the Citadel. “You’ll need them if you want to make it to the Goblin City safely. Chosen or not, there are many creatures and enemies between Gollush and Vaugner’s tower that I wouldn’t want to face unarmed.”

Delia sat on a bench, wrapped in freshly laundered brown robes as she examined a glowing Shadow Elf dagger.

Lilae, Liam, and Rowe tested weapons that caught their eye.

Liam knew quite well about the enemies Pretica spoke of. During his time in the Order, he’d fought Shadow Elves for longer than he cared to recall. They already swarmed much of Kyril. He just hoped his mother, Queen Aria was safe from the increasing threat.

“Thank you, Pretica,” Lilae said.

Liam watched Lilae sheath a Valhorian long sword into her new finely crafted scabbard, and a dagger in each boot. She looked fine in her new, clean Shadow Elf light armor. The form-fitting brown leather clung to her curves. A silver breastplate covered her full bosom, over a tunic that was tucked into soft hide pants. Even her boots were impressive, hard and covered in more silver armor.

Liam was certain Lilae would look attractive in anything she wore.

“You’re welcome. I hate to admit that there are more enemies in the woods than allies. Nostfar creatures can be treacherous.”

“I’ve come face to face with a basilisk from Nostfar before,” Lilae said. “I still have the scar.”

“At least you have your life,” Pretica added.

"These are fine weapons," Rowe said. He tested the weight of multiple axes.

Liam raised a Shadow Elf sword. A cast of his Tryan power into its steel made it glow a dim yellow. He made sure to use very little power, just to test whether or not it was safe to use his Enchant without breaking the blade.

"You don't have to hold back, Liam. Our steel is one of the strongest in all of the realms. Only the Silver Elves can rival our weapon forging. Our gods are sisters after all. It isn't a surprise that their people would have such similar qualities."

"Aden is known for creating complex gods," Delia stuck a dagger in her belt. "I dare say Ellowen has the most varied gods in all of the worlds."

"Indeed," Pretica said with a nod.

Liam poured more of his power into the sword, testing the steel's limits. Each surge of his essence made the sword's glow change color. It went from yellow to orange to blood red. At it's maximum input, the sword glowed a deep blue.

Liam's brows rose. "This sword can now cut through stone like a knife through softened cheese."

"I approve of this ax," Rowe added, his ax burning a deep red as he gave it a swing through the air.

A smile came to Pretica's face. One of the first they'd seen on the otherwise serious woman. "I am honored by your approval."

Pretica nodded to the map in Lilae's side purse.

"The map will show you the fastest route to where The Barrier between Nostfar and Eura once was. After that, you'll follow the river to the Goblin City. We haven't been able to document much of the path through Eura, but I believe there is one human town between The Barrier and your destination."

Lilae cried out, and everyone stopped what they were doing.

She fell to her knees with a pained look on her face, and Liam met her on the floor, catching her in his arms.

"Lilae?"

Lilae clutched his neck. "Help. The pain. My skin!" Her thin fingers struggled to take off her armor. She cried out again, a scream so blood curdling that it gave Liam chills.

Delia was on her feet in seconds, helping Lilae remove her clothing. Liam took a dagger from Lilae's boot and cut through the fastenings of her armor and the buttons on her tunic.

When she fainted, Liam's mind turned to the worst possible outcome.

She cannot die. Please. Not her.

Opening her clothing revealed cream-colored undergarments stained with fresh blood. Delia touched Lilae's odd black tattoos of symbols Liam vaguely remembered from his studies during his time in the vaults as a young boy.

Lilae's tattoos started to bleed as if the symbols cut and burned her skin. Blood dripped onto the floor and onto Liam's hands.

"Holy Elahe," Pretica gasped. "Those tattoos. I've seen those symbols in the old temple ruins." She pointed at Lilae, stepped away. "She's marked by dark magic."

"Magic from the Underworld," Delia said. Her glare lifted to Pretica, her white cheeks reddening with fury.

"How?" Pretica stepped away from Lilae as if the tattoos would infect her somehow.

"Dragnor did this," Delia snarled. "He's collecting on his promise to make Lilae suffer no matter how far she runs. He is a vengeful soul, one that I cannot wait to get my hands on."

Liam clenched his jaw, vowing to end the Shadow Elf's life the first chance he got. But now, he needed to help Lilae. He collected her writhing body in his arms.

His heart raced as she cried out in pain. Her eyes rolled into the back of her head, showing only the whites.

"I'm not letting him harm her. We've healed each other before," he said to Delia, desperate for some kind of confirmation that what he had said was true. "Maybe I can heal her now."

"Maybe." Delia's eyes widened as she nodded her head. She touched Lilae, withdrawing her hand as if Lilae's skin had burned her. "This magic is strong. You can certainly try."

"Take her to the infirmary. Maybe one of our clerics can help her as well, though we know nothing of combating dark magic such as this."

Liam nodded, looking down at Lilae's pale face as she hung lifeless in his arms. "Show me the way."

WAKING UP IN AN EMPTY ROOM was jarring.

Lilae sat up in her bed as heat filled her legs, like when she'd run for too long with Pirin and the twins.

She rubbed her legs in an attempt to ease the lingering pain. All she remembered was darkness, agony, and Dragnor's face.

But, to her delight, Liam was there, waiting for her to wake up.

"How do you feel?" Liam handed her a warm cup of tea. "The healer retired for the evening. I refused to leave you here all alone."

The corners of Lilae's lips lifted as their eyes met. She accepted the cup, a ragged cough coming out instead of words of gratitude.

Liam put a hand on her back and started gently patting it.

"I'm okay," Lilae said in between coughs. She winced, an unsettling rush of heat filling her once again.

Liam sat in the chair beside her, watching with concern-filled eyes. "Do you need anything else?"

Lilae shook her head. The coughs ceased. "Thank you, Liam."

She tried to steady her hands as she took a sip of the dark liquid, delighted by the surprisingly sweet and minty flavor. She let out a long breath as she leaned back against the wall.

"What happened?"

He folded his arms and leaned his back against the door. "The tattoos Dragnor put on you. He used them to hurt you."

Remembering his face in her dreams horrified her.

What was Dragnor up to?

Could he truly hurt her from so far away?

Lilae's face paled. "I almost forgot about his promise. He'll never let me be."

"The Gollushan healers were able to suppress its effects with a little magic of their own. We just don't know how long it will last."

"So, I am at his will again." Lilae lowered her eyes to the symbols on her arm. She wished she could claw them off.

"I hate to see you suffer. There has to be something I can do."

"You can relax. I'll be okay." Lilae forced a smile despite the anger boiling inside of her. "I'm stronger than I look."

"I don't doubt it. We have to stop the Shadow Elf that did this to you."

"I know. I should have killed him when I had the chance."

Liam stepped away from the door and knelt down before Lilae's bed.

"Give me your hand," he said, a curious smile on his face. "I want to try something."

Lilae sat up a little straighter when Liam took her hand into his own. She bit her lip as he placed the palm of her hand against his cheek.

He was so warm, and his scent was nearly intoxicating. She would be happy to be close to him always.

She eyed his full lips as he closed his eyes.

"Relax," Liam whispered.

"Okay. I will try."

Lilae was sure he'd hear her heart beating and tried to slow her breaths.

She jumped when a flood of cold filled her. The sensation was unlike anything she'd ever felt. It was as if Liam replaced her blood with cold water. Curious, she watched his face, seeing the glow of his skin fading. Her eyes widened when she noticed that her skin started to glow.

The pain started to lessen.

"Oh my," Lilae breathed.

"You felt that?"

That would be an understatement.

"Yes. I still do."

"Splendid." His eyes brightened. "How do you feel?"

"I could kiss you," Lilae joked. "I feel amazing."

Liam didn't reply. Instead, he leaned over and kissed Lilae on the cheek.

He stood, and Lilae's hand touched the spot his soft lips had touched.

"I've never used my Enchant on a person before," he said. "Hopefully, its effects will last." He opened the door. "And if the pain returns, I'll use it again."

Lilae nodded, watching him with disappointment as he began to leave.

"Don't go," she whispered.

Liam paused. "What was that?" He looked back at her.

Lilae swallowed. "Stay with me. Please."

"Are you sure?"

"I am."

Liam nodded. His face turned serious.

Was he was conflicted by her request?

Doubt filled Lilae. Did she really just say that? Her mind raced. She'd never been so forward before. But Liam gave her courage, and she now understood just how short life was.

Too short to hide one's feelings and desires.

Lilae took a breath and pulled the quilt aside so that he could climb into bed with her.

"Please." She offered a smile.

Sharing a bed with a man before marriage wasn't proper, but she cared nothing about such things. She just needed Liam's company and perhaps his protection.

Nothing more.

She didn't want to be alone—not with Dragnor threatening to invade her dreams. Liam was her dream man. Perhaps just being near him would fight that Shadow Elf's evil.

Liam closed the heavy door and took off his boots. She scooted and let him under the quilt with her. Her heart raced. Having him so close excited her. Turning her back to his chest, she melted into his warm embrace.

Bliss.

"I do hope you get to meet my mother one day, Lilae," Liam whispered. "I think she'd adore you."

"I've never met a queen before. What is she like?"

"My mother is kind, wise, and always made sure I knew she loved me."

"Lucky," Lilae said, closing her eyes as sleep began to overtake her. "I wish I'd had that growing up."

Liam held her close, his warmth relaxing her into oblivion. "You can have that now."

Lilae drifted to sleep with the sound of Liam's breathing and the feel of his breath on her hair.

"Goodnight, Lilae."

SOON SONA WOULD FACE the woman that had once looked at her with love. The mother of the man she had loved with every ounce of her being.

Aria had no idea what was coming.

The look in Liam's eyes when she'd stabbed him still haunted her.

Now, she had to ruin his mother.

Sickened by her own deeds, Sona walked through the abandoned manor with her swords down at her sides. Despite the current state of Oren, the manor she had grown up in looked virtually untouched.

Even as the green fog lingered in the air, seeping into the large building, one could clearly see the glory of what it once was. Beautiful tapestries still hung on the stone walls. Lush carpets still stretched unruffled along the quartz floors.

Once she entered the main hall, she slid the swords into their harness against her back. Emperor Kavien's words still circulated within her mind.

There was something about that man she just couldn't understand. She wondered if his insanity was for the good of the new world, or if there was someone better to take his place. Someone like her.

She heard something, footsteps, and turned around. A servant peered around the corner of the wall at her. He was sickly, barely more than a pale skeleton.

Sona raised an eyebrow. He looked afraid. He was all alone. She met his eyes and slowly took a small knife out of her belt. He glanced down at her hand, and she threw it at him, tossing him backward as the blade impaled his skull.

Leave no one alive.

She felt a lump in her throat as she listened to the silence. His small body lay sprawled before the grand archway leading into the main hall.

She'd killed her entire family.

She looked up at her father. He hung from his neck at the top of the staircase.

Lord Rochfort had made her what she was. Even then, his soulless, lifeless, eyes frightened her. She stared at him, half expecting him to come down and scold her for ruining their plan. He would beat her, making sure to leave her face untouched. That face was his only chance to gain influence in the Orenian palace.

Sona was his sixth daughter, the only one bred to possess Charm. Children were like a lottery to him, always anxious to see what skill they would be born with. Five children were born with nothing. Sona was born with a skill that would ruin any shred of her virtue.

Charm was something that could either be a blessing or a curse, depending on how it was used. Lord Rochfort made sure Sona never knew what a childhood or even a true moment of love was like.

Now, he was dead, and Sona had killed him. She'd wrapped the rope around his neck and kicked him off the banister. With her increased powers, he'd been defenseless.

"Did you have to have everything?" Sona stared up at him from the bottom of the staircase.

He couldn't hear her, and yet she expected an answer. He was one of the wealthiest men in the realm. Why couldn't he be happy? Still, even as she contemplated such things, she knew she was just like him. She had inherited his blind ambition and wanted more than just influence in the Orenian palace.

Sona wanted the world.

Something dripped onto her forehead. She looked up at the ceiling. Blood was splattered and pooled everywhere. She hadn't shown mercy to even the lowliest scullery maid. She wiped the blood with the back of her hand, smearing it across her pale, white, forehead.

This is what I've become, she thought. *Death is my best friend.*

"Sona?"

Sona tensed at the unexpected voice.

"Is that you?"

Sona turned around and looked blankly at Claus, her grandfather—the last member of her family. She had once thought of him as a friend.

He looked weak, his skin hanging off his face. Just another Tryan affected by Wexcyn's devastating plague. His bloodshot eyes looked on in horror as he noticed the carnage all around her. Dismembered bodies littered the floor.

"What's happened here?"

Sona didn't speak. She slowly crossed the room towards him. Claus reached out for her, as if to embrace her.

She almost felt sad.

Almost.

It didn't even cross his mind that she was the monster that he feared. To him, she was still that sweet little girl who used to beg him for sugar cubes meant for the horses. In the darkness of the large front room, he couldn't see that she was soaked in blood. Her black leather concealed the evidence.

Claus met her blue eyes and she cringed. His tear ducts were bleeding red tears.

He's crying. Why?

Such an emotion seemed odd to her. Did he actually care about those people she had slain? They had always treated him like nothing more than the servant that he was. Perhaps seeing what she had become saddened him.

She raised an arm to hug his neck. With one touch, he was hers. He melted into her arms.

Charm was funny that way.

She sighed. It was better for Claus to feel something similar to love in his last moment.

He smiled at her, rubbing her smooth cheek as he had so often when she was a child.

"Good bye, Claus," she whispered reaching for one of the swords secured to her back.

It glowed green with her touch. With a single, powerful, swipe, Sona sliced his head off.

Claus's head fell, and his body followed.

Sona looked down at his body. He was the last. She could feel the power of her ancestors pass onto her. Centuries of Tryan knowledge and skills radiated through her. She was the last of the Rochfort clan—a Legacy.

Her Charm and the powers of her entire clan would be unstoppable.

Her smile stretched across her pale face. One chapter of her life had ended, and now, another more ruthless and unforgiving one would begin

Chapter 20

"IT'S NEVER LASTED THIS LONG." Queen Aria stood on her covered balcony watching the storm rage on, its waves looking more like a wall of water prepared to crash into her castle.

The waves of the sea roiled and crashed along the silver rocks behind the Orenian palace that hovered in the sky, hundreds of feet above land.

She looked on in horror. The waves were higher than she'd ever seen. She feared that they might actually reach the palace.

"Are you seeing this, Yoska?"

"I'm sure it'll pass." Yoska's white wings reflected the light of the moon as he flew to the balcony and stood on the stone railing. "I do find it odd that I didn't encounter the storm until I reached Oren."

"Is Oren the only kingdom affected by this storm?"

"I can't say for sure. But, it does seem that way. I'd have to go investigate to be certain."

"What is happening?" She turned to walk back into her bedroom, and Yoska followed. He flew past her and landed on her plush red lounge chair.

"What did Liam say when you went to him?" Aria wrapped a soft, blanket around her shoulders and pulled her legs under her.

"After I told him about the girl being The Flame, his determination was renewed."

"The Ancients were right. Liam and Lilae are bonded. Out of all the other Chosen, they are the most connected. We've never heard a single word from the Silver Elves. When will they reveal who The Steel is?"

"Perhaps something is keeping them from stepping forward."

Aria sat on her chair and picked up a cup of tea. She nodded and sipped the ginger spiced liquid. "I'd very much like their support. This war is as much theirs as it is ours."

"Indeed."

She took another sip, hoping it would settle her stomach. She winced, and Yoska moved closer to her. His dark eyes searched her face. For a moment, Aria thought that he looked worried.

"What is it? Are you ill?"

Aria shook her head. "It's nothing," she assured him, ignoring the pain in her belly. She sat the cup down and rested her head on the back of the chair.

Banging on Aria's outer chamber sent chills up her spin. After a quick glance at Yoska, Aria was on her feet. She hurried over to the door and opened it. Four of her soldiers waited outside.

Her brows furrowed, as she looked the soaked soldiers over. "What is it?"

The leader stepped forward and bowed. "Sergeant Strongbow, my Queen. Please forgive us, but it simply couldn't wait."

"Come, let's get you some tea," she motioned for them to come inside.

They stepped into her sitting room with muddy boots.

"Mindy," Aria called. "Get more cups and some fresh tea. And send for Lord Franco."

Mindy gave a quick bow and hurried to obey her orders. Aria watched her scurry down the red-carpeted corridor and turned to the soldiers.

Each man was visibly shaken, his body tense, eyes wide.

She propped the door open and entered her study.

"Please sit. Tell me everything."

Strongbow cleared his throat and looked at her with deep-set blue eyes. "Elders, my Queen. We saw them outside the gates."

Aria's face paled. "What?" She slumped into the nearest chair.

"Nearly a dozen Elders—in their true form stand outside the gates."

"Like shadows," a soldier said, looking up at Aria. "Horrifying sight, Queen Aria."

The Ancients had told her nothing about the Elders roaming the lands. Why were they congregating outside her city?

Wexcyn had destroyed the majority of the Elders years ago. Only a few had escaped his takeover of the Underworld.

"It's unheard of for the living to see them," Yoska said.

It could only mean one thing.

The Elders were waiting for death. A lot of it.

Mindy entered the room with a tray. The soldiers accepted hot cups of tea and nodded thanks to her.

Lord Franco arrived in a huff. He stood in the doorway, his staff pointed at the soldiers.

"This is unheard of, your highness," he called to Aria. His face was twisted in disgust as he looked at the soldiers. "It's simply improper to host men in your chambers like this. Especially soldiers. Who told you that you could come up here?"

"Calm down, Franco. They know the rules, but I commend them for coming straight to me."

Lord Franco pursed his lips. He was much older, with long gray hair and a thick gray beard. His blue robes swished as he stepped inside.

"What could be so urgent?"

"Elders," Aria answered, and his bushy brows stood up in surprise.

"They wait outside the gate, in the darkness of the forest. They don't speak. They don't move. They simply wait." Strongbow looked toward the open door that led to Aria's sleeping quarters. They could see the sky brightening outside her balcony.

"Aria," Yoska said. "I hear something coming."

"What is it?"

Yoska tilted his head. "I'm not sure. I will go check it out." He lifted himself into the air without a word and flew from the room and out the balcony door.

Not yet. Please. Not yet.

Her eyes fixed on the storm outside. Thunder crashed, and lightning followed.

Aria didn't want to admit it, but it was happening—one of her worst fears.

Wexcyn was making his move.

Lord Franco shook his head. He rested both hands on his staff. "Elahe save us."

The sky became green, two layers of clouds crossing paths, highlighting a faint light from the moon. A sound even louder than the thunder resonated throughout the entire kingdom. It sounded as if the entire world was cracking into two, and it was.

The ground split below, and they trembled above.

Doom had arrived to make her people suffer, and Aria could do nothing about it.

Everyone rose to their feet.

Their hands went to the hilts of their swords, but Aria knew that weapons would be useless against what was coming to destroy them.

A roar came from the sky.

The ground rumbled, and Aria tensed.

Please. Don't abandon us now.

Silence.

The Ancients had warned Aria.

There would be no more communication between her world and the Overworld.

The palace shifted, sending everything from the shelves on the wall to the floor as the palace continued to make its descent to the ground. What once floated serenely close to the clouds met the soil, crushing those who were beneath it in the courtyard.

"Wait," Lord Franco said. "It might not be over."

Another blow never came, and Aria crawled to the balcony.

She had to see what had assaulted her ancestral home—the home Liam would one day rule.

Aria stood at the stone railing of her balcony and looked from the calm sky to the sea. The palace was at the edge of the sea and level with the ground. Soldiers and servants waited, watching the sky in a daze, and her gaze followed theirs.

Aria held her breath.

There was a hum as a cloud of smoke descended upon Oren until it was lost in a thick fog.

PART TWO

Chapter 21

FAINT CHANTING MADE Emperor Kavien risk opening his eyes.

Exhaustion had taken over days ago, but he would try to reach Lilae once more. He needed her, but he knew it wasn't Lilae chanted those words. It continued as if to taunt him with its haunting beauty.

While his body remained frozen in a death-like curse, he still controlled one of his powers. Therefore, he peered outside of his mind to places only his mental powers could reach. *Any* escape from this nightmare was worthwhile.

He stood up from his place on the cold, wet floor and pounded his fist into the wall. His hand bounced away from the wall of visions, and he stumbled back disoriented.

He pounded on the wall of his own mind's Sight, a place of darkness and dread, where The Horrors awaited.

Kavien's mother would lock him in an empty wardrobe and make him stay there in the dark. He had been five years old the first time—right after Wexcyn first visited him in his dreams.

Young Kavien would sit there miserable in the dark for hours, with those voices, trying to focus. Not until he could see her and speak to her when she was halfway to the other side of their home would she let him out.

"What are you doing?" Kavien asked as he finally located the source of the chanting.

Sona stopped abruptly. "What was that?" Realization filled her blue eyes. "Oh. It's you, Emperor."

Kavien watched Sona straddle a man in the middle of an abandoned street somewhere that looked much different from Avia'Torena.

A tight grin formed as she plucked an eye from the young man's head, all the while ignoring his shrill screams of terror.

"Why haven't you arrived with the antidote yet?"

"Wexcyn needs me here in Kyril. You will have to wait."

Just as he'd feared. His father was going to make him suffer.

Punishment. That's what this curse was.

Kavien slumped to the floor.

The curse Sister Eloni had put on him had ruined his plans of escape with the woman he loved. Now, he had no idea if Lilae was alive, dead, or if she truly knew how much he cared about her.

"Why are you tormenting that man?"

His eye sockets were congealed with crimson blood. She dug a finger into the pool, and his body began to jerk.

"Nikolaj deserves everything I've done to him. I wouldn't expect you to understand."

Sona stood and kicked the dying man with a booted foot. Nikolaj didn't make a sound. She looked to the sky as her muddy heel crushed the young man's throat. Then, she rubbed her hands together, smearing the blood over her knuckles.

"They say that you are the presumed ruler of the entire New World. And yet, you cannot control your own mind. What do The Horrors say to you, Emperor?"

The Horrors were the voices that had haunted Kavien since childhood. A weaker man would have been driven mad by now. He thought he would have been lost to the world if Lilae hadn't taught him to resist their constant torment.

He watched Sona glance over her shoulders at the dead bodies strewn over the dirt roads. A green fog that enveloped her, making her look like a ghost as she stood there white as snow and dressed in all black. Her black hair, wild and loose, blew away from her face in the wind.

"Where are you?" Kavien looked out into the world she was in.

His body was paralyzed back in the palace, and people he didn't trust were left to roam his palace unchallenged.

"This was Evans Glade. It's a small city on the outskirts of Oren. It's where I grew up. I'm almost done here. Then I shall head to the capital of Oren." Sona paused and looked up. "Emperor?"

Kavien looked out at the sun setting above her. The world outside taunted him. "What?"

"I killed The Storm—even though I loved him. Why didn't you kill The Flame? Did you love her? Were you too weak to end her life?"

Kavien was silent. Perhaps he was weak. He let Lilae get under his skin and into his heart.

Still, despite his current plight, he didn't regret it. Love was a mysterious thing to him. But, Kavien would do it again.

"I've been ordered to kill her." Sona's eyes started to glow for just a moment as she fingered her dagger's blade.

His fists clenched at the thought of anyone harming Lilae. Still, he kept silent. It would be unwise to reveal his plans and thoughts.

Somehow, he would protect the woman he loved.

Kavien broke the connection between their minds, unwilling to hear her speak ill of Lilae any longer.

The darkness of his mind let the fear return. It crept onto him like a spider, making his flesh tighten as he listened to the silence.

The silence didn't last long.

Scratching on the floor sent shivers up his nude body. The distinctive scurrying of feet made him tense. Cold, slimy hands reached and grabbed him.

Kavien held his breath as if he was going under water.

His eyes widened in terror as those hands began scratching and clawing at him.

"Get off me."

The laughing became more of a roar that made his skin crawl with such dread that tears burned his eyes.

"Kah Vi Ennn."

The voices were no longer just voices.

In this cursed place—the darkest depths of his mind—The Horrors were real.

Chapter 22

"TRY SOME LAKTI SAUCE on your lamb," the Shadow Elf woman said to Liam with a smile of pride.

Nearly as tall as Liam, with shoulder length red hair, the older woman stood behind a serving table filled with bowls and serving platters of food that all looked new to Liam. Everything smelled appetizing, so he nodded.

"I'll try it," Liam said.

"Trust me, you'll enjoy it. It has just enough mint to bring out the truest of flavors."

Standing in the serving line of the Citadel dining hall, Liam and Rowe simply let her ladle the sauce onto their lamb and bread.

"Food is food," Rowe said as they carried their oval iron bowls to the seating area. Elves of all ages came to the Citadel daily for food and drinks.

It had been nearly a week since they'd arrived in Gollush, and the elves were getting used to them being out in public, mixing in with their culture.

Liam even wore a traditional Valhoran tunic. Rowe, on the other hand, washed his heavy Orenian clothes daily, citing that the Shadow Elf clothing wasn't tall, or wide, enough.

They sat together before an open archway that looked out on the green river that flowed through the cavern. Women and children dressed in white clothing bathed in its waters, pouring the cool water onto each other and swimming back and forth.

The men sat on the rocks on both sides, fishing for the mystical red-sparkled fish that resembled lizards.

"Makes you think of the Silver River, doesn't it?"

Liam nodded and took a bite of his bread. It was soft and chewy, with a nutty flavor. "It does. I do miss home sometimes."

Rowe nodded. "We will return when all of this is over."

"Yes, we will. And Cammie will have your little one in her arms, ready to hug Papa Rowe," Liam said with a chuckle.

Pretica entered the dining hall, and everyone grew quiet.

Liam was broken from his thoughts when she sat next to him. He looked up from his half-eaten plate to see her heading straight for them.

He sat up, his forehead creasing. "Everything okay?"

Pretica, dressed in a dress instead of her usual pants and simple shirts, sat beside Liam. She hooked her legs over each side of the row seat, the sides of her dress clinging to her thighs.

"Thought I'd join you two," Pretica said before motioning for one of the ladies that poured the drinks.

"Of course," Liam said. "We were just finishing up. I was going to check on Lilae."

"You should let her rest," Pretica said. "She is in good hands."

"She is," Liam agreed. "Still, I like to check on her myself."

Pretica dipped her finger into Liam's food. "I see you tried our famous Lakti sauce," she said, using her long tongue to lick the dripping sauce from her long finger. Her eyes met Liam's. "What do you think?"

"It's quite bland," Rowe said, breaking Pretica's focus on Liam.

She shrugged. "Can't please them all, can you?"

A young woman with long black hair braided into two braids bowed to Pretica, her head nodded down to her knee and hands stretched behind her as she did so.

"What would you like, Chief Pretica?"

"Three mugs of ale for myself and the Tryans."

Liam and Rowe exchanged looks.

"I don't drink ale," Liam said.

"Well, mead? Wine?"

"None. I'll take more water, please," Liam said to the woman.

"I'll take his ale," Rowe added.

"Very good," she said and hurried off to fulfil their order.

"A man that doesn't drink anything but water," Pretica said with a light laugh. "That's something I've never heard of. You are an odd one, Prince Liam."

"That's what they all say," Rowe said. "He is. And that's what makes Liam here a gem amongst stones."

"I can see that," Pretica said, tapping her long nails on the table.

"Any news about your stolen sister?"

Pretica stopped tapping the table and gave Rowe a heated glare. "No, and I would rather not have her mentioned."

Liam's brow rose. "Why?"

Sadness filled Pretica's eyes. "I need to be strong for my people. Thinking of what those nasty Bellens are doing to her makes me lose sight of our plans. Ayoki is strong. She will survive. And I have faith in Vaugner's assassin."

Liam's face softened. He could understand that. The role of a leader was a difficult one. Showing any signs of weakness could be disastrous for morale.

"There is comfort in that," Liam said. "I'm sure she's all right. She is the Seer after all."

"Right," Rowe said, pulling Liam's plate over to his end. "You're done?"

Liam grinned. "Yes. Go on," he chuckled.

Rowe took a bite of Liam's leftover lamb. "I understand all that," he said with a stuffed mouth. "But why didn't her Seer powers help her against the Bellen's? They're just a bunch little ladies with a bit of magic." He chewed and swallowed. "Nothing like what a Chosen is supposed to be able to do."

Pretica grimaced. "They are more than just a bunch of little ladies with magic. And it is complicated. Ayoki refuses to use her power."

That last bit intrigued Liam. "Why?"

Pretica glanced at him. "Enjoy your meal, gentlemen. I'm needed elsewhere."

Liam nodded, but he suspected that Pretica hid something from them as she got up and walked back out the main entrance.

The young woman returned with three mugs of mead and set them on the table.

"Enjoy," she said.

"Ah," Rowe said, pulling all three mugs before him. He took a hearty gulp of foamy ale and licked his lips. "To be drunk in the afternoon."

Chapter 23

WILEM COVERED HIS EYES against the bright sun. The bright light seeped through the slits of his fingers.

He missed his large, plush bed stacked high with satin pillows stuffed with feathers. The soft covers that kept him warm nights when the fire in his bedroom went out. The milk and biscuits his nanny would bring into his room most nights before bed.

His mother's love.

Dread filled his belly whenever he thought of her. One day, they would meet again. In the Underworld and Wilem would apologize and tell her tales of his adventures.

Tears stung his eyes. When would the pain of losing his family fade?

He feared it would be some time before their faces stopped making him wish he could vanish from the world.

Wilem sat up with a deep sigh and glanced back at Vleta. She lay curled up on the edge of the mountain peak that looked over the Silver River.

Vars said that it would be safer to stay high above ground—where they could see in all directions. They didn't want any Shadow Elves sneaking up on them.

Vleta agreed and stayed outside of the amulet to look after everyone.

Wilem doubted that anyone, or anything, would come near them with a dragon around. Her scaled belly was red with heat that warmed Wilem and Jorge.

Jorge stirred in his sleep.

Wilem wondered if he missed his mother as well. He never spoke of the palace cook.

"Morning, Wilem," Vleta said, uncoiling, sitting up, as tall as the trees that used to make up Raeden's forests.

"Good morning, Vleta."

"The fairies left to go find fish."

Jorge sat up and rubbed his eyes. "Breakfast?"

Wilem grinned. "I thought you were asleep?"

Jorge yawned. "I heard Vleta mention food," he said with a shrug.

Wilem chuckled. "Did you sleep well?"

"We are lucky to have a dragon to protect us. She makes me feel safe and warm like the stove I used to sleep next to. Thank you, Vleta."

Vleta licked a talon. "You're welcome."

Jorge drank from his water flask. "I was dreaming about beef stew and fresh bread. But, fish is fine with me."

"Beef stew," Wilem said, leaning back to rest on Vleta. "That does sound good. Your mother's red sauce and noodles were my favorite."

Jorge pursed his lips and nodded. His voice lowered, his blue eyes looking down at the Silver River.

Wilem sighed. He wished he hadn't brought up Jorge's mother up. "How long before we make it to the Silver Elf realm?"

"We are not far. Alfheim is just beyond the White Plains of Ilwisone. It is going to get colder, little master."

Wilem nodded, already chattering despite Vleta's body heat. He had the power of Creation, and he wished he could make something to keep them warm.

Jorge didn't even have on shoes, let alone warm cloaks.

Wilem patted Vleta's belly. He forced a smile. "At least we have you to keep us warm, Vleta."

Jorge stood and walked over to the woodpile. He tossed sticks from a pile onto the waning fire. He knelt before it and warmed his hands. Leaves and twigs stuck out of his brown hair that had grown past his ears and into his eyes.

"More fire, please," Jorge said.

Vleta extended her neck toward the fire. "Step back, please."

Jorge moved backward, careful not to get too close to the ledge.

Wilem ran his hand through his own hair. He was lucky that no one would see the King of Raeden with tangles in his hair and dirt on his face.

"Ah," Vars said as he and Ved flew back from beneath the ledge, fish hanging from a string. "You're all up just in time for breakfast."

"We caught enough fish for everyone, even the dragon," Ved said, pride on his face as he pulled up a long string of shining green fish and placed them next to the smooth stone beside the fire. "And I found some frost berries."

"What is a frost berry?" Wilem rose to his feet to get a better look at the berries that Ved pulled from his side pouch.

They looked like blueberries encased in ice.

"They are good," Ved said, his gray eyes meeting Wilem's. "A bit sour like green apples, but tasty nonetheless."

Wilem popped one into his mouth. The burst of flavor made him wince.

"They are sour," he said, puckering his cheeks.

Vars chuckled. "Eat up. They will give you energy. We have a long day of traveling ahead."

Wilem took a handful and sat next to the fire.

"I'd say we will be in Alfheim in a few more days. We just have to follow the Silver River to the white gates. All of the fairies are welcome in Rargard."

Wilem raised a brow. "How? Why? Silver Elves are not our allies."

Vleta used a talon to take a fish and use her teeth to pull it from the string. She swallowed it whole. "We aren't going to the Silver Elves, Master."

Wilem ate more. He chewed them, blue juice running down his chin. "I don't understand."

Ved sat beside him, stringing the fish up on a spit. "You didn't know? Rargard is a city full of hybrids."

"What is a hybrid?" Jorge folded his arms across his chest for warmth.

"You two must not listen to your lessons," Vars said with a laugh.

"In this case, the hybrid we speak of is a mixed race of fairy and elf. Before the Great War, fairies and elves were friendly with each other."

Wilem's eyes widened. "Holy Elahe. I didn't know such a thing was possible."

Ved put a hand on his shoulder. "In Ellowen, anything is possible."

Chapter 24

DELIA LED THE WAY, her staff outstretched before them, casting a glow that lit the overgrown path beneath her and Liam's feet.

Though Lilae rested, seemingly peaceful, Liam worried that he shouldn't have left her side. Rowe was there; he would protect her. Liam had to be content with that fact. There was no one he trusted more than his old general.

How many times had Rowe saved his life, stood by his side in dire situations, and left his family to accompany him on the most dangerous journey of their lives?

Gollush's front gate was far behind as they walked farther into the surrounding dark woods. The charred trees were tall, the tops fading into the night sky. The air was hot and humid, filled with the sounds of nocturnal creatures.

"Just a little bit farther," Delia whispered.

Liam's eyes scanned the left and right. He had the distinct feeling that they were being watched. He had faith that Delia knew where she was going, but the hairs on his flesh rose at the thought of unknown creatures that waited in the darkness, ready to strike.

After crunching on dead leaves and twigs for what felt like much longer than they'd actually been trekking, Delia led him to an old, abandoned temple.

"Here it is," she said, stopping just before the old stone steps.

Liam waited beside her, his eyes taking in the sight of the ruins. Crumbled stone, broken pillars, and dark windows awaited them.

"This is it?"

Delia turned her gaze to him and nodded. "It is." She rested her weight on her staff and sighed. "This is where Dragnor was born and raised. He trained here and ultimately became the temple's grand master."

Intrigued, Liam took his first step onto the stairs.

"Careful," Delia warned. "Dark magic still lingers here."

Liam looked back. "Wasn't he dead for centuries before Wexcyn brought him back?"

"Yes. But dark magic can remain alive until the end of the world. It is not to be trusted or taken lightly."

"What am I supposed to do here?"

Delia pointed her staff to the front door that looked as if it had been broken down. The light shot toward the inside, illuminating the entire building.

"Inside, there should be a black book made of elven flesh. Find it, and bring it to me."

"You aren't coming?"

"I will stay behind and keep watch." Her eyes turned to the forest that encircled the ruins. The trees rustled as a breeze blew from the mountains. "There are many that do not want us here."

Liam rubbed his hands together and nodded. The air felt tight as if it urged them to leave. Not even the forest wanted them there.

"Right," Liam said under his breath. "I can do this."

Delia lifted a quizzical brow. "You have to. Lilae may not survive without that book." She took a step toward Liam, her finger pointed at his face. "We must attempt to counteract the curse he's drawn into her flesh."

The notion of Lilae not surviving was enough to send Liam running up those stairs, but he had to be cautious. Dark magic was not something he was used to meddling with.

The power inside of him was god-given and pure, not a spell contrived from darkness and evil—not the kind of arts the Bellens practiced.

Quiet filled his mind as he tried to tune into his senses. He stepped over stones and deteriorated wood as he entered the temple. Delia's light cast a glow on everything, making it easy to navigate his way into the main room that closely resembled the temples in Oren.

A red altar stood before a black wall with symbols much like the ones of Lilae's tattoo painted over every inch. Tattered rugs were scattered on the floor for people to sit and listen as the Dark Clerics gave their speeches.

Statues of the Shadow Elf god, Inora, lay in pieces on the stone floor. He looked up, following vines that had wrapped themselves around the columns and beams to the domed ceiling that had a gaping hole in it.

The air was thick with the smell of mildew and a faint hum—as if someone was right behind him, breathing in his ear.

Liam tensed.

He was certain that someone other than Delia watched him, and it made his skin crawl. Liam looked around and saw nothing but artifacts strewn about.

"Try to be quick," Delia called from outside.

Liam looked back at her. She sounded farther away than she was. Her voice was muffled.

Warnings filled Liam's gut.

Go.

Liam's eyes widened. A smile crossed his face at hearing his old friends.

The Winds.

"Go where?"

He spun around as if he might catch sight of one of the spirits who had guided him since childhood.

Lilae. Go.

Liam pursed his lips. His back straightened.

"What about Lilae?"

Delia's light went out, leaving Liam in darkness.

Something creaked behind him: A loose floorboard, or a door. Liam glanced back to see a shadow cross past the archway at the back of the room.

Fear gripped Liam's throat.

Dark magic.

It wasn't something he was prepared to meddle with.

But Lilae. She needed him.

Liam ran the palm of his hand down his face and sucked in a deep breath.

He looked back.

Delia was gone.

Liam ran for the door, and some unseen force grabbed him by the shirt and threw him far across the room to the archway where he'd seen the shadowy figure.

"Delia," Liam called, getting to his feet. He drew his sword, not quite sure what use it was against an evil spirit.

Silence.

Liam held his breath, listening.

Delia's light returned, and with it the vision of a Shadow Elf standing before him.

The color drained from Liam's face as he beheld the being. There was no doubt in his mind that the elf was not alive.

Dark eyes, dark skin, a svelte body under black robes with long black hair.

And a snarl.

"You're The Storm," the Shadow Elf said. He lifted his head, looking down his nose at Liam. "I expected more. Not the frightened boy before me."

Liam's heart pounded—not with fear—but with realization.

Realization turned to rage.

His eyes glared at the elf.

"Dragnor."

The Shadow Elf took a step forward. "You've heard of me," he said. "And yet you still came to my temple. My house. I should kill you right now. The spells I've left behind will do it for me. And then I can kill that temptress in Gollush."

Liam pointed his sword at Dragnor's nose. "You touch her, and I will skin you alive," he said through clenched teeth."

Dragnor grinned. "But you can't, boy. I'm not here with *you.*"

Liam lifted a brow.

"*I'm with Lilae.*"

A gasp escaped Liam's lips. He ran through Dragnor's body as if he were composed of nothing but cold air. The room was empty when Liam spun around.

Lilae!

Once outside, he saw Delia standing there, a look of surprise on her face.

"What is it? Did you find the book?"

"Forget the book," Liam said. "Dragnor has Lilae."

He ran into the forest, unsure of where he was going and hoping Delia would hurry and lead the way, when a blast behind forced him to stop.

No, Liam thought with dread.

Lilae. Go.

The Winds had tried to warn him.

Delia sped past Liam.

"Come," she said, seeming to float on air as she headed toward Gollush.

Liam nodded and ran into the darkness of the forest as the temple burned.

Chapter 25

"YOU WILL WISH YOU WERE DEAD," Dragnor hissed into Lilae's ear.

His hot breath made her shudder.

Strapped down to a cold stone altar, Lilae wanted nothing more than to get up and run, but her body wouldn't obey.

This dream—or whatever alternate reality this was—terrified Lilae.

Once again, her greatest enemy had the ability to manipulate her and do whatever he pleased.

Why couldn't she wake up?

She winced as his sharp dagger traced the tattoo he'd etched into her skin. She watched the blade trail from her breastbone to her navel. The tattoos burned as if her skin had been removed and she'd been patted down with salt.

Dark eyes met hers as he leaned down, an inch from her face.

"If you do not come back to me, Lilae," Dragnor purred. "You will regret it. I will not stop until I have you back."

She twitched, refusing to cry out as the pain increased tenfold.

"I will not," Lilae said through clenched teeth. "You will be the one to wish you were dead."

"Is that so? What about those you love and care about? What if I exert my rage on them?" His breath was hot on her ear. "What if I kill Kavien while he sleeps?"

Her door burst open, waking her.

"*Kavien*," she said into the darkness.

"Lilae," Liam called. "Are you all right?"

Lilae's eyes popped open.

Lilae's entire body tingled with the after effects of Dragnor's curse. Her stomach churned, as she processed what she'd just learned.

Her breaths came out too quickly as she sat up in her bed. She ripped the blanket off, desperate to cool her sweaty skin.

"Liam?"

"I'm here," he said.

"Where is Delia? Dragnor—" Lilae paused, shooting up in bed to search the room. "He visited my dreams." She tried to get out of bed.

"No," Liam said. "Please, lay down and rest. You need to conserve your energy."

Delia stepped inside the small room. She knelt down beside Lilae and took her hand into hers. The lines in her forehead were creased as her blue eyes looked over Lilae's face.

"What is it? What happened, Lilae?"

Lilae tucked a chunk of red hair behind her ear, shaking her head.

"I don't know, exactly. From the first night, I could feel something…like an itch trying to get inside my head."

Liam folded his arms across his body. "Why didn't you tell anyone?"

Every night since her escape, Dragnor was there.

Waiting.

And each night, Liam was by her side.

Protecting her—healing her the same way he did in their dreams.

"I wasn't sure what it was," Lilae said with a shrug. She wiped her forehead of sweat. She fixed her eyes on her hands. "But, tonight was different."

Her eyes flickered up from her hands, past Delia to the dim light out in the hallway. "Dragnor was here. He hurt me. He threatened me, and it *all* felt real."

Delia and Liam shared a look.

"What?" Lilae sensed something had transpired while she was recovering from the affects of the curse.

Liam sighed as he rubbed his chin. "I'll tell you all about it," he said, turning to Delia. "Can I speak with you outside?"

Lilae pursed her lips as Delia and Liam left her room.

She stretched her legs, tired of being bedridden. It had only been a week, but she hated feeling so useless. Dragnor wanted her. She needed to find a way to free herself from his curse.

"Lilae," Liam called when he returned.

"Where did Delia go?"

"She went to bed," he said, taking his shirt off.

Lilae averted her eyes but didn't say a word.

"Delia and I went to a temple tonight. Dragnor's temple."

Lilae's eyes widened. "What?"

"Yes," he said, taking off his boots and setting them neatly beside the door.

The only light came from a candle whose light was moments away from burning out. Liam's sculpted body made it hard to think straight.

Darkness.

Curses.

A handsome half-naked man is in my room.

She wasn't sure what vexed her more.

"We were looking for his old spell book so that we could destroy it. But, he knew we were there, and destroyed the temple and everything inside."

The revelation was startling. The only hope for breaking Dragnor's curse was probably nothing but ash.

Liam crossed the small room and got into bed with her.

Despite everything that had occurred in her dream, Liam's presence alone made it all melt away. Lilae looked down at Liam as he rested on his elbow. His bright blue eyes were full of concern, and she wanted nothing more than to lie back down and cradle her head in his arms.

She bit her lip, conflicted by having Liam in her bed while her heart broke for what Dragnor threatened to do to Kavien.

"Delia knows we've been sharing a bed," Liam said.

Lilae nodded. "She knows everything. It's fine. I should have told her. We aren't doing anything wrong. I just feel safe with you. During all I went through, you were always there for me."

Liam reached for her, helping her back to the feather-filled pillow.

"There is nothing he can do to hurt you, Lilae. He can try his best to scare you, but you are stronger than that. Don't let him affect your waking hours."

Lilae sighed. "You're right."

"Why did you say Kavien?"

She tensed, avoiding his eyes.

"When I came in, you whispered his name."

Could she tell Liam the truth? Was she naïve enough to think Liam felt anything for her beyond their predestined bond?

He is *in my bed.* She met his eyes full on. *He has to feel something.*

But was she certain of how she felt?

"Dragnor threatened to kill him unless I came back to Avia'Torena."

After a moment of silence, Liam's eyes narrowed.

"Lilae."

"Yes?"

"Do you care for Emperor Kavien?"

She turned away from him, unable to face his question. Her eyes fixed on the flickering flame of the candle as it began to die. The question was so layered that she truly didn't know what to say.

Kavien was her first kiss.

He was also the man who kept her in a chest beside his bed.

The man who let Dragnor put the curse on her.

The man she missed despite it all.

"You're not going to answer me?"

"I do—I did. I don't know," she said, her words not making sense. Her stomach churned again, and she squeezed her eyes shut. "He was kind to me in the end. He wanted to leave the empire behind. With me."

She couldn't look Liam in the eyes.

"Lilae," he said, taking her hand into his. "Look at me."

Trembling, Lilae looked at Liam. "Yes?"

He stroked her cheek with his thumb. "I understand. Don't be ashamed by what happened to you or your feelings. I thought I would spend the rest of my life with Sona. At least Kavien didn't betray you and try to take your life. You are fortunate, and don't ever apologize for it."

Lilae's lips parted.

Who was this man before her?

Was it possible for anyone to be so good?

She leaned down and pressed her forehead to his. She closed her eyes, and they remained like that for a moment, before Lilae took a chance and kissed Liam on the lips.

Nothing mattered at that moment, just the feel of his lips against hers. And then he pulled her onto his body so that she straddled him.

Liam's arms wrapped around her in a tight embrace as their kiss deepened, erasing any doubts she had in her mind that Liam was the one her heart yearned for.

Still, she cared for Kavien and wanted no harm to come to him. She loved him still, but this—what she felt for Liam—filled every crevice of her heart with joy, a joy she'd never feel ashamed to reveal.

She moaned as he parted her lips with his tongue, tasting her mouth. Warm and wet, his tongue tasted of cinnamon and sugar from the pastries Valhorians were famed for baking.

Heat raced up her body as he cradled her head in both hands. Places that had only been awakened once before ached with need. This ache was different. As Lilae's most sacred spots pulsed—she enjoyed it.

She craved more.

Liam placed her on her back and rested on his elbow beside her, his face in his hand as he looked down at her.

Lilae's chest rose and fell with quick breaths.

He smiled at her.

"I wanted to do that the moment I saw you at The Barrier."

Lilae nodded, captivated by his eyes. "I did too."

He leaned down to kiss her again and then pulled her body into his.

"We need to rest," he said. "Tomorrow is our last day here."

A part of her wanted him to continue, to kiss her until dawn, but he was right.

Lilae nodded, closing her eyes.

Lilae's body relaxed. She'd never felt so safe and sure in her life, even as a little warning in her gut threatened to wedge its way into her confidence.

Chapter 26

LIAM RESISTED THE URGE to hold Lilae's hand and help her from her chair with wooden wheels.

He watched her stand, tense and ready to come to her aid. But, she managed to come to her feet gracefully.

"How are you feeling today?"

Rowe asked the question that Liam had been thinking since Lilae decided she was ready to join the Council in Gollush's meeting hall.

"I'm fine," she said, taking a deep breath as she took in the setting before her.

The eyes of seven high-ranked Shadow Elves joined Liam in watching her stride from her chair at the entrance of the massive room to the circular stone table in the center.

Liam pulled out a chair for her and sat back in the seat beside her.

"Are you sure you're okay to be up and about again?"

"I am starting to feel like myself again, Liam. Thanks to you."

Lilae's smile reminded Liam of the moment he'd never forget. Simply lying in bed with her had been a true gift. The smell of her hair would be a welcome scent he would never forget.

Rowe gave Liam a wink and a nudged him in the side of his ribcage.

"We are pleased that The Flame is able to join us," Pretica said. She remained standing after the other men and women sat around the large table. "Today, we have Chief Matsuharu, Chief Keiko, Grand Master Neru, Lord and Lady Song, Chief Altan, and Master Soh. Elder, Delia has brought together Liam: The Storm, Lilae: The Flame, and Rowe— a Tryan warrior."

Liam couldn't help exchanging a smirk with Rowe.

Tryan warrior, indeed.

How *elite* Pretica made him sound.

Liam shook his head. He knew better than most that Rowe was much more than just a warrior.

"Please bow in a show of mutual respect."

Everyone bowed their heads. Then, they resumed sharing curious looks at one another from over full goblets of wine and water.

Liam took each Shadow Elf in—watching their every move. He still wasn't sure if Shadow Elves could be fully trusted. Any one of the assembled councilmen could be spies or assassins.

"Elder, Delia has some news she'd like to share."

Delia stood and tapped her staff on the table.

The eyes of the Shadow Elves widened when Delia's staff sent a glow into the center of the table and opened into a flickering scene that looked much like a hazy dream.

Liam leaned forward. His eyes narrowed.

"Is that Oren?" Rowe's question was laced with disbelief. The usual humor in his voice was gone. His face turned ashen as his eyes widened at the scene before them.

Delia pursed her lips and nodded. "It is. Oren is just one of the many kingdoms under attack."

The blood drained from Liam's face as he looked at the dead bodies strewn around the streets of his kingdom. Soldiers and citizens in brown uniforms worked to remove the bodies, tossing them into carts. He rose from his seat, leaning across the table for a better look.

"Klimmerick's Row." Liam swallowed back a lump in his throat. "What is happening?"

"What you see here is Wexcyn's first stage of an attack on Ellowen," Delia said, her voice grave. "A plague has been set free. Sickness will spread through all of the major kingdoms of our world.

Until the weak are gone, and the strong are weakened. This is how he will reduce the number of those opposing his rule."

"We have to do something," Liam said, his heart thumping in his chest. His people were dying. He looked away, his troubled eyes meeting Rowe's. "We have to go back and help them."

Rowe nodded.

"There is nothing you can do for them right now, Liam. The sickness will spread and do its job. What we must do is find an antidote that will cure those who suffer from this affliction."

Imagining his mother laying in her bed, ill with a deadly plague made him want turn, leave, and find a horse. Oren was an ocean and thousands of miles away and, yet he would find a way.

Liam tried to keep his composure. "How?"

"We were brought together for a reason. I left my mountain home and vow of solitude to stand against this evil," Grand Master Neru said. His bushy white eyebrows rose. "I am willing to offer my fighting skills and potions to the cause." He folded his hands on the table, his thin eyes narrowing to slits. "My knowledge of potions is only surpassed by Vaugner's knowledge of curses."

"Exactly. Vaugner is proficient in the dark arts of the Underworld. We need a combination of both to stop the plague that threatens our entire world."

"We are lucky to have him on our side then," Lilae said, everyone's attention going to her and her soft voice. She looked down at the table, her long hair covering her face—shielding her.

"That is correct," Grand Master Neru said with a nod. "I believe we can make a stand against this threat with his help. When are you going to meet with him?"

Delia took her seat next to Lilae. "We leave tomorrow, Grand Master Neru. I believe it is a few days time on foot. With Lilae strong enough for travel, we have much ground to cover to make up for lost time. Wexcyn and his agents certainly aren't wasting a second while we organize."

He gave the table a single tap. "I'm going with you," he said. "I know Nostfar quite well. I can guide you to where The Barriers used to stand, and together we can enter the Goblin City."

"We welcome you on our journey, Grand Master Neru," Liam said.

"Please, call me Neru."

"Very well." Delia nodded. "We'd be honored to have you accompany us."

Lady Song leaned forward, her bosom pressed against the table. Regal and beautiful in her purple gown, she fixed her dark brown eyes on Delia, her gray skin flawless like porcelain.

"How long before the plague reaches Nostfar? Do we have time to prepare for an outbreak?" Lady Song's thin brows lifted as she looked from Delia to Lord Song, a white-haired elderly Shadow Elf. "We haven't seen a widespread illness since the 2nd century when the dragons passed their fire disease to the Shadow Elves of Evorn."

Delia turned her indigo gaze to Lady Song and lowered her staff, ending the scene of Oren's plight.

"It's already here."

Chapter 27

LILAE FOLLOWED LIAM INTO THE crowd of Shadow Elves. Her stomach was twisted into knots at seeing the fate of Liam's kingdom and the news of the plague.

She had no allegiance to any kingdom. The wild was more her home than any particular place.

"Liam," Lilae called, hoping he would slow down so she wouldn't have to run to keep up with him.

Liam stopped but didn't look back at her.

"Wait," Lilae said, ignoring the incessant burning in her legs.

The Shadow Elves made a path for her as she stepped down the stairs that led from the meeting hall to the main level, which was alive with music and loud chatter. Lilae was well aware that the elves feared her. The tattoos on her skin were a sign of evil, even if it had been applied against her will.

She clenched her jaw, used to ignoring judging looks.

"Are you all right?"

Liam's shoulders slumped. "I just wish there was something I can do. What if my mother is one of the dead?"

Lilae's brows furrowed as she stood in front of him. She took his face in her hands, warmth filling her at their touch. Her heart broke at the sight of tears shimmering in his eyes.

"You'd feel it," she said. "You'd know if your mother was dead."

He lifted his chin and took her hands into his. "Do you really think so?"

"I do. There is no use feeling grief for something you are uncertain of."

Lilae sighed and stepped even closer—so close that her chest was pressed to Liam's. Her eyes sparked with determination as she looked up at him. "We will make things right. I swear it."

Liam's forehead creased as he stared down at her.

Lilae would give anything to know what went through his mind as he looked at her like that. The sounds of chatter at rushing water seemed to dull as they shared a look. She hadn't realized just how close they stood to one another, close enough to feel and hear his soft breaths. Her hands were still within his, and she feared they'd start trembling at any moment.

A flush crept up her face as she imagined him leaning down slightly and kissing her fully on the lips. How she wished, he would.

"I need a drink," Rowe's voice boomed, breaking Lilae from her thoughts. "What do you say, Liam?"

She stepped back and took a deep breath.

"Enjoy, lads. I'm going to try to get some rest."

"Don't go," Liam said. He reached for her hand. "Come, you've been resting for days. We leave tomorrow. You should stretch your legs out a bit."

Lilae glanced down at his hand, a smile threatening to take over her face. "If you insist."

"Of course," Liam said, and she slipped her hand into his.

He held her firmly, and Rowe's eyes lingered on their hands. He flickered a glance from Lilae to Liam, and his forehead creased.

"Did I miss something?"

Lilae chuckled, her cheeks reddening as Rowe stared at them, crossing his arms across his chest.

"Where are we going?" Lilae cleared her throat, hoping to detract from Rowe's quizzical look at her and Liam. "I admit this place is like a maze to me. I haven't been out to explore."

Her eyes scanned the surroundings, feeling tiny amidst the tall buildings that stretched toward the ceiling, which had to be hundreds of feet high. Thousands of Shadow Elves dwelled in Gollush, and at that hour, many of them were out on the city streets, enjoying what were considered their evening hours.

Without a shred of sunlight to be seen, it is hard to distinguish the time. Lilae and the others were beginning to adjust to this new schedule.

Soon, however, they'd be out within the world once more, where danger lurked, and their journey was certain to be filled with peril.

Lilae almost wished they could stay within the safety of Gollush's walls just a bit longer.

She never expected to feel safe around Shadow Elves.

"There is a tavern on the third level, near the west gate," Rowe said, stepping through the path the Shadow Elves made for him. Some elves were almost as tall as Rowe. Still, he towered over them as they passed by. "Just follow me. I'll show you a good time."

Lilae smiled. The promise was alluring. With Liam by her side, there were no doubts that her evening would be better spent at the tavern than in her lonely bed.

With the nightmares.

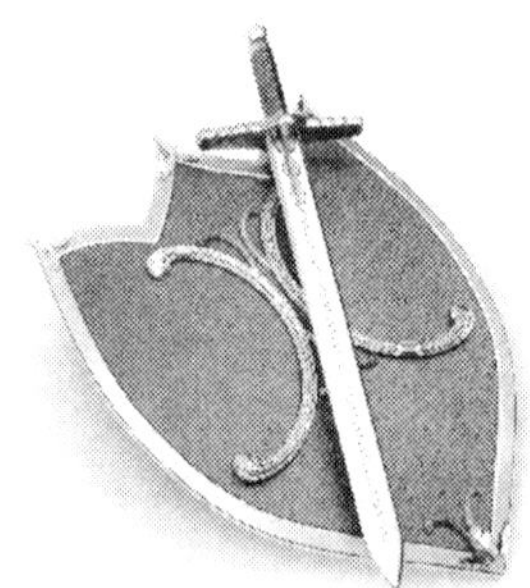

THE INNER CITY OF Gollush bustled with energy. Shadow Elves crowded the streets. Venders were out, setting up shops and carts. Young Shadow Elves stayed together in packs, arms locked and smiles on their faces as they socialized with one another.

Lilae realized that she might actually miss Gollush. She still wasn't used to being stared at all of the time, but Shadow Elves were much friendlier than she'd ever anticipated.

"Would you like a shawl, miss?" A tall shopkeeper in an evergreen dress called to Lilae, her hands outstretched to reveal a beautiful blue piece of fabric embellished with silver embroidery. Her wide smile seemed to take over her oval-shaped face.

"No, thank you." Lilae eyed the garment, almost tempted to touch it. She did miss nice clothing. Growing up as a nomad didn't afford her with pretty dresses or anything of the sort. She and her family lived a simple life, but as a slave, she'd worn only the best dresses and garbs.

"Come now, try it on," the shopkeeper insisted.

Lilae smiled and shook her head. She kept close to Liam as they traveled along a narrow road between two rows of shops that housed what had to be hundreds of families. She noticed that many of the elves were trying to get a better look at the foreigners: she wished they could hurry to their destination.

Having people so close that they could touch made Lilae uncomfortable.

After being in Avia'Torena for nearly a year, Lilae had seen heavily populated areas, but this was different. Gollush was built upward while Kavien's empire was sprawled over an expansive space.

"We have to show her the river," Liam said to Rowe as they stopped at a dead end.

Lilae stood back as they came upon a fork in the road that stretched outward from a fountain with a giant statue of a wyvern in the center, its wings outstretched as if it were about to take flight.

On either side were more roads, shops, and Shadow Elves camped out wherever there was space, chatting and eating from long skewers stacked with delicious smelling meats and vegetables.

"Grand idea," Rowe said. "They say it's good luck to make a wish at the river."

"There's a river *inside* the cavern?"

"Yes." Liam nodded at her, smiling like an excited child, joy at sharing something with her in his eyes. "It is unlike anything you've ever seen."

Lilae put her hands on her hips. A coy smile lifted the corners of her mouth. "How do you know what I've seen? I've been from one end of Eura to the other."

"We'll see then." Liam took her hand, pulling her into his body. In front of everyone, he placed both hands on either side of Lilae's face, fingers laced in her hair, and kissed her.

Lilae's eyes closed as she breathed him in, the kiss sending a flood of cold into her body.

Every kiss from Liam was pure magic.

Liam pulled back and smiled at her, a sparkle in his crystalline blue eyes as his thumb caressed her cheek. For a moment, no one else existed.

"Shall we?" Liam looked at Rowe as he hooked his thumb in his belt.

Lilae blushed as the world returned around her. The sounds, smells, sights had vanished during her magical kiss.

There was no hiding it. Liam was not ashamed of whatever had developed between the two.

Sucking in a breath, Lilae glanced at Rowe.

A smirk was on his face. "This way, you two," he said, leading them down the white stone walkway to the left of the fountain.

Lilae could be lead to a cliff, and she wouldn't have noticed. She floated through the city, a smile fixed on her lips, her cheeks flushed with a deep pink, and a flutter in her belly and heart.

This—what she shared with Liam could never fade. She'd fight for it until her last dying breath.

Her stomach ached then, with fear that something would rip the small glow of happiness from her.

As it always did.

Her face morphed into one of sadness, so much that she almost shed a tear for the prospect of something or someone taking Liam away from her.

Chapter 28

LILAE TOOK OFF HER SHOES and dipped her feet into the river.

"It's cold," she said, yet her smile grew.

Liam sat beside her on the rocks, watching the rushing green water create foam against the large stones that peeked through the surface.

Moonlight spilled into the cavern from a two large holes that resembled nostrils in the low ceiling above. There were several holes like that, all over Gollush that let in just enough moon and sunlight to always light the city, even when the torchlights that littered the streets and window were put out during sleeping hours.

Some days Liam would walk the deserted streets during the day when Shadow Elves were fast asleep in their homes. It was another world during those times. Quiet and serene.

He watched Lilae play in the water, like a child, her wild red hair bouncing as she kicked and splashed.

"What would you wish for? If you believed in that sort of thing?"

Lilae glanced at him. She sighed, shrugging. "I don't know. The only thing I want is my family. I'd wish to bring them back."

Liam nodded. "That is a good wish. I'd wish for Wexcyn to be punished in the land of the gods, once and for all. They say the

Goddess of Law is strict, with enough power to destroy even the most powerful gods."

"Do they?" Lilae splashed water with her feet. "Delia never told me much about the land where all of the gods come from. It does sound exciting."

"I caught one!"

Lilae and Liam turned to Rowe. His pants were rolled up as he stood knee-deep in the river, a sparkling redfish in his large hands.

Lilae giggled as a group of young Shadow Elf women rose from the riverbank and clapped their hands at Rowe. They whistled and laughed, making eyes at the Tryan that towered over their men.

"You did. Looks like we have our dinner," Liam said, clapping his hands.

"And Rowc has some admirers," Lilae added.

Rowe nodded, a grin on his face as he held the fish up into the air. He winked at the group of women dressed in white bathing dresses.

"I'll get the cook at the tavern to fry it up for us. With butter," Rowe said, stalking out of the rushing water. "Lots of butter."

Lilae pulled her feet out of the river. "Sounds good. My stomach is starting to grumble."

"Yes." Liam scratched his chin. "We should get going. We don't want to stay out too late. We have an early start tomorrow."

"Gollush is a beautiful place," Lilae said, turning to him. She sat on a smooth surface and reached for her boots. "But I look forward to reaching Vaugner. He taught Delia. He must be incredible. We can learn so much from him."

"I agree. How many get to meet the original Gatekeeper?"

He stood, and waited for her to put her shoes back on, and extended a hand down to help Lilae to her feet.

She smiled up at him, sprinkles of water on the bridge of her small nose, and reached up to take his hand.

There was something special in her eyes, something Sona never had. The memory of Sona's betrayal made Liam clench his jaw.

It hurt. Even though Sona had merely used him, and never loved him, Liam *had* loved her. For many years. That fact remained, and yet he didn't care anymore.

Liam would do everything he could to keep that loving look Lilae gave him as she accepted his hand and allowed him to pull her to the rocks.

"Thank you for showing this to me," she said, motioning to the river. "I used to swim every morning when I was in Sabron with my family. It was much colder, but not nearly as magical as this water."

"I told you," Liam said.

"Yes, you did." She glanced back at the water, watching red fish rushing through the water, their glittering scales making the water look enchanted.

Rowe approached, dripping with water onto the gray rocks as he held the dead fish with both hands.

"Ready, you two?"

"This way," Liam said. "The Red Room Tavern is close."

He paused when two of the cheering women approached them, covering their giggles behind their hands. They had to be in their early twenties, one with an auburn ponytail that reached the back of her neck, the other with long black hair braided into thin braids that wrapped around a bun on the top of her narrow head.

"My friend," the one with the braids said in between giggles. "Would like to touch your muscles."

Liam snorted. "You hear that, Rowe? Your muscles are more famed here than any title Lilae and I have."

Rowe's face turned red. He lowered his voice as he spoke to the young Shadow Elf women. "You can touch, miss. But that is all. I'm a taken man."

"Oh bother," the shorter one said. "He's *taken*."

She didn't hesitate, wrapping both hands around his bicep. Her green eyes widened.

"It's hard," she exclaimed, and in a tirade of giggles, they ran back to their friends, delighted to have touched the giant Tryan man's muscles.

Rowe looked ahead as Liam chuckled. "Not another word out of you, Liam."

Chapter 29

THE RED ROOM TAVERN was busy and much bigger than Lilae anticipated. Her heart thumped in her chest as she looked at the dozens of Shadow Elves that were packed inside.

Chandeliers hung above, casting a warm light onto the large room. Young and old elves stood in groups or filled the long bench seats on either side of thick wooden tables covered in mugs of cold ale. Attractive women dressed in short belted tunics scrambled to remove tables of empty glasses and refill the mugs of boisterous men and women.

"Table's free at the back," one of the barmaids shouted over the commotion. "I'll swing by in just a bit to tell 'ya the specials of the day."

She sucked in a breath as Rowe and Liam walked in without a care. She was reminded of her first time in The Blind Pig with Anic, the blacksmith's son.

As they crossed the room to one of the only empty tables, Lilae breathed in the smell of roasted chickens and fresh flatbread mixed with the odor of burning red candles as tall as men, standing in pots like flowers.

Beneath the wooden table, Liam put his hand on Lilae's knee and gave it a gentle squeeze.

All sounds seemed to fade as heat rose to her ears.

Lilae tensed, not expecting such a touch. She held her breath as her eyes flickered up to his. Color filled her cheeks as she tried to avoid thoughts of his hands touching more of her, under her clothing. Lilae licked her bottom lip, words evading her.

She tilted her head as their eyes met. The blue of Liam's eyes never ceased to stun her. Such magic should be outlawed, for they always left her weak and conscious of her appearance.

She ran her hand through the tangles of her red hair, missing the ladies that used to groom her in the palace.

The life of a slave wasn't always awful.

"Thank you for joining us," he said, withdrawing his hand to pick up his drink. "We've missed your company while you've been recovering."

Lilae hid her smile with her mug. Rowe had no idea Liam had been joining her in her bed most nights. Just having him near was enough to chase away the evil that threatened to creep upon her each night.

She nodded and took a hearty gulp of her drink. The bitter ale filled her mouth as she drank. She'd made the mistake of drinking too quickly once before.

Now, she took smaller sips, not wanting to lose her senses. She couldn't make a fool of herself in front of Liam, not while he drank cider.

Rowe slammed his mug down and called for the barmaid.

"Another round," he said. His eyes went to Lilae. "Drink up now," Rowe told her, nodding to her almost full mug.

Lilae peered into the amber-colored liquid, the smell strong and acrid.

"I'll try," she said. She couldn't understand why anyone enjoyed the flavor; although she enjoyed the way it relaxed her frazzled nerves. From the smiles and laughter from the other patrons, they seemed to enjoy its effects as well.

"I believe in you, Lilae. You can do it. Just pour it in," Rowe advised with a chuckle. "I'll make a pro out of you."

Lilae shook her head with a smirk. "I'm not sure if that's something I want to be a pro at."

She watched two young elves, maybe slightly older than she, drink from tiny cups. They slammed their cups onto the long wooden tables once they were empty. The young men erupted into laughter.

With all of the ale going around, the Shadow Elves barely glanced at Lilae, Liam, and Rowe. They seemed to be in their own world.

"Cammie will survive," Rowe sputtered, downing his third mug. "I just know it. She's a strong one, you know?"

Liam drank water. He nodded.

"She is, Rowe. She's one of the strongest women I know."

"I'm sure she and the baby made it out," Rowe added. He looked down into his mug, his brows furrowing, deepening the lines in his forehead. "I would very much like to meet my son or daughter. If I could hold it just once, I'd be a happy man."

Rowe has a baby? Lilae hoped he was right. She never imagined having children herself, but the thought of losing one saddened her.

"You will," Liam said.

Lilae nodded. "I hope I get to meet your baby too."

Rowe raised his mug. "Come on," he said. "Raise your mug to my child. Someone to pass my Legacy power to when I die."

Lilae grinned. "I'll raise my mug to that."

"Here, here," Liam said, lifting his water cup.

"No," Rowe said, shaking his head. He called for the closest barmaid. "You are not celebrating my child with water. You will have a man's drink."

Liam chuckled and set his water down on the slick wooden tabletop. "Fine. Just this once."

"Another round of ale," Rowe said to the young barmaid. "And one for my friend here as well."

She nodded with a quick bow and entered the crowd to make her way to the bar.

Lilae smiled. She couldn't imagine what Liam would be like after a drink of Gollush's potent ale. Musicians played their drums loudly. Lilae tapped her toes to the festive beat.

Tomorrow, they would leave this beautiful place, and reenter dangerous territory. She would enjoy this night and worry about their journey ahead later.

The barmaid returned with three more mugs.

Lilae groaned. She didn't know how she would finish both mugs. Her mind already started to blur a bit. Her shoulders and arms felt warm and weak. Ale was like a toxin, one that relaxed and made her anxious at the same time.

"All right," Liam said, lifting his mug. "To your healthy and happy little one."

Lilae grinned. "To Little Rowe," she giggled.

Rowe winked at her, and they all clashed their mugs together before drinking the ice-cold liquid.

Lilae wiped the foam from her mouth and laughed. "I am sure your wife has some good stories about you, Rowe."

"I have some stories about Rowe here," Liam said with a grin. "But I doubt he'd let me tell them."

Rowe finished his first mug of ale. He nodded. "That's right. Not if you don't want a knot on your head.'

Liam chuckled and took another drink. "You're the bigger man, but I have the lightning."

"You can't summon any blasted lightning if you're knocked out with one of these," Rowe said, lifting his giant clenched fists.

Lilae covered her mouth as a loud laugh erupted from her throat. She spoke between hysterics. "But you'd have to take on both of us," Lilae said. "And you wouldn't hit a girl, would you?"

"Is that what you are? A girl? I thought you were a bit more than that."

Lilae began to retort when a Shadow Elf man sat beside her at their table. The table went silent.

She and Liam shared a look, smiles fading.

The tavern was packed; perhaps he simply needed a seat.

But when he turned to Lilae, she knew that wasn't the case.

"Are you really The Flame?"

Rowe and Liam quieted at the young man's question.

Liam's expression darkened.

"Who are you?"

"Kenichi," he said.

Lilae licked her lips. He was starting to blur before her. "Hello, Kenichi. Yes, I am The Flame."

He leaned close to her, his voice a low whisper.

"Where is Ayoki? Are you guys going to do anything to save her?"

Lilae sat up, although her body felt heavy. She cleared her throat. "You're the first person to express any concern about Ayoki, besides Pretica."

He pursed his lips. "Because she means more to me than even her sister."

"Were you close?"

He nodded, his eyes flickering down to the table. "I was the father of her unborn child." He bowed his head.

"Child?" Liam's eyes narrowed. "No one mentioned a child."

Kenichi's head shot up, his eyes blazing with fury. He spoke through clenched teeth. "Because no one knew about our child. How could they? Pretica locked her away once it was known. She killed our child." His voice broke.

Horror flashed in Lilae's eyes. "What?"

"With her poisons," he added. "She killed our child. And I am not going to let her get away with it."

Lilae covered her mouth. No. They'd been tricked. Warnings filled her entire being.

Kenichi took Lilae's hand. His eyes were full of worry and pain. This was the truth, and she scolded herself for not seeing the lies within Pretica's eyes.

"Please," he said. "Come with me to rescue her. Before Pretica kills you as well."

Lilae nodded, biting her lip. "Let's go."

She stood, Liam and Rowe following suit.

The tavern went from loud and boisterous, to a hush, as Pretica, Master Soh, and Chief Keiko stepped through the doors.

There was nothing friendly about their faces as they met the eyes of Lilae, Rowe, and Liam.

They were all armed, Pretica with daggers, Master Soh with his red sword, and Chief Keiko in light armor that fit her curvaceous body. Her hands were held out, encased in a weapon that Lilae had never seen before. Wires were wrapped around her fingers and around her hand, with spikes and curved steel set with sharp blades.

Chief Keiko looked ready for a fight, a grin on her pouty mouth. Cocky and sure of herself, she lead the group, her eyes fixed on Lilae.

The tavern quickly began to grow quieter as everyone started to leave.

Kenichi gave Lilae's hand a squeeze. "We are too late."

Something warm trailed down her chin. Not taking her eyes from Pretica, Lilae took her hand from Kenichi's and wiped her mouth.

Blood stained and dripped from her white fingers.

Ancients help us, she thought as the world began to spin.

Chapter 30

LILAE'S HEART THUMPPED, her breaths quickening as she fought to stay out of the darkness that threatening to overtake her.

No. Not this time. Whatever seeped into her blood was met with flames as she willed her body to stay awake— to not miss the fight.

Liam's gaze met hers, his brows scrunching.

"Do you feel that too?"

Lilae nodded, her movements slower than normal.

"Poison," she said, looking back at Pretica.

Pretica placed her hands on her hips, the hilts of her daggers protruding from her waist belt. "I should have made the barmaid slip more Vorgren in your ale."

"I'd prefer a fair fight," Master Soh said, his dark eyes glowing in the dim torchlight. "There is no honor in weakening your opponent before a battle."

"We don't have time for honor," Pretica said, drawing her daggers.

Lilae's eyes narrowed as the air seemed to move around Master Soh.

"Very well," he said before turning to a pair of women hiding beneath one of the tables. "If you want to live, you will leave," he said to the remaining patrons that stood watching. They didn't have to be told twice. Everyone escaped through the double doors, leaving the tavern empty.

Kenichi stood tall. "Are you really going to do this, Pretica? Do you want the world to finally know what kind of woman you are? A traitor? A disgusting fiend?"

Pretica laughed. "I don't care what the world thinks of me. I didn't do any of this for the world. I did it for myself and for Wexcyn's new order."

She put her hand on Liam's arm, clutching him.

"Fight it, Liam."

He nodded, wiping blood from his mouth. He took Lilae's hand into his own, his Tryan power sustaining them both.

"Enough pretending. I want Gollush destroyed by dawn. Kill them," Pretica said. "Kill them all. Even *Kenichi Kamarue*."

Rowe finished his beer. All eyes turned to him as he stood and pulled his ax from beneath the table.

Why hadn't the poison affected him?

"Right." Rowe swung his ax up to rest on his shoulder. He cracked his neck. "Who wants their skull bashed in first?"

Chief Keiko's green eyes went from Lilae to Rowe. "I'd like for you to try," she purred, tossing her short white hair from her eyes.

Keiko's wide grin looked odd on her small, heart-shaped face. However, something about her that warned Lilae that this Shadow Elf woman was not to be underestimated.

Lilae held onto Liam, basking in his power, buying time until the pain of the poison subsided—recharging for the battle that was seconds from beginning.

Liam gave her hand a squeeze. She was grateful to have him by her side. Together, they were invincible.

Keiko made the first move, darting to Rowe at a speed that made her Shadow Elf brothers and sisters look slow. Lilae could barely follow her with her eyes, but Rowe, a Tryan with eyes equipped to trace the speed of a Shadow Elf, caught her by the neck.

Keiko's eyes went wide as Rowe slammed her down onto the table so hard that her armor made a shrill screeching noise.

Liam let go of Lilae's hand as Master Soh charged for them.

Lilae took in a deep breath and braced herself. Pretica stood back as if waiting for her. She gritted her teeth. Pretica had lied to them, tried to poison them, and now sought to kill her new friends.

Not this time.

None of her loved ones were going to die today.

Rowe kicked a table into Master Soh's waist, launching him backward.

"I told you, Liam," Rowe said. "Never leave your weapons behind. Now look at you. Caught off guard with nothing but your looks."

Liam ran his hand through his black hair. "I don't need weapons."

"Here," Kenichi said, giving Liam a dagger.

Liam shook his head. "Keep it for yourself."

Kenichi offered a single nod and readied himself. "I'm with you," he said. "I'd rather fight with foreigners than traitors."

"You can die with the foreigners as well," Pretica said.

"I will not be dying today," Kenichi said. "Grand Master Neru only trains the strong."

Master Soh slashed at Kenichi only to connect his sword to that of Kenichi's dagger. The young elf met the attack with such grace that he made it seem effortless. Still, Master Soh apparently had years of experience ahead of Kenichi, meeting every attack with a counter-attack.

Pretica threw a glowing dagger at Liam's head. Liam smacked it away, sending it flying into the fire. His face turned white and his nostrils flared.

Master Soh held Kenichi with one hand and used the distraction to slash Liam across the chest, drawing blood.

Pretica sucked her teeth. "I missed."

"I didn't," Master Soh said, his white grin flashed and vanished as he spun out of Liam's reach, Kenichi still held in a subdued move that kept him frozen in pain.

Lightning erupted from Liam's body, so loudly that Lilae winced and took several steps away. Her back pressed against the wall beside one of the hearths.

Ropes of power slammed into Master Soh's chest.

He let Kenichi go, the elf's body falling stiffly like a statue.

To Liam and Lilae's surprise, Master Soh's armor absorbed the ropes of light. The steel breastplate was illuminated by Liam's lightning, glowing even after the power faded.

Master Soh's hair was wild after being tossed back by the table, but his face was calm, quiet, determination in his eyes.

"You should listen to your friend," Pretica said. Her eyes met Lilae's, and she pointed the sharp tip of her other dagger at Lilae's face. She closed one eye. "We came prepared."

Lilae gasped as Pretica sprung from her place on the floor. She crashed into Lilae. They both fell to the ground, as Pretica straddled Lilae, her dagger slipping in and out of Lilae's stomach.

"You aren't invisible," Pretica spat at Lilae.

Lights flashed behind Lilae's eyes as she coughed up blood. Fear flooded her when she realized she couldn't sit up.

"You and The Storm bleed just like the rest of us."

Liam. Where is Liam?

A sharp pain left Lilae without a voice as she sucked in a breath. She bit her lip, red-hot rage consuming her, and Pretica raised her dagger to stab her again.

She grabbed Pretica by the neck and squeezed with all of her might, mustering every ounce of strength to slam the Shadow Elf over her head and into the stone floor.

Pain didn't exist as rage took over. Liam called for her, but the rush of blood to her ears drowned out the sound..

Pretica still breathed air. Lilae wanted to fix that. Her eyes burned down at Pretica as she flipped over and sprung back onto her feet.

Lilae knew nothing about fighting Shadow Elves, but the Ancients had equipped each race with the tools to defend themselves.

While Pretica's body shot through the room, daggers ready, Lilae let out a long breath and activated her Focus.

And all was clear.

A low chuckle rumbled in Lilae's chest as Pretica ran to her. She used her Evasion to swiftly change positions and grab Pretica by her hair.

Pretica gasped as Lilae swung her by her hair into the air and back to the ground in one adrenaline fueled move. Lilae's fist met Pretica's jaw the moment the elf attempted to get to her feet again.

She held both of Pretica's hands down beside her head as the elf bucked and tried to get Lilae off of her.

Pretica growled as flames raced up Lilae's arms and burned her skin.

"Stop!"

Lilae held her down, watching the flames melt Pretica's dark skin away.

"I thought you were prepared," Lilae hissed.

A deafening thud caught everyone's attention. The tavern shook, sending Lilae and Pretica into the air and crashing back to the ground.

Lilae cried out as her head hit the stone floor. Lights flashed beneath her eyelids as she rose to her elbows and pushed herself to her knees. Pretica had rolled out of the way and run out the door.

"Lilae," Liam called for her. "Are you all right?"

Lilae held the back of her head and winced. She nodded. "I'll be fine. Don't let Pretica get away."

Liam nodded and chased after Pretica.

Lilae looked over to see Master Soh's body on top of the bar, impaled with Rowe's.

Rowe pulled his ax from the elf's chest, swinging blood onto the floor.

"Where is Chief Keiko?"

Rowe nodded to the body that hung from the rafters above.

"She did try," Rowe said with a shrug as he eyed the small woman. "Not very hard, though."

Chapter 31

LIAM FOLLOWED PRETICA as quickly as he could, her shadow erratic as she ran through the winding streets of Gollush. She shot darts from the gauntlets around her wrists, and Liam smacked each sharp blade away. The sound of the steel striking stone filled the alleys.

A young man found himself in Pretica's way. She crashed into him. A frustrated growl escaped as she swung him around and tossed him into a nearby wall.

Liam's jaw dropped as he watched the young man's head crash against the stone, and his dead body fell to the ground.

How was Pretica so strong? She threw the man as if he were a child.

"My sister's power makes yours look like an amateur magician," Pretica said over her shoulder. She flashed him a wicked grin, still running as fast as the wind. "I am *not* impressed."

"Is that why you sold her?"

Liam watched Grand Master Neru walk into the empty town square.

Pretica screeched to a halt as Grand Master Neru stood directly before her. Every time she tried to run around him, he was there, before her, his face free of emotion.

Pretica swallowed, giving up her attempts at escape. "It was a wise decision—one that Wexcyn will reward me for."

"I am disappointed in you, Pretica," Grand Master Neru said, folding his hands before him. "You lied to us. And we came here to help you in a time of need. I've watched you and Ayoki grow from babies. I would never have guessed you'd betray her and your people."

"Then you know that she had to be stopped. She would have destroyed us all." Pretica tilted her chin upward. "I was smart enough to benefit from stopping her. You would have done the same."

Liam didn't have siblings, but he couldn't imagine betraying someone he was supposed to love in such a way.

Neru shook his head, his long white hair stark against his gray skin and simple red belted tunic. "You are sorely misguided, child."

Pretica shrugged. "I had to think about myself for once. For years she was the center of attention. Then, she killed our parents with her power. I am putting the balance back into place by having her killed. Justice."

"The world will punish you for this. You have no right to judge anyone."

"You're saying you won't? You're just going to let me go."

Neru nodded. "I don't have to punish you. Like I said, every action warrants a reaction, and you will meet your judgment."

"I'm glad you think so," Pretica said, drawing her daggers. She lunged at him, teeth gritted as her guttural growl filled the room.

Grand Master Neru sidestepped her—like magic, so quickly that the air blurred around him. Pretica stumbled, and Neru struck her in the back of the head with such force she flew across the floor and slid into the side of one of the stone towers.

"I granted you mercy that you clearly do not deserve," he said.

Pretica scrambled to her feet, gasping for air.

"You want me to punish you?" Neru drew his sword, a ringing sound filling the air. The black steel marked with white symbols much like lightning began to glow. He held it ready, one arm folded behind his back. "I will oblige."

Liam took a step back, watching as Pretica stood there, her face ashen, her hands shaking as she held out her dagger.

Neru's eyes met Liam's.

And before Liam could blink, Pretica's crumpled body lay lifeless on the stone, a gaping hole in her chest.

Neru appeared beside Liam, a stern look on his face as he wiped the blade of his sword clean.

"We should leave now," Neru said.

Liam's eyes locked on Pretica's body, as were those of hundreds of Shadow Elves who had stayed hidden during the fighting.

"Yes. We should."

Apparently, the Chosen were not the only ones with remarkable abilities.

GOLLUSH TREMBLED, summoned lightning. It whipped from the darkened sky and into all of the holes of the cavern. There was a hush inside as the lightning lit up the entire ceiling.

Still, it did nothing to make an entrance.

"Looks like she locked us in here," Rowe said, slamming his axe into the stone door for what must have been the hundredth time. "Is every exit sealed like this?"

"It seems that way." Liam's chest rose and fell from the exertion of commanding his power for hours.

Lilae called her flames back, seeing that they did nothing to penetrate the sealed exit. "Why would she do this? She didn't want her people to be free?"

"Pretica was not always like this. She used to be kind and honorable. Evil can corrupt the best of us," Grand Master Neru said.

"I shouldn't have trusted her," Delia said.

"You had no way of knowing that she sold her sister and planned the attack on you all," Grand Master Neru said.

"What a revolting woman," Lilae said.

"Well," Rowe said. "It looks like there is only one way out." He nodded to the sealed door.

"What about the people of Gollush?" Lilae asked. "She betrayed them as well."

"She will betray her people no more," Neru said, stepping over rubble.

"Is she dead?"

"Yes, Elder. She is."

"Good," Lilae hissed.

Kenichi ran to them. "Have you found a way out yet?"

"We have," Liam said with a nod. "Go on, Rowe. Do it." Liam took a step back.

Rowe nodded. "Right."

He stood with his legs spaced apart and clenched his fists. Everyone watched in silence, curious as to what the big Tryan man was up to. How would he free them all?

Rowe's Tryan glow intensified and shot outward to form crisscrossing circles that spun and flew up and down his body.

"Step back," Rowe said, his voice taking on a deeper tone unfamiliar to the others.

Liam, however, had heard and seen Rowe like this before. Only twice, when all hope seemed lost. This—the power of a Legacy wasn't something Rowe chose to exploit. He was humbled because it came from the deaths of his entire clan, and he would not seek advantage at their loss.

The ground shook, rubble and stones vibrating. The walls of the cavern trembled. An indentation within the floor surrounded Rowe as his glow grew so bright that Lilae and the others shielded their eyes.

Without warning, Rowe took off. Like a Raeden bomb, he shot through the Citadel, burning a path into the floor, bursting straight through the steel door.

The boom that echoed throughout the entire city shook the cavern. A hole remained in the door that had once trapped the people of Gollush and Liam's companions like prisoners.

The remaining Shadow Elves rose to their feet, hesitant and afraid.

"Can we go?" a female elf asked. Her eyes were wide with terror as she clutched her little boy to her chest, shielding his face from falling debris.

"Yes," Liam said. "It's okay. You are all free."

Still, some of the others seemed reluctant as the mother and her child ran for the opening. They looked around at one another.

"Go," Lilae shouted at them. "Don't wait for the ceiling to collapse on your heads." She led the way, leaping over fallen columns and dead bodies.

Liam followed behind, still appalled by Pretica's destruction of her own home.

Once again, Liam left a falling city behind.

Chapter 32

DRAGNOR TAPPED THE TABLE as the harem girl poured his wine. Her hands were shaking, causing splatters of red liquid to spill onto the maps and plans he studied.

Dragnor grabbed her by the hair, yanking her onto the table.

"Useless," he spat and pushed her from the table to the floor.

The fire in her eyes startled him for a moment, and he half expected her to strike him back.

Where was her fear?

He was so used to everyone fearing him that he hadn't seen true defiance since Lilae escaped, and Kavien was cursed.

Dragnor folded his hands before him as he rose from his seat behind the drafting table.

"What? Were you going to say something? Do something?"

Faira was the most beautiful of the harem girls in the palace and Kavien's favorite before Lilae arrived. Dragnor was in agreement with the woman's dark beauty. She was almost as attractive as a Shadow Elf woman, with curves and eyes that could melt his cold heart.

Still, he hadn't returned from the Underworld to seduce women. That didn't keep him from requesting her company now that Kavien was unconscious.

Faira bit her bottom lip as she glared at him. He could tell that she wanted to speak but knew her training, and kept quiet.

"Speak freely," Dragnor said, lowering his voice.

"I have nothing to say," Faira replied, her shoulders squaring as she stood to her full height. The tension in her face lessened and she feigned her usual compliant expression.

"Of course you do," he said, calmly. "Sit down, Faira." He motioned for the pillows on the granite floor near the low table where Dragnor dined.

She straightened her clothes and did as she was told, her flawless face blank.

"Where are you from, Faira?" Dragnor asked as he sat down at the table, opposite her.

He motioned for the mousy attendant to come into the room from her position outside the archway inside the study where Dragnor kept his piles of scrolls and artifacts.

"Bring some meat, cheese, and bread," he told her.

Faira's nose scrunched for a moment as she mulled over Dragnor's question. "Why?"

Dragnor leaned over the table, his dark eyes narrowing. "Just answer the question."

"Vol'Mavi," she answered flatly, fixing long wavy black hair that hung over her right shoulder.

"Ah, yes. Most of the harem girls come from surrounding cities. Besides your beauty, why did Kavien choose you?"

She shot a look at him before looking down at her hands.

"Yes. I know that you all inherit a special ability. No need to fear Kavien's punishment when he awakens," Dragnor said. "Just tell me what your ability is?"

Faira took a deep breath and met his eyes straight on. "I can sense the powers of others."

"Remarkable," he said. "I can certainly use you then. Can you detect a Bellen from a crowd of humans or Mithrani?"

She nodded. "I can."

"Good," he said. "Perhaps you aren't so useless after all. Maybe at pouring wine, but you're much more valuable than such menial tasks."

She huffed. "I could have told you that."

"Let's not become insolent," he said. "I respect your power, but you will not forget that I am your master until Kavien awakens."

Hope filled her eyes at hearing of Kavien awakening.

"When will that be?"

"You will know when the time comes. What do you know of Lilae?"

Faira watched the attendant return with the food Dragnor requested. He saw her swallow and avoid his pointed gaze.

"Kavien loves her. That's all I know and all I need to know."

This love word vexed him. He'd never loved anything or anyone in his entire life. How could anyone be so ruled by such a simple emotion that did nothing but cloud the judgement of both involved?

Not even his mother had taught him love. Dragnor had been sent to the temples as a baby, where he'd been trained as a soldier and a sorcerer.

Where was *love* back then, when Dragnor was left to sleep in the cold and rain every night since childhood?

Dragnor discovered that hate was much more powerful than any delusion of love. When he'd risen as High Cleric of the Temples of Bain, he'd made sure every elf felt the effects of his hate.

"Did she bewitch him somehow?"

"No," Faira said, her brows furrowing. "She was different. Men like different."

He was wrong about Faira. She was useless after all.

"Come now," he said, wrapping meat and cheese into a piece of fresh baked flat bread. "I'm sure you know more about her than you let on. Tell me more."

She shrugged. "Nothing to tell. She's a plain Northerner with a strange accent, and my Master chose her over me."

"Oh. I detect a little jealousy there."

"I've never been jealous of anyone."

"Until Lilae stole the Emperor from you?" Dragnor chewed his food and watched the array of emotions play out in her eyes. That was a soft spot for her.

"No. She was my friend."

Dragnor rolled his eyes. "Friends? No such thing. There are those that pretend to care for you—that will betray you to protect themselves, and there are those that let you know their intentions up front. There is no in between."

She pursed her lips and kept silent.

"She left you, Faira. Her friend. Am I right? Wouldn't a friend at least take you with her when she escapes?"

Faira frowned. "You're wrong. I had no reason to escape."

"You're telling me the harem girls enjoy being Kavien's toys?"

Faira nodded. "Yes. Now, can I go?"

"No," Dragnor barked, slamming his fist into the table. "You will go when I dismiss you. And that will not happen until you tell me everything you know of Lilae. Everything."

She shivered and leaned away from him. "I don't know anything."

"You'd better give me something before I send that sister of yours to my torture chamber," he snarled. "I hope that jolts your memory."

Faira raised the hands to him. "No. Please! Leave Rahki out of this."

She got on her knees, her gray eyes widening. "I don't know much at all. I just know that she was awfully saddened by the loss of her family. She spoke of her father and sisters often. She didn't reveal much more of her past to us," she said quickly, her brows raised as she pleaded. "Please. Don't hurt my sister."

Dragnor nodded, his memory jolted by the day he'd killed Lilae's father. A smirk came to his face. How could he have forgotten the other portion of that day?

The twins.

They just might be the key to unlocking Lilae's mysteries.

Chapter 33

"LET ME DO IT," Risa whispered into her twin sister's ear as they crouched low to the smooth granite floor.

Jaiza looked over her shoulder at the torch-lit hallway that led back to the main house on the Duke of Avia'Torena's grounds. A soft breeze drifted in through the archways that looked out over the tall grass surrounding the compound and briefly diminished the heat of the outer corridor.

Fluorescent cicada's buzzed outside. The noise the glittering insects made seemed too loud when their mission required silence.

Jaiza suppressed the urge to cringe at the purple bruise that encircled Risa's left eye. The swelling had begun to go down, but it didn't lessen Jaiza's anger.

Their master promised to never bruise their faces.

The Duke was a liar.

"Come now, Jaiza. Let me kill him," Risa said as she clenched her fists.

Risa had as much as a claim to the Duke's life as any of the other slave girls, but Jaiza had made up her mind at the beginning of this scheme. Risa's black eye was punishment for speaking her mind and for trying to protect her sister.

Kelsi, a girl from the village where they were captured from nearly a year ago, wrung her hands in worry. She glanced over her shoulder to make sure no one had followed them. The halls were clear.

When she looked back at Jaiza, sweat dripped from her forehead.

"No one is coming," Kelsi whispered.

With a nod, Jaiza turned her attention back to the Duke's corridor.

"Be careful," Kelsi said.

Jaiza didn't look back at her. This would not be the first man that either twin had killed.

Their father, Pirin, had trained them since childhood. Even though he'd only agreed to teach and protect the heir to their human god's throne, he spent an equal amount of time preparing Risa and Jaiza for battle.

Lilae.

They both missed her. Not a day went by that Jaiza didn't think of her.

Jaiza peeked around the corner once more. She had to force herself to get up and make the walk to the Duke's private quarters. She felt exposed as she rose to her feet.

The archways within the corridor looked directly out into the duke's private gardens. The guards were passed out on the ground.

Yuvorias, a small exotic purple stemmed tree with great blooming yellow flowers, were planted in intricately embellished clay pots. They lined the walls, secreting fragrant opium-like aromas that altered the senses once inhaled.

"Risa," Jaiza murmured. "You couldn't sneak up on anyone if your life depended on it, and this time, it does." She twisted her blonde hair into a bun at the top of her head and tied it.

The large stone doorway at the end of the hall was open as Jaiza stood made her way down the corridor. Sheer curtains floated into the hallway as the open windows let a gentle breeze into the manor.

Sweat dripped between Jaiza's breasts as she drew in a deep breath and looked back to see that Risa and Kelsi watching her in anticipation.

The Duke of Avia'Torena was a cruel master and from the darkness, Jaiza glared at him, wishing she could exert the same punishment on him that he'd used on them on him.

Jaiza slid the dagger from her sleeve and stalked into the spacious room decorated with nothing more than the Duke's bed and two tall torches. Not a floorboard creaked, nor was a footstep heard.

They had chosen the perfect night. The entire compound's staff was drunk on whatever concoction the cook put into their soup.

The cook's part in this mission was irreversible. She'd already set the other slaves free.

Everything hinged on this moment. Rumors about a slave—one with red hair and enough power to kill dozens of soldiers traveled quickly throughout Avia'Torena.

Jaiza and Risa were now certain that Lilae was alive.

There was hope.

Their destiny was not to live as slaves for the rest of their lives. They were to be at Lilae's side, saving the world.

Without a sound or hesitation, Jaiza clamped her hand over the Duke's mouth and slit his throat. She watched his eyes pop open, and the blood began to gush from his neck, soaking into his bed.

A gurgling sound came from beneath her hand as the Duke struggled. He deserved every moment of agony for what drudgery and perversion he'd put his slaves through.

When the light faded from his eyes, she turned and left his sleeping quarters without a sound.

It was done.

Jaiza hurried back to her sister and Kelsi and motioned for them to follow. Down the long, labyrinth-like, hallways they went.

Each elaborate room they'd been forced to clean and serve the Duke's friends and family in could burn for all they cared.

Outside the kitchen, the cook waited, a look of worry creasing her forehead as she watched them approach.

"Is he dead?" Emirra's gray hair was pulled into a messy ponytail, and her face was smeared with soot from cleaning the hearth.

"Yes," Jaiza answered. "We told you we could do it."

"Good, we better get moving." Emirra grabbed her sack from behind the kitchen's heavy wooden door.

The other girls went to the cupboards and pulled their own bags from the shelves. They had already packed essentials: food and a change of clothes from the Duke's wife's wardrobe.

Risa and Jaiza stood ready. They were used to such nights when everything was left behind. Never had they been more willing to leave a place.

"This way," Emirra motioned for them to follow her, and down the dark hallway they went.

Jaiza's heart thumped in her chest. The fear of getting caught plagued her. That only meant that she and Risa would have to kill more people for their freedom.

Nearly a year ago, Jaiza had thought she'd seen Lilae at the port. The girls had been on separate ships but once they reached Avia'Torena, Jaiza was sure she'd seen Lilae. Her red hair had captured the light.

Jaiza had cried out for Lilae, praying that she would look their way and know that they had all made it out of Lowen's Edge alive.

She'd suffered a swollen lip in return. Life would never be the same.

She began to wonder if any men left in the world had a shred of compassion or empathy. Brison, the man she was meant to marry, had faded from her memory a long time ago.

Those days all seemed like such a blur. She could barely remember happiness. The days of a slave were all the same, dark and full of suffering.

The memory of being summoned to the Duke's bedchamber made her clench her fists. Those nights alone with him, she would bury so deep that she prayed she would forget, forever.

Once outside, the air was just as hot and thick as inside. They all held their breath once they stepped foot outdoors. The sleeping guards were armed.

The twins were wary. There was a lingering fear if Emirra's concoction was strong enough to keep those men asleep long enough to escape.

Risa knelt down before one of the guards. His chest heaved up and down with his steady breaths. She watched him, focusing on his closed eyes as she gently pulled his sword free from his scabbard.

The steel scrapped against the brass scabbard. Risa held her breath. Her eyes widened as he stirred. Worry filled her eyes as Risa glanced at Jaiza. When she looked back at him, his small, dark eyes stared back at her.

Risa yanked the sword free and stabbed him in the chest. The tip of the sword slid through his body and stopped at the clay molded wall on which he leaned. He began to shout, and she quickly clamped his mouth with her hand.

She shook, hoping the other men wouldn't awaken as well. They would have an all-out battle on their hands if those men saw them trying to escape. And they knew they would lose the moment they called for the Duke's own private sector of soldiers who weren't too far away.

He reached for Risa and grabbed her neck with his rough, callused hand and held tight. She held her breath, hoping she could outlast him. Sweat dripped from her forehead as she waited for him to die.

Jaiza reached an arm across Risa and slit his throat with one sawing motion, ending all struggle.

Risa took his sword and together they ran from the other sleeping guards.

The tall yellow grass reached to their waists and scratched them on their exposed legs. Once the manor was out of sight, they all took a breath of relief.

"You just couldn't resist, could you?" Jaiza scowled at her sister.

"We needed this," Risa said with a shrug, her hair brushing her shoulders.

Jaiza let out a harsh breath and shook her head.

"Ok girls," Emirra began. "We must separate now."

Kelsi hugged Jaiza tight to her chest, sniffling. Risa was next for an embrace. The three girls had been through so much together. Before the massacre in Lowen's Edge, Kelsi had been a different person—snobbish and full of spite.

Nearly a year of slavery had changed her.

"Go with Emirra," Jaiza said.

Tears trailed down Kelsi's freckle-splattered face, and Jaiza wiped them away with her thumb.

"Don't cry. Emirra will take good care of you. You're free now."

Kelsi would have a difficult time blending in with the people of Avia'Torena. Her auburn curls were hard to tame, very different from the raven-haired women native to the land.

Jaiza and Risa would have to keep their blond hair cloaked.

"Why can't I go with you?" Kelsi wrung her hands. "I saw what you girls did that day the soldiers came. I've never seen anyone fight that way before. I would feel safer with you."

Risa put a hand on her shoulder. "It's too dangerous, Kelsi. You have to go where it's safe. Flee Avia'Torena and start a new life."

Kelsi tilted her head as her eyes went from Risa to Jaiza. "You're going to find Lilae?"

They nodded.

Kelsi stepped away toward Emirra. "I hope you find her well."

Jaiza kissed her cheek. "Thank you. Take care of yourself."

"I'll do my best."

"Girls, don't forget," Emirra said. "Vaugner is a great friend to anyone in need. He makes potions that heal people, and he has always been charitable to those who seek him with a pure heart. Only those who are evil shall fear him."

"We won't forget," Risa rolled up her dress' sleeves.

Emirra nodded. "May the Ancients guide and protect you."

Jaiza took her sister's hand as they watched Emirra and Kelsi head down the opposite path toward the thick jungle that led toward the north of the empire.

"We did it," Risa said, a smile forming on her full lips.

"I won't feel safe until we are far from this place."

"Do you think the Ancients know we are out here? Do they even care about us?"

Jaiza shrugged, and together they looked at the night sky as a warm breeze blew strands of their blonde hair.

The Ancients had never guided them before. It was Delia that spoke to them.

"I really don't know."

The twins would be on their own, yet they were confident that nothing would keep them from reuniting with their sister.

A goblin city awaited.

"We are coming, Lilae," Jaiza whispered.

THE RAIN OVER OREN BEGAN to lessen for the first time in weeks since that horrifying night Queen Aria's palace was sent crashing to the ground.

The fog, a mixture of green and gray, was thick as ever and smothered Oren like a blanket.

Queen Aria tightened her hood, and still, her face got wet from the soft droplets of rain on that cool evening. Her leather boots splashed in puddles no matter how careful she was to avoid them.

A troop of armed Tryan guards followed at her sides and behind as she walked the streets that were in danger of becoming flooded.

The series of winding stone roads and alleyways were abandoned. The sun hadn't shone in days.

Horrible deaths, mysterious illnesses, crime, starvation were all that seemed to fill Oren as of late. The cheery city was nothing more than a shell of its former glory.

News of a plague had drawn Aria from the palace. Against her advisor's judgment, she wanted to see for herself. She was tired of reports. Aria needed to help her citizens, not sit in her comfy palace hoping someone else would do something.

If only she had someone there that could guide her. Her parents would have known what to do.

From their windows, Tryans watched her walk by, some brave enough to step out into the heavy rain to get a better look of their Queen.

Aria offered a reassuring smile, knowing that she was lost as to what she would actually do to keep the Orenians alive.

"Watch your step, my Queen," one of the soldiers warned.

Aria paused. Her eyes went to the crack in the road. She'd discovered that many of the roads had been damaged by the quakes.

Cottages and shops had been toppled and even though Aria had teams of men sent out to repair those homes, the people were still on edge.

It was apparent that Oren was under attack.

It was just one that no one seemed to know how to fight.

When they reached the home of the latest infected family, she paused before the door. She looked back at her men, who she knew were fearful of contagion.

Sucking in a deep breath, Aria knocked on the door.

Inside, she heard someone run loudly down the stairs. The door was ripped open and before her stood a tall young man that looked to be in his late twenties. He wore a tattered, blood-soaked tunic and wool pants. Glossy, red-rimmed blue eyes looked at her. Even his Tryan glow was dimmed.

Oily, stringy black hair hung to his shoulders. From the smell of him, he hadn't bathed in ages. Sweat beaded on his pale forehead, saturating his cheeks and neck as well.

Aria's throat went dry as she began to speak. "Mr. Triston?"

Her eyes widened at seeing the blood that dripped from his hands. Aria was not a warrior monarch like her son would be; she had never seen a battle. The sight of blood turned her stomach.

He wiped his hands on his already soiled tunic. "Aye, Queen Aria," he replied, his voice quavering. "I 'poligize for the mess."

Aria swallowed hard when he lowered his face. She could see the tears trailing down his cheeks. It was obvious that he'd tried to hide them from her.

Mr. Triston wiped his chin on his shoulder and turned towards the stairs. "This way." He motioned for her to follow.

The darkness inside that door was intimidating, and Aria feared what she was about to walk into.

Aria looked back at her men once more. “Stay here,” she ordered. Despite standing in the rain, she could tell they were grateful for her orders.

Aria entered the small cottage. Her hand shot up to cover her nose and mouth when the putrid smell of decomposing flesh hit her. Her stomach churned, but she followed closely behind.

“My ma and pa died first,” he explained in a whisper. He glanced over his shoulder as he headed up the old staircase. “My wife died this morning.”

The old floorboards groaned beneath their weight. “I haven’t had a chance to clean out her room yet. I’ve been too busy caring for the girls.”

She followed him up to a narrow hallway. There were two doors, and he went straight to the one on the right. Light shone from the uneven doorframe.

The door creaked open. The horror Aria witnessed cut straight to her heart, nearly crippling her.

Hot tears stung Aria’s eyes as she looked in to see two little girls laying in a bed that was low to the floor.

Holy Elahe. Help us.

The two little ones laid there with their eyes closed. Blood stained their pale white cheeks and the corners of their dry, crusted mouths. The smell was repugnant, but the sight was heart wrenching.

“Carrie,” he called, and the girl on the left stirred. “Suessa,” he added, and they both opened their eyes and tried to sit up.

Such a task was taken for granted as Aria realized that the two girl’s eyes were sealed shut, blood seeping from their tear ducts.

“Oh my,” Aria croaked, covering her mouth. The line in her forehead deepened. “What has happened to them?”

He shook his head. “Same as the other folk that died last week. Something’s got a hold of my entire family. I’m shocked that I’m still able to care for them,” he paused, his voice growing hoarse. “Something’s killing my babies, Queen Aria. It isn’t right for a man to bury his entire family. To bury his children who haven’t had a life of their own yet.”

“Who’s that with you, Papa?” Carrie asked. Her bloody eyes tried to see. “Is it really the Queen?”

"Yes, girls. The Queen has come all the way from the palace to see you two."

"Oh, Papa!" Suessa squealed before going into a fit of coughing that shook her entire body. He knelt down at her bedside with a cup of water from the side table. She wheezed and tried to catch her breath.

Mr. Triston put the cup to her mouth, and she took a tiny sip. When the coughing fit finally ceased, she tried to speak again. He wiped her mouth with a dirty rag. "Is she wearing a pretty dress?"

"Yes, Suessa."

"With gold trim? Like at the fair?" Carrie asked.

Suessa's bloodshot eyes sparkled. "And shiny gold shoes?"

Mr. Triston looked at Aria in her muddy leather boots and plain black cloak. "Yes," he answered, his tearful eyes not leaving Aria's. "She is wearing a gold gown and gold shoes for you girls."

"Oh, Papa," Carrie smiled. She tried to wipe her eyes with her sleeve. "Can we play with her?"

"Please. Please. We feel all better." Suessa went into another coughing fit. She nearly choked on the red phlegm that splattered onto the dull gray quilt.

Aria's jaw hung. Her eyes widened in horror.

Enough.

Her heart broke at seeing those girls in that state. She ran down the stairs and out of the house as though something chased her. She was grateful for the rain that poured once more. It washed away her tears as she faced her men.

"Send for the palace physician, a healing fairy, and an herbalist."

Aria balled up her fist, her eyes fixed on the desolate city street before her.

"Send for them all."

THE SOUND OF SOLDIERS woke Jaiza. Her eyes opened to the jungle canopy. It was dawn, and traces of sunlight beamed through a ceiling of thick leaves.

Jaiza's senses were heightened, so much so that the sound of the soldier's boots broke her from her slumber. Her body tensed, the blood draining from her face.

How close are they?

She activated her Accuracy—a trait common to humans, but useful in situations such as this. Usually, Accuracy was used for making precise shots with her bow and arrows, but it had its other uses.

The trees became a blur, as her sight extended far ahead. Tall soldiers, clad in Avia'Torenan armor of gold and bronze, patrolled the wide merchant road a few yards away from where she and Risa slept.

Jaiza gave Risa a gentle push.

"What?" Risa yawned and opened one eye to peak at Jaiza's face. "It can't be time to wake up yet."

The soldiers stopped near the sign stuck in the ground to have a drink.

Turning her gaze to Risa, Jaiza's brows furrowed.

"Soldiers," Jaiza whispered. "I can see them with my Accuracy."

Risa shot up from her spot on a bed of leaves, holding her breath. Her eyes widened.

"Calm down. They aren't that close, but close enough to make me uncomfortable. We better get moving."

"How many?"

"Eight."

Risa let out a long breath and laid back down as if eight soldiers wasn't much of a threat. "Maybe we should wait until they are farther away," Risa suggested with a half shrug of her shoulder. "I was dreaming of Mother's winter porridge. You know, the kind with chopped pork."

"No," Jaiza said, her eyes glazed over as she used more energy to focus on the soldiers. "I want to keep to the Parthan River and put more distance between the soldiers and us. If we are quiet, we can avoid detection."

"Couldn't we just sleep for a bit? That would *also* avoid detection," Risa said as she picked long blades of grass out of her braided blonde hair.

"What if one of them decides to come into the forest to relieve himself?"

Sighing, Risa nodded. "Fine."

Risa pushed herself up to her feet and started gathering their scant supplies.

The rushing waters of the Parthan River returned as Jaiza deactivated her Accuracy.

"I'm tired of running."

"I am too," Jaiza said as she stretched her arms. "But we can't stop until we get there. I promise we can rest then."

"But we've been running all of our lives."

Jaiza noted the sound of fatigue in her sister's voice. "We can't afford to stop now. Lilae needs us, and we need her."

"I know. But, what if Lilae is dead?"

"Don't you *ever* say that again," Jaiza said through clenched teeth.

Risa waved her hands. "I'm just saying. What if she's gone?"

"She's not."

"I'm sorry," Risa said, sucking her teeth. "I'm just tired. I'm hungry. My feet hurt. This stab wound still itches."

Risa scratched her belly through her clothes. The wound had healed, but Jaiza told her it was just in her mind, reminding her of her one moment of weakness. They shouldn't have been taken that day in Lowen's Edge.

They should have protected Lilae.

"Haven't you learned anything? I'll never complain again as long as I am free."

Risa wrapped her arms around Jaiza. "You're right. I don't know what's wrong with me."

"You're scared."

"I am. I don't like feeling like this. I just miss Mother, Father, Lilae, and even Delia."

"I'm scared too. But we are strong. We can do this." Jaiza stroked Risa's cheek as they pulled free from their embrace. "You better not let that tear slip."

Risa bit her lip and sucked in a breath. She shook her head as if shaking off the sadness.

"Are you kidding?" Risa forced a smile. "Risa, daughter of Pirin, does not cry."

Jaiza searched her wet eyes and nodded. "Good girl." She picked up the stolen sword, missing her bow and arrows. They were lucky that their father, Pirin, taught them to fight with more than just their weapon of choice.

"Let's go. We're close to the Goblin City. I just know it."

Risa nodded and pulled her pack on. They began their trek along the side of the river when a piercing scream filled the jungle.

Jaiza put a hand on Risa's, stopping her. Her blood ran cold.

A woman in trouble.

Risa's eyes met hers. "It's not our business—" She started to shake her head when the scream came again.

Terrified.

Desperate.

Jaiza closed her eyes, sighing. She couldn't turn her back on women in need. She rubbed her temples and took in a deep breath. As she opened her eyes a thought came to her.

What would Lilae do?

They both knew the answer and drew their swords.

Chapter 36

THE PATH WAS OVERGROWN WITH tree roots, old leaves, and sun-bleached weeds that reached their knees. Ayoki and Mai followed behind Luc, still mystified by this new world, yet worried that they took a route so out in the open.

Eura was beautiful, bright, and full of light. The sky was so calm, with birds fluttering above, seemingly singing as they flew from tree to tree.

As Ayoki wiped her face of sweat, she yearned for the safety the underground provided. The sun, with its intense rays of light, bothered her eyes, and its heat was almost intolerable. The cool comfort of a cave was still preferable to this bright world.

"I hear you were taken by Bellens," Luc said, breaking Ayoki from her thoughts.

"We were," Mai answered, giving Ayoki a sidelong glance.

Ayoki was grateful for Mai's discretion. She could have killed every Bellen within seconds, but fear kept her held in submission.

Visions of being poked and prodded, tested and experimented on was not nearly as disturbing as the memories of her childhood.

Pretica's face kept trying to wedge itself into her mind, but Ayoki pushed it back. She didn't want to remember, but one memory in particular, wouldn't be silenced. It fought to return to her, and each time it appeared, she placed her hand on her belly, where comfort awaited, and the memory vanished into the dark recesses of her twisted mind.

Everything would be better once her child was born. Ayoki was certain of it.

Her jaw hardened. She simply prayed that her child wouldn't be born with her power.

Ayoki kept her eyes fixed on Luc's back. She knew Mai was still upset with her for being a coward—for not fighting back when they were taken.

She should be ashamed to call herself The Seer.

"What was it like?"

Mai glanced at Ayoki. "It wasn't pleasant."

Luc turned to face them, walking backward with a quizzical look on his face. "They've been taking girls since before any of us were born. You two were lucky to have been rescued."

"Lucky?" Mai said with a smile. "I'd say so…Luc."

A grin crossed to Luc's face, one that neither of the Shadow Elf girls had seen since Hartwig sent them off with him.

It was a nice smile, warm, and perhaps a little shy.

A whistling sound made Ayoki pause on the worn road.

The blood drained from her face as an arrow shot into Luc's shoulder and poked out the other side.

Mai's scream filled the entire forest, shrill, desperate, and laden with terror.

Ayoki slapped a hand over Mai's mouth, silencing her, and whipped her around to run. Mai recovered quickly, keeping up with Ayoki as they darted into the trees.

Luc.

They hadn't the time to look back. Another new friend would be no more.

Soldiers. The sounds of their boots haunted her as they ran into the forest.

The underbrush was thick, making it a feat to run without getting caught by roots, vines, and fallen logs. Each step took them farther away from whoever shot that arrow.

No other race was as fast as a Shadow Elf.

Ayoki's eyes widened when a man appeared before her, out of nowhere. He materialized at such a speed that his body was a blur.

What trait was that?

He was human. Tall, with a clean-shaven face, bright green eyes, and a wicked smile that turned her blood cold.

Evasion? Is that what this power was? Ayoki was unsure, she hadn't studied the humans as closely as Pretica. Now, she wished she had.

They wouldn't be able to run. Not from these soldiers. More materialized before Ayoki and Mai, all with smug smiles on their faces, seemingly pleased to have stunned the young Shadow Elf girls with the traits of their race.

"What do you want from us? We have nothing," Mai shouted, already in tears.

The leader stepped forward. He grabbed Mai by her neck.

Mai screamed again.

Ayoki tensed. Her right eye twitched.

This wasn't going to go well.

"Shadow Elves, Captain Marick," a soldier said, folding his arms over his chest. He was a big man, with muscles that rivaled the statues of Wexcyn himself. No one in Gollush had muscles like that.

Human men were all built bigger. Solid. Strong.

Ayoki wondered if she could defeat them with just her physical strength.

Two human girls with wispy yellow hair ran from the trees, swords ready, determination on their identical faces.

Ayoki crouched low as an all-out battle ensued around her.

She watched as the twin girls fought as fiercely as any warrior she'd seen in Gollush.

The clash of steel against steel rang through the forest. Birds squawked and flew from the trees as the noises of battle grew louder. Ayoki wished she could drown it out.

Too loud.

But the girls fought for them. That was odd.

Why would a human defend them?

"Jaiza," one of the girls called. "Use your Accuracy. They have Evasion."

Ayoki's eyes narrowed as she tried to follow the standoff before her. Evasion against Evasion. It was a scene from a dream as one of the human girls went from soldier to soldier, her image flickering erratically as she shot from one end of the battle to another, clashing steel and flesh to fist and boot.

Excitement filled Ayoki as she watched. Mai crawled over to her. “Let’s go,” she whispered, her eyes wide.

Ayoki raised a finger. For a second she considered helping the human girls. From the looks of it, they could take care of themselves.

Ayoki nodded and started for the forest while the soldiers were occupied.

Again, the man they called Captain Marick appeared before her, his smug smile nowhere to be seen. He reached for Ayoki, grabbing her by the hair.

No.

This was not going to go well.

A STARTLED GASP ESCAPED Ayoki's lips as she found herself before the captain's sun-scorched face.

She slashed him across the cheek with her nails, drawing crimson blood.

A punch to the jaw took Ayoki's breath away, sending her gasping to her knees. Dirt and pebbles embedded into her flesh as she squeezed her eyes shut against the stinging pain.

"Let her go!"

Mai struggled against two men as they pinned her arms behind her back. The twin girls were captured as well. Disheveled and covered in blood, they didn't look fearful.

Anger seethed in their large blue eyes.

The battle was quick once it was realized that all of the soldiers had special, human traits that would take more than two well-trained human girls.

The soldiers that held Mai shoved her down until her face was pressed against the dirt.

Mai's face was ashen, her eyes wide as she looked at Ayoki for help.

"Risa," Jaiza said through ragged breaths as she was bound and forced to her knees. "Are you okay?"

Risa didn't reply. Calm, she bent to her knees and glared at the soldiers.

Jaiza's eyes met Ayoki's, hard, yet filled with tears.

Something stirred within Ayoki—an anger that she was unused to. Rage boiled in her belly, threatening to burst forth.

They were going to die.

All of them.

"Bring the male over. We will make this quick," Captain Marick said.

Though bleeding from his mouth, the soldiers brought Luc to the lineup. Luc's already ash-colored skin was paler than normal, his eyes sunken in as blood dripped from his wound and face.

Still, he was stoic, unflinching in the face of death.

Ayoki wished she could be that strong.

She wiped fresh blood from her own mouth, not liking the salty taste or the sting of her wound. It would have been easy if the soldiers would have listened to Mai.

Marick drew his dagger and forced Ayoki back up to her knees. She grunted as he placed the blade to her throat, the other soldiers following suit to each captive in the clearing.

Her body shook.

Not with fear for herself.

But for them.

Ayoki would have begged them to run far away if she had a voice.

Go. Just go. I will forgive you if you run now.

Her eyes clouded with tears.

At the end of the line was Luc, yet he was first to meet his end.

Ayoki gasped as Luc's throat was slit, crimson blood spilling onto the dirt.

"No!"

Mai's scream radiated through Ayoki's body.

Too late.

A flutter in Ayoki's body made her tense. The life inside deserved a chance. It was above her self-loathing and fear.

"Ayoki," Mai cried through terrified gasps for breath. "You are The Seer. Please."

"Seer?" White fingers curled under Ayoki's chin, tilting her head back so far that her long ponytail brushed against the small of her back. Marick was prepared to show Ayoki the same fate as Luc.

Ayoki sucked in a long breath.

And closed her eyes.

A soft buzz—like a swarm of bees came from the ground as purple smoke crept up Ayoki's wiry body. Her skin cooled as the smoke—the power—filled her.

A hum filled her chest, clutching her lungs.

It had been so long.

"Ahhh," Ayoki breathed, mystified by the sound of her own voice.

Marick's fingers left her chin as if caught on fire. He looked down at his hand and shot a glare back at Ayoki's face.

"Kill them. Now," he ordered, raising his dagger.

"What's happening, Captain?" The soldier seemed unsure, his eyes watching the rising smoke as it laced around their feet and up their legs.

Ayoki opened her eyes and raised a hand toward Marick. His dagger was ripped from his grip by an unseen force and shot to Ayoki's open palm.

"You're all about to die," Ayoki said, her voice echoing through the trees.

Mai's eyes widened.

She'd never seen this side of Ayoki, devoid of fear—the side that took Marick by the hand and thrust him to the dirt.

It happened within seconds, too quick for most eyes to see, or for anyone to retaliate.

Captain Marick groaned as Ayoki's boot pressed against his throat.

"Mai," Ayoki called.

Cool.

Calm.

"Girls," her eyes going to the fierce set of twins that had risked their lives to save a pair of Shadow Elves they didn't even know.

She'd spare them.

Mai looked from Captain Marick to Ayoki. Her lips trembled at seeing the whites of Ayoki's eyes blacked out, her feet hovering above the ground and she folded her arms across her chest, Marick's dagger still in her hand.

"Go and wait for me in the trees. Far from the circle."

The purple smoke began to cover the ground around them like a thick fog.

Mai nodded, shaking as she came to her feet and darted into the forest.

"Hurry now," Ayoki purred.

There was no room for fear when The Seer power filled her and took control. She'd never felt more confident in her life.

Mai ran, crunching dead leaves beneath her quick steps. The two human girls followed, desperate to keep up with Mai's speed.

Good girls, she thought.

Once Mai and the twins were far from Ayoki's area of effect—the range of her power, Ayoki cracked her knuckles and sucked in a long breath.

"Now," she said, exhaling. She tilted her head, her sullen eyes fixed on Marick's. "We shall begin."

Chapter 38

A DARK POWER WAS UNLEASHED—one that not even Ayoki completely understood.

No one trained her.

No one warned her.

The gods deemed her worthy, and she had no choice but to be that which destiny named her.

As purple smoke lifted, creating a funnel that spread. The trees within range bent backward as if bowing in reverse—or cowering.

Everything was consumed: Ayoki, the soldiers, and the traces of life that sprouted from the dirt.

Ayoki removed her foot from Marick's throat and watched her power at work.

Their screams could chill the bones of Wexcyn himself, and Ayoki trembled—torn between disdain and a sadistic form of pleasure.

A burst of light shot from the ground, in a circle that trapped them all.

The first wave immobilized Marick and his men, gripping them with some unseen force.

The second, slow yet precise in its purpose, burned their skin. Pink flesh, ripe with fresh blood was revealed and exposed to the elements.

The screams grew louder, more panicked—agonizing as the acrid mist of the funnel covered them.

Ayoki lifted her arms and looked to the sky.

"Is this what you wanted?" Her chest heaved. "Is this all that I am?"

Her question to The Ancients went unanswered, and yet the part she was most afraid of—the sequence of her power that horrified her—didn't relent.

Ayoki saw things.

Things that would never leave her.

But for now, it comforted her to know the true evil of the men that she was about to slaughter.

Later, however…

Ayoki closed her eyes. Later was another thing altogether.

Her victim's darkest deeds were revealed.

Women screamed as their men were massacred, their virtue stolen without remorse. SO many women. In their homes. On the road to safety. None were safe.

Then the children.

Ayoki choked on tears.

Children wept and screamed, wide-eyed, and afraid as their innocent lives were stolen.

Ayoki's eyes opened as she growled in rage.

The third wave was green, and the funnel spun as it ate at the soldier's muscle until white bone was revealed.

Most of the men were dead by then, from shock, loss of blood, and utter terror.

Ayoki wasn't done.

Not until the bone was turned to dust and dust carried away by the funnel of despair.

Seeing was all that was left as her funnel returned to her body, purple smoke, bolts of light, and all.

Ayoki fell to her knees. The images of depravity and evil haunted her. She covered her ears with both hands, desperate to stop the sounds of screaming and sorrow.

Why couldn't *that* go away with the funnel? Why did she have to *See* those deeds for the rest of her life?

Cries of anguish escaped her lips.

Her voice had left her once more—with her power, but the crippling fear returned.

The Dark Princess of Death.

That title had followed her since she was a child and had mistakenly killed all of her friends one dawn after a game in the woods outside of their cavern home.

The Ancients warned her parents.

Let us assign her an Elder. Her power must be contained. She cannot be allowed to live untamed.

They hadn't listened, wanting nothing but to keep her close and safe from the violence and chaos of the world

She'd killed them as well. Such guilt couldn't be erased, no matter how hard she'd tried. However, the love of a man had eased the pain by a small measure, and now she didn't even have him anymore.

Ayoki's eyes flickered up, remembering that Mai still watched in the distance. She looked at her through a blur of hot tears.

There.

Fear—it shone on Ayoki through Mai's eyes. Even the human girls stared at her with unblinking, widened eyes as the sun's light cast an eerie glow on them, highlighting the dust of the dead men.

Ashamed, Ayoki curled into a ball and sobbed into the silence, surrounded by tiny pieces of bones and blood.

The flutter in her belly no longer comforted her. The confusion of such loss was melted away as a rush of memories flooded her.

Ayoki's eyes widened as visions of blood and pain came to her.

She couldn't breathe.

My baby. My future, and second chance at happiness.

The flood of realization overwhelmed her.

Pretica, with her greed and jealousy, had stolen everything from her.

Ayoki had tried so hard to forget, to cling to the hope that her baby had given her.

And now, she was left with nothing.

Why couldn't Elahe—creator of all of the gods and Ancients just take her—let her die and vanish from all existence?

She knew she'd never be that lucky.

Chapter 39

FRESH AIR WELCOMED Lilae as she stood before the desolate city of Gollush. The cavern was nothing more than an empty shell.

A memory.

Liam held her hand as they watched the final Shadow Elves leave their homeland to join the others beneath a stone staircase that led up to a sentry post.

Chief Matsuharu stepped up to the post and presided over the thousands of survivors.

"People of Gollush," Chief Matsuharu began, his black hair blowing as the wind picked up. "All of you are welcome to follow us back to Koravi. You will be safe and treated like family. We will join forces as allies against the evil of Wexcyn. The betrayal of your former leader will not tarnish our ties nor our resistance toward what the fallen god wants for our world. In Koravi, we will rebuild, and our alliance will grow stronger because of it."

Lilae and Liam stood side by side as the sun beamed down on them from the tall, charred trees, watching the Shadow Elves gear up for a trek to Koravi.

Cheering arose from the masses, and the elves pulled their quickly packed bags onto their backs and armed themselves.

Lilae sighed. She couldn't help feeling guilty. Gollush might have still thrived if she and the others hadn't stirred up such political drama with the enemy clans.

"No use lingering," Delia said. She pulled the hood of her cloak over her black hair and glanced at the darkening sky. "We should get going. Vaugner will need to hear of Pretica's betrayal. I fear what has become of the Seer."

The sun that had just warmed Lilae's face was now hidden behind gray clouds. Fat raindrops began to fall, splashing on her face, and she closed her eyes against the coolness of the water.

"We need her on our side," Lilae said.

"Precisely," Delia said.

Kenichi stepped closer to their circle. "She is nothing like Pretica. Ayoki is good. She would never betray her people. Or me."

"Good," Delia said. Her brows furrowed. She nodded to the sky as she eyed Liam. "Are you doing this?"

Liam followed her gaze and shook his head.

"I learned to control my emotions a long time ago," he said. "I'm afraid I'm not bringing this storm."

"Let's get a move on then," Rowe said, stashing his flask in his bag. "I've had enough of Nostfar. I draw the line at being poisoned. This place puts me on edge."

"Why didn't the poison affect you?" Lilae asked, still stunned that it had no effect on him.

"One of my Legacy traits makes me immune to posion."

"Oh," Lilae said. "That's amazing."

Rowe shrugged. "I'm just a big back of tricks," he said, giving her a wink.

Neru left the congregation of Shadow Elves to join them. He'd collected his traveling gear and a bag of wyvern eggs from the Citadel.

Lilae lifted a brow. "Brilliant idea," she said as he handed each of them an egg. She touched the smooth purple outer shell and felt a pulsing heartbeat beneath her fingers. "This will save us so much time."

"Bloody brilliant," Rowe agreed.

Neru held his wyvern egg in the air. "First, you must whisper to the wyvern and ask its name. You cannot summon one without permission *and* a name. Then, just toss it gently, and say your wyvern's name, and it will appear."

"This has been my wyvern since I was a young man. So, I already know her name."

Everyone watched as Neru tossed the egg into the air. "Qynn," he said, and a large, slender white wyvern broke from the shell.

Qynn stretched her leathery white wings. She was much bigger than the wyverns they'd rode to Gollush. Her long snout was smooth, yet rows of sharp silver teeth were revealed when she yawned and gracefully lowered herself to the ground beside her master. She purred and knelt her head at his boots.

Neru stroked the shimmering scales on her neck that reminded Lilae of the crystals she'd seen in the Avia'Torenan palace.

"Remarkable," Liam said, letting go of Lilae's hand to examine his wyvern egg. He looked down at Lilae. "This reminds me of Vleta, the dragon Wilem commands."

"Really?" Lilae had only ever seen drawings of dragons and had never seen a wyvern before Pretica approached them. "I've been told that dragons are much like wyverns."

Neru nodded. "Yes, they are similar. But, dragons have four legs while wyverns only have two."

Liam nodded. "Ah, yes. That's true." He lowered his voice to speak to his egg.

Lilae did the same. She pressed her lips to the cool shell. "What is your name?"

"Triste," a familiar voice called from inside. "My friend, you may summon me."

A smile shone on Lilae's face. Having Triste again was a welcome surprise. She remembered their conversation as he flew her to Gollush a week ago.

She tossed the egg. "Triste."

The black wyvern revealed himself just as Liam's, Rowe's, and Delia's did the same.

Even though they had met only once, Triste was like an old friend, a welcome one that promised an escape from the disaster she and her party were leaving behind.

"I will meet you at the Goblin City," Neru said as he flew up with Qynn. "I must make sure the people of Gollush make it to Jordan."

Delia nodded and climbed onto her wyvern. "Safe travels," she said and held onto the reins with one hand and her staff with the other. She looked as though she'd ridden wyverns for years.

Graceful and sure of herself, Lilae attempted to mimic her, hopping onto Triste's back and grabbing ahold of the reins.

"To the Goblin City we go," Delia said and rose into the sky.

QUEEN ARIA FOLDED HER HANDS in her lap as she sat on her throne and listened to the crimes of her people. It was a dark time for Oren, where crime was on the rise, yet Aria knew she must remain stoic and resolute to keep order and peace.

Meetings such as this used to take two hours a day, but now there were so many crimes that Aria had to listen to the cases for half of her day.

She remembered sitting at her father's feet as he oversaw criminal cases. He also had the ability to read the thoughts of others, and such a gift made it easy to deem who was guilty and who was innocent.

Still, Aria had been intrigued how even the most guilty man or woman would try to lie their way out of their punishment. She sentenced the last man to death for killing another man for his coin purse.

Desperation was rampant, but Aria would not allow order to be lost. They needed to stay civil, now more than ever.

Yoska sat beside her on the arm of her throne, his eyes watching her as she rubbed her temples.

"Just a few more," he said. "And we must meet with Franco to discuss the famine in the countryside."

Aria glanced at him and nodded with a sigh. Dark circles had developed beneath her eyes. Sleep was a privilege she was no longer used to. Her people were hungry, afraid, and desperate, and it kept her up each night.

"Maybe we can finally make a plan to keep the people outside the city fed."

Her face blanched at the sight of the next guest. She sat up in her chair and leaned forward for a better look. Her eyes had to be deceiving her.

It wasn't possible.

"Next case," David, the palace secretary, announced. "Lady Sonalese Rochfort."

Sona.

Aria rose to her feet, eyes widened as she watched the young woman walk past the long rows of seated attendants that awaited their turn or simply wanted to spectate.

"Where is Liam?" She couldn't stop herself from blurting the question that ripped at her insides.

She looked past Sona, expecting to see her son follow her. When he didn't arrive, she shot a look at Sona.

The look on Sona's face struck fear into her heart.

Cold eyes. Clenched jaw. Barely healed scars.

What happened? Aria feared the worst.

David's eyes shot to Aria after he read from the scroll. He swallowed and looked back down at the writing on the cream parchment.

"Lady Sonalese Rochfort accuses Queen Aria of treason against the people of Oren."

Silence filled the room as Aria covered her mouth with a trembling hand.

David swallowed, his eyes blinking, as he went on. "And for causing the death of her son, Prince Liam Marx."

When her voice returned to her, Aria fought through tears to speak.

"What do you mean? Liam is not dead," she said. "He can't be."

Sona stepped forward, tears in her eyes. "He is, and you killed him."

Aria watched Sona turn to the crowd of onlookers. Dressed in a simple black gown with a red satin sash and black boots, Sona played the part of grieving widow.

"Queen Aria has lied to us. There are no Shadow Elves in our territory. Only militia that *she* sent out to not only destroy the Order but kill her son—our future King." Sona's eyes narrowed as she pointed a thin finger at Aria's face. "Just like she killed her husband before her reign of lies."

The whispers that followed stunned Aria. How could anyone even begin to believe such an accusation?

Their thoughts revealed their feelings.

Fear.

It was a powerful emotion that could cloud anyone's judgment.

Aria's heart thumped in her chest, so loudly that she feared everyone in the room could hear it. She didn't want to hear their thoughts, but the power within reached for those of one.

Sona, she thought as she read the secrets of the young Tryan woman's mind. She clenched her fist as bile filled her throat.

Images of Liam falling into the sea struck Aria's heart, nearly choking her. Blood stained hands and a bloodied dagger appeared.

Sona's hands.

A whimper escaped her lips as she looked Sona in the eyes.

What have you done?

ARIA LOOKED OUT THE WINDOW of her carriage as she and Yoska rode along the rocky road to the old Temples of Dyone.

Two large black wolves rested at her feet, snoring, as the carriage rose and fell with each bump in the dirt road that cut through the Dyone countryside. Aria's brows were furrowed as she held a wolf pup in her lap as she struggled to accept the fact the Sona had killed her son.

No amount of tears would bring him back, but that didn't stop her from shutting herself in her chambers and sobbing into the night.

Tragedy was what defined her.

Aria's parents died when she was just a girl, making her the youngest Queen to ever rule Oren.

Her husband was killed in a battle with the wild men of Harthon from the west of Kyril.

Now, her son had been murdered by the woman he loved.

Aria bit her lip and squeezed her eyes shut.

Why had The Ancients done this to her? She deserved better.

Everyone she'd ever loved was gone.

"Are you all right?" Yoska asked her from across the carriage. "You've been very quiet."

Aria shook her head. "No," she said. "I'm not all right. But, I will be."

Bitterness filled her mouth as she thought of the young woman. She clenched her jaw, imagining her vengeance.

I will destroy her.

"Try not to get too ahead of yourself. Cyden will be able to tell us the truth of what you saw in Sona's memories. We do not know if what you saw was real."

"We'll see," Aria said as she stroked the tiny pup's white fur. She kissed the top of his head and watched the meadows pass her by. "My gift has never been wrong. If Sona has found a way to lie in her thoughts, then I'll be both relieved and amazed

Farmlands lay desolate, abandoned by owners that now lay in their graves. Diseased cattle were piled high in ditches and burned.

Back in the capital, there were nonstop requests for more money to help feed her citizens.

For the first time in twenty-two years, Queen Aria was at a loss for what to do. There were two individuals that she trusted more than anyone in the world.

Yoska.

And her uncle, the prophet, Master Cyden.

The carriage emerged from the forest and approached a stone temple set in the middle of a flat field of rose bushes that stretched for miles on in every direction. A faint outline of mountains was visible in the distance.

If she hadn't been stricken with grief, she might have smiled at the sight. Memories of her childhood holidays being spent with her uncle, Master Cyden came to her, but the best she could do was relax her jaw.

"We're here," Yoska said. "I think it's best if I alert him of our arrival."

"That's probably wise," she said and Yoska flew out the open window and into the bright sunlight of midday. She watched him fly over the simple gate that stood before the temple. There wasn't a need for a strong defense when it came to Cyden and his disciples. An intruder would never dare step foot onto her uncle's property.

Not if they wanted to remain sane.

The carriage stopped and Gwevern hopped from one of the horses that pulled the carriage along to open the door for Aria.

"Take care with your step, my Queen," Gwevern said, reaching a hand out to help Aria out of the carriage.

She held onto her skirts to keep from stepping on the white lace as she carefully made her way onto the road. The smell of roses overwhelmed her as she and her wolves walked to the gate.

A young man dressed in robes with long black hair pulled into a single braid waited at the gate. He bowed as he held the gate open for Aria.

"Welcome, Queen Aria," he said, keeping his eyes and head low as Aria entered the courtyard filled with young Tryan men and women sitting in rows with their legs crossed and their eyes closed. "Midday meditation will be over in just a few minutes. You can go right in if you'd like."

Aria nodded, watching Cyden's disciples. There weren't warriors like the Orenian Order; these Tryans had reached a new level of mental awareness. The young women and men within the temple could control parts of their minds and power that most ordinary Tryans didn't even know existed.

All Tryans had the potential to tap into their common gift of Enchantment, but most never had the training to do so. The disciples could do things that would make common folk believe them to be gods amongst men.

As Aria stood inside the gate, she folded her arms across the square cut neckline of her lace gown. She remembered the time studying with her uncle when she was a child. Her desire to control the voices inside her head had made her grow up faster than most little girls.

Discovering that those voices were the real thoughts of the people around her had made her train even harder. Somehow, she felt at peace around the disciples. Just being in the temple had already calmed the parts of her mind that made her want to use her power in ways she'd never imagined.

"This way, Queen Aria," the young man said softly so as not to disturb the disciples.

They walked along the narrow white walkway. There was a sea of black sand on the left side and white sand on the right, and as a bell chimed, everyone bowed their heads to the sand and the silence continued.

Aria almost wished she could return to her life as a disciple. The quiet that surrounded her was exactly what she needed. The skill it took to free one's mind from troubling thoughts was impressive, and everyone in the temple could do so.

Why hadn't she come back sooner?

No thoughts to read.

Pure bliss.

The white archway gave way to a steep set of stairs that led into the temple's tall double doors.

Aria hadn't expected to do so, but as she looked up to see Master Cyden at the top of the stairs, long black hair reaching his waist, wearing brown robes, and arms outstretched to her, she couldn't help herself.

Tears welled in her eyes, but a smile also came to her lips.

"Welcome home, Aria."

ARIA FOLLOWED CYDEN to the temple vaults.

The dark corridors were simply lit by scant torches which only increased the eeriness that Aria felt when they went so deep underground.

"I knew you'd come to me one day."

"You could have come to visit at any time."

"Oren is too big. The people don't want someone like me in their business."

"Think of how I feel," Aria said, raising a brow. "They know I can read their thoughts, and yet they still love me."

Cyden paused, glancing over his shoulder. "Aria, you think they love you?"

The question, and the way he said it, sent shivers along her arms.

She swallowed. "Well, yes. I do."

"Naïve. Don't be that."

Aria pursed her lips. Cyden was more straightforward than she was used to back at the palace. The more she thought about what he said, the more she appreciated it. She needed someone to be blunt with her.

"You have no idea how bad things are," Aria said.

Cyden glanced over his shoulder, pausing in the middle of the dim corridor, almost as tall as the low ceiling.

"I am a prophet. Do you really think I don't know what has been going on? Like I said, I knew you'd come to me." He lifted a finger, his brows rising. "And it's a good thing you didn't wait too long."

A sigh slipped through Aria's lips as she followed him to the end of the corridor. A thick door stood between them and the vaults.

She wiped a stray black hair from her face, waiting as Cyden pulled a long key from his pocket and turned the heavy iron lock.

The lock clicked and Cyden pressed his palm against it, making it creak open to darkness. Once he stepped inside, a low hum buzzed in Aria's head.

Candles began to flicker with flames. The grooves in the floor and walls were lit with orange light.

Aria entered the large room, her eyes following the light as it traveled higher and higher up to the ceiling etched with an ancient mural. The ceiling was much higher than she'd anticipated, stretching almost as tall as the temple.

"We must be really deep underground," she whispered.

Cyden nodded. "We are. Almost sixty feet. The Dyone Disciples built the temple at the end of the Great War, right before The Barriers were built. They knew that what would be kept down here would be very valuable to someone one day. And dangerous to those that would use this information to do harm."

Aria's throat felt dry as she walked along the narrow path that was set amongst the pillars. Instead of bookshelves lining the walls, pillars stood in rows, each with a scroll encased in glass set upon its surface.

"Good girl," Cyden said, turning to face her. "Stick to the path. Don't touch anything. Magick lives here, and it must be approached with respect."

"I understand," she said, clasping her hands before her.

"Do you remember how to clear your mind?"

"I do," Aria said with a nod. Her eyes met Cyden's. They were a murky blue that reminded her of the sky before a storm. "Clearing my mind has helped keep me sane. You can't imagine hearing everyone's thoughts, all of the time. Not everyone thinks about good. There is so much evil in the minds of others."

"I know, Aria. You're a strong woman to have such a power and not use it for evil."

"Maybe. But what I saw in Lady Sonalese Rochfort's mind has me rethinking my kindness." She chewed her bottom lip and looked away from Cyden's intense gaze. "If she truly killed my son, there is *nothing* that can protect her from my wrath."

"We will find the truth in what you saw. Clear your mind, and come with me," he said, turning back to face the path that led to a faraway wall.

At the end, Aria could see a pillar set away from the rows. It was encapsulated against the wall in a thick plate of glass that looked fused to the stone wall. A golden lion's head was placed above, its mouth opened in a roar.

A faint breeze swept through, cooling Aria's ankles as she walked. She paused.

Aria, something whispered. It wasn't just an eerie whisper; she could feel a warm breath on her ear, making her tense and hold her breath.

"Cyden," she said in a low voice as she looked to the left and the right. "Something just called my name."

"Magick. Ignore it." Cyden stopped and raised a finger. "Unless it tells you to leave. Then, let me know. We don't want to tempt the spells left behind, but they do like to have a bit of fun with the living whenever they get the chance."

Aria swallowed and continued to follow Cyden. "They must not encounter the living very often."

"Almost never these days. I have no use for these scrolls most of the time, and Magick takes care of the upkeep of the vault for me."

Aria. You've come to see me, haven't you?

A gasp escaped Aria's lips, and her face paled when a shadowy figure with burning white hair that stood straight up blocked her path. Its hair was much like the flames on a candle's wick, wavering like fire.

She shivered as the tall figure opened its arms and stretched them above its head.

She couldn't tell if it was a man or woman, but a simple face with wide black eyes, thin lips, and a hollow nose set upon translucent skin appeared on the figure before her. The figure looked like the beginnings of a person, yet one that was unfinished as there were no other distinguishing traits. Arms fixed to a thin body without legs, but rather a block-like gown that hovered a few inches above the path before Aria.

Too afraid to move, Aria spoke in a soft voice. "Cyden?"

"Yes?" He didn't glance back; he simply drew something on the glass on the wall with his finger.

"Something is blocking my path."

"I told you, Aria. It's Magick. Just be kind, and it will let you pass."

Aria's eyes widened. "Magick is a…person?"

"No. Magick is an ancient being. Not a person," he said. "Magick. Let my friend pass. We haven't come to play."

Magick's creepy grin widened as it floated closer to Aria, so close that its face was an inch from hers. The eyes widened.

"But, I've been so bored. I want to play with her," Magick said this time with an actual voice that sounded like a mixture of a little boy and a little girl's.

Aria yelped when it lifted her arms. She tried to pull away, but it was too strong.

"Do these come off?" Magick asked, tugging Aria's arms forward, before spinning with her.

"Magick," Cyden shouted in a stern voice that resonated throughout the entire vault.

Magick hissed, letting Aria go as if she were on fire. It flew away, fading into the air like a mist.

Shaken, Aria rubbed her arms; still feeling as though hundreds of spiders crawled all over her skin. She scrubbed her arms, trying to make the sensation go away.

"I'm sorry, Aria. Magick shouldn't have touched you. It got a bit too excited."

"I'm sorry," Magick said, peeking its head from around a pillar. Its hair now burned blue. "Will you forgive me, Master?"

"You are forgiven. Just mind your manners."

"Will you forgive me, Mind Reader?"

Aria shot it a glance, but kept her lips pursed as she nodded.

"I want to show you something."

Aria hurried over to Cyden as Magick watched from behind a pillar.

"What did you find?"

Aria stood beside Cyden as the glass shield slid into the wall, revealing an old book with a brass binding.

"Rochfort history," Cyden said to the book.

The pages glowed, and then flipped to the page they wanted. Cyden peered down at the text, and his eyes widened at a particular line.

"What do you see? Right there?" He pointed to a line at the bottom of the page.

Aria squinted as she read the line. To her surprise, Sona was actually in the book.

"What is this book?"

"It's the Chronicle of Past, Present, and Future. It tells us everything about the Tryans of Kyril, and even some of the other races."

She nodded, and read along.

Lady Sonalese Rochfort, daughter of Lord Rochfort. Warrior with the Charm trait.

Aria's eyes shot to Cyden's.

"She possesses the Charm trait."

Cyden nodded. "It seems your problem stems from a crafty little liar."

Chapter 43

CYDEN BLEW OUT ALL OF the candles in his temple sanctuary Yoska flew in and landed beside Aria on one of the smooth stone benches lined up before a raised stage.

She stared at the stage, remembering times when she and the other disciples would exhibit their new skills before an audience of their peers.

Those were good times, times when Aria was more than just the Queen of Oren.

Times when she was young and full of unlimited potential.

"What did I miss?"

Aria sighed and rubbed her temples. "Apparently, Sona has the Charm trait."

"Dear Elahe," Yoska said. "I never suspected."

"Right. Neither did I. She's very good at what she does," Aria said with a shake of her head. "Her father put her up to it. I'm sure. But, why did she have to kill Liam?"

"Did Cyden see anything to confirm if Liam is truly dead?"

"No," Aria said with a sigh. "Nothing about Liam will come to him. I know what that means."

"I'm sorry, Aria," Yoska said.

Aria pursed her lips and looked down at her folded hands in her lap.

"This is more serious than I thought. Sona is much more powerful than I thought."

Aria looked to him. "Clearly. She fooled us all. Apparently, swords aren't her only weapon."

Yoska's eyes widened. "We need to hurry back to Oren."

"Why?"

"You left a skilled Charmer in your Kingdom, one that wants to see you executed."

Aria's face paled. He was right. She wrung her hands. Not only did Sona have the power to turn her entire Kingdom against her, but her family was in direct line for the throne through ancient bloodlines.

"All of this time I truly believed that she loved my son. I was ready to welcome her into our home and family." She wiped a tear. She hadn't felt such bitterness and sorrow in a long time.

"I know, Aria. I am very sorry about all of this. You don't deserve such pain."

Aria cleared her throat. She lowered her voice, her eyes fixed on Cyden. She was ashamed to be brought to tears yet again, but Yoska was her dearest friend. He had been there every time tragedy crossed her path.

"I had dreams of little grandchildren running through the palace. Now, I dream of watching her blood pool into the grooves of the chopping block."

Fury filled her belly, yet she kept it contained. She gritted her teeth, hands folded as she watched Cyden pace the room in deep thought. Her hopes were that Cyden would be able to guide them.

With limited options, she knew that there was so much at stake that she couldn't risk a single mistake.

"Cyden," she called, tired of waiting. "Do you see anything?"

Cyden shot an eerie look at her. "I do," he said, his voice almost as low as a whisper.

"What is it?" Aria's brows knitted into a frown as she watched Cyden step from the stage platform.

"We must leave. Right away."

Standing, Aria nodded, eager to take action. "All right. We are ready whenever you are."

Cyden rubbed his hands together before rubbing his chin. "I will gather my disciples, and we can head out within the hour."

Brows furrowed, Aria watched Cyden head for the archway that led outside.

"Why do you need to bring the disciples?"

"Why would I leave them behind?"

Aria shrugged. "What are you planning to do?"

"Leave Oren," he said, glancing over his shoulder at her.

"What?" Aria's eyes widened as she walked over to meet Cyden near the exit. "Why would we leave Oren? I need to save it. Not abandon it."

"I fear it's too late to do anything for Oren. We need to leave immediately. This plague is spreading, and it will consume everything and everyone in its path if we do not get out of its way."

"What? I can't just leave my Kingdom in the hands of that psychotic woman."

"You must," Cyden said, his eyes darkening. "If you want to live."

Speechless, Aria watched him leave the room.

Yoska flew to her. "What are you thinking?"

"I don't know," Aria said, her shoulders slumping as she looked out to the garden as Cyden walked along the path to his disciples congregated outside.

"We go home," Aria said. She turned to Yoska. "I cannot let my people down. No matter how bad things get."

Chapter 44

SOON, THE EMPEROR WOULD be awakened, and a sliver of fear hid inside Dragnor's mind. His jaw tightened as he thought of what would happen the moment Kavien's eyes opened.

Dragnor had cursed him yet again, and now Sister Eloni was dead.

Time for a new ally.

Faira's revelations about Lilae had led him to a dead end. The twins had escaped, and it brought up the same anger he'd felt each time he'd catch up to Lilae just to have her slip through his fingers.

He'd find them. The cook he'd captured would speak, eventually.

Dragnor stood at the open window, looking out onto the city as the sun bathed the creams and beiges of the tall buildings it in its orange light. Avia'Torena was too bright for his tastes, but even he could appreciate its beauty. The sandy dunes in the distance however, should be flattened and covered with the black trees from his home.

"Where are you taking me?" A young woman with dangling bracelets piled onto her arms yelled as she struggled against two guards.

The men dragged her into the center of the small conference room with chairs set in rows that faced a hanging map of Eura.

"I'm talking to you!"

Dragnor shot her an icy glare that made her swallow her protests. She was forced to her knees and stared at him in horror.

"It's you. The Shadow Elf. What do you want with me?"

Dragnor ignored her question and circled her, noting her brown skin and ethereal hazel eyes. Her hair was long, and black, reaching her ankles. She hid it with a red scarf that shimmered in the rays of the sun. Red silk was wrapped around her body and draped over her shoulders like the customary dress of the Avia'Torenan nobility.

They were at least making an effort to blend.

He smiled as her large eyes met his. She swallowed and looked away. Yet, he could feel the power radiating from her. She was perfect.

"What is it you want?"

Her voice was a little calmer now.

"You know exactly what I want. You can stop pretending now." Dragnor waved the guards away and she waited silently until the room was cleared.

She rose to her feet and pulled out a small brown rod from her satchel. She yanked the rod forward and it clicked, lengthening into a staff.

She no longer looked at Dragnor with fear.

Dragnor stood there regarding her with a look of respect. She had hidden so well.

"You have one minute to speak your business with me. I am a busy woman, and I do not appreciate being taken against my will."

Dragnor shook his head and met her eyes. "You have this meeting all wrong. I have nothing but great respect for you. But, I also know that you don't want your cover blown."

She didn't flinch. "What do you want, Dragnor? We are tired of your empty promises and lies. Unless Wexcyn came to ask for our aid, we no longer have any business with you."

He grinned—something rare for him, yet he was truly pleased. The Bellens were the key to many things. They were what he needed to gain an edge over The Chosen.

This woman might be the key to finding those that posed a threat to Wexcyn and their plan for a new world.

"I want to make you an ally, Eyshe."

"Really?" She put a hand on her hip and squinted her eyes. "After what you allowed to happy to Sister Eloni, I am not sure I trust you. My sisters and I no longer want to be a part of your scheme."

"But think of all of the souls you can have. The immortality that comes with those souls…and the young recruits we would give you."

"We don't need your help. We've been claiming souls since the beginning of time, and never needed a Shadow Elf's help."

Dragnor sat down in a chair, and crossed his legs. He wrapped his hands around his knees. "But your leader. Tell me she doesn't want to make a Bellen of The Flame."

Eyshe's eyes widened for a second, and then her face became a blank canvas once again.

"Our leader will not be beguiled by your false promises." She turned to leave. "You cannot offer such a thing. The Flame slipped from your fingers. And now no one knows where she is. Sorry, Dragnor. It was a valiant effort."

"But, I do, Eyshe," Dragnor said. "I know where she is going."

Eyshe glanced back at him, a brow raised. "And how do you know where she is going?"

Dragnor grinned. "I found the cook that helped her sisters escape."

She pursed her lips, but turned back around. "Go on."

"They are heading for Torgrid, the Goblin City," Dragnor said. He raised a long finger. "The Elder will lead Lilae there, right to us. *If* we can make a deal. Come now. You know you want to…and that your leader dreams of an opportunity such as this."

"How do you know she will go to Torgrid?"

"Vaugner rules Torgrid. I am certain that the Elder is leading The Flame and The Storm to the Goblin City."

Eyshe's eyes brightened. "Two Gatekeepers. In one place. Holy Elahe, Dragnor. Imagine the power."

"Yes," Dragnor said, nodding. "You know where I am going with this."

"I do. Two Gatekeepers can Gate more than we ever could." She sat down in a chair, wrapping her legs with her long skirts."

Dragnor's grin widened. "Exactly. Forget using the soul of one poor girl to travel to the different realms. *They* can Gate an *army*."

"But," Eyshe said. "As much as I want to invade Auroria, I have a better idea that can accomplish two goals at once."

Dragnor leaned forward in his seat. "What is that?"

"Oh," she purred, her eyes widening. "I think it will please both of our masters."

"Tell me. Don't be coy," Dragnor said.

Eyshe smiled. "I know how we can free Wexcyn. If we free him, we won't even need the Elders to Gate us anywhere. We can stride into every territory we choose."

Dragnor drew in a breath. *Yes. This is it.*

He nodded. "I'm listening."

Chapter 45

THE GOBLIN CITY OF TORGRID was a stronghold of darkness. Bleak stone structures and metal made up the city, and black gates and a towering wall protected it from outsiders.

Lilae held tight to Triste's reigns as they emerged from the clouds and flew over the city. Her eyes roamed over the landscape. It was hidden by the thick forest, miles from any other towns or villages. A river stretched across the right side, feeding a distant ocean.

"Follow me down to the clearing," Neru said, leading his wyvern to the black stone path before the gates.

Lilae swallowed. She leaned forward, her chest pressed to Triste's neck as she spoke to him. "Follow Neru to that smooth clearing."

"Yes," Triste said. "Thank you for not making me land inside. The goblins frighten me."

Lilae smoothed the scales on his neck. "They scare me too," she said, although she'd never seen a goblin, and still didn't see a trace of any as the moon cast a hazy light on the sleeping city.

Once they landed, everyone dismounted and summoned their wyverns back to their eggs.

"Keep them," Neru said. "They will be loyal to you forever if you treat them right."

Lilae smiled, despite her fear of standing before the mysterious Goblin City in the dark. To have her own wyvern was like a dream. She'd never been given such an amazing gift.

Delia approached the gate and two goblin guards faced her from behind the thick black bars.

Wearing armor that covered their small bodies and faces, they looked over the group of foreigners with cool disdain.

"What's yer business?"

"Vaugner," Delia said, her staff's tip glowing. "We have been invited by your leader."

The guards watched the glow of her staff, taking a step back.

"Elder," one said. "We didn't know it was you."

"It's fine. Please, just let Vaugner know we are here."

"'Course," he said and went to unlock the gate. "Come right in."

The other held the gate open as Lilae and the others filed in.

"We've had so many strangers come to us of late. Not too long ago we 'ad an intruder fly right in on one of those flying lizard things you came in on. Very suspect, I'd say. But, he had his comeuppance."

"An intruder?" Neru asked.

"Yes," the goblin said. He scratched his fuzzy chin, his eyes squinting as he looked down at Neru. "And he looked much like you, old fella."

"Dragnor," Lilae whispered.

"Don't know 'is name. But Master Vaugner gave him quite a fright. He ran from here as if 'is arse was set ablaze," he said with a chuckle. "We don't get much visitin' round here. Most know betta."

"What did he want?" Delia asked, exchanging a look with Lilae.

The goblin shrugged as the other closed the gate and locked it.

"Dunno. Ask Vaugner. He knows everythin', doesn't tell Wick or Frew anythin' but what ta do."

"Right," Delia said. "Take us to him, please."

"I can't leave me post, miss. But, lemme call someone that can."

The goblin whistled and a goblin riding a brown horse came trotting over from down the road that led through the city of towering buildings that were nearly as tall as those in Gollush.

"So," Liam said, folding his arms across his chest. "This is the lost race."

"Lost race?"

He nodded. "I read about them in my studies as a young boy. Goblins, fairies, and mermaids don't have Ancients like we do. They are neutral."

"Well," Rowe said. "The fairies do have an Ancient now."

Liam nodded, his eyes darkening at the memory of Nani. "True. That does change things a bit."

"What happened to their god?" Lilae asked, her eyes watching the horseman as he leaned down to the goblin guard. He nodded, his eyes scanning them, and turned to deliver the message.

"They died, left, or sacrificed themselves to sustain their race."

Delia turned to Liam. "I am impressed by your knowledge, Liam."

He shrugged, yet his cheeks flushed. "It's nothing. I only spent half my life devoting my days to reading, memorizing, and studying the ancient texts."

"All of Oren doubted he existed for the longest time. We never saw his face without it being glued to a book," Rowe joked, clasping a hand onto Liam's shoulder. "He knows more than anyone I've ever known."

"That's nothing to be ashamed about," Delia said. "A scholar is always of value."

Liam smiled, and Lilae wrapped her arm around his waist. "You'll have to teach me some of what you've learned someday."

He looked down at her and nodded. His eyes locked with hers, and he unfolded his arms to pull her into a brief embrace. "Of course. I'll teach you everything I know."

Lilae's grin faded at the way Delia looked at her. Something in her eyes seemed troubled, but the Elder said nothing of it. She simply turned the other way and whispered something to Neru. She nodded, and they stepped away from the group and continued their hushed conversation.

Lilae chewed her lip. She wished she could hear what was being said.

"You didn't lie about an adventure, Liam," Rowe said. "I may need to write all of this down when we return to Oren. Better yet. I'll let you write it for me."

"I'd be honored," Liam said. "You'll have to wait until I've bathed in the palace bath house and eaten as much roasted pork as I can manage. I truly miss the palace cook's food."

"No," Rowe said, shaking his head. "You've never had Cammie's cooking. You're coming to dinner at my house, and I guarantee you'll never want to eat that pompous palace food ever again. Country cooking. That's what you need."

Liam chuckled with a half shrug. "Whatever you say."

Lilae smiled, but somehow the thought of Liam returning to Oren worried her. Where would she go once everything was over? That was assuming they won and peace would follow whatever war Wexcyn waged on Ellowen.

She twirled the ends of her red hair around her finger. "I wonder where I will go once everything is over."

Liam and Rowe looked at her.

"I don't have a home," she said, softly, her brows furrowing at the center. "I never have."

Liam reached for her hand. "You'll come home with us. I already told you that you needed to meet my mother. You're welcome in my home, Lilae."

She smiled up at him, and he leaned down to kiss her lips.

What Liam said made her happier than she'd been in a long time. She realized then that he was the source of all of her happiness since her escape from the Avia'Torenan palace.

That realization made her hold onto his hand a little tighter. Fear struck her heart.

No.

Not again.

Everyone she'd ever loved had been ripped away from her in the most brutal and devastating ways. How could she go on if she lost Liam?

She sucked in a breath.

"Thank you," she said, but her heart ached for a loss that hadn't even occurred yet. She hated that feeling. Why couldn't she just live in the moment and enjoy him while she had him?

She knew why.

She loved Liam. More than anyone.

That made the stakes higher. She clenched her jaw.

She'd fight to protect him with her dying breath if she had to.

No one was going to take him away from her.

"I'd go anywhere with you," she whispered.

"You mean that?" Liam asked.

She nodded, on the verge of tears.

He leaned down to whisper to her. "We will never part, Lilae. I promise you that." He kissed her again and stood tall to look ahead as the horseman returned.

She beamed. It was as if he had read her thoughts, felt her insecurities, and squashed them with just a few words and a tender kiss.

"Vaugner invites you to come to the Keep. He's been waiting for your arrival," the horseman said, his small rubbery green face taken over by a friendly smile.

"Thank you," Delia said. "We will follow you."

"Perfect. I'm Dunstan," the goblin horseman said.

"Nice to meet you, Dunstan. I am Delia and this is Lilae, Liam, Rowe, and Neru," Delia replied. "Thank you for your kind welcome."

"Same. Truly," Dunstan said, and turned the horse to walk at a steady pace down the stone slab road lit with short lamps set on either side. "The goblin population is asleep, but tomorrow, the city will be energized after hearing of your arrival. We've been anxiously awaiting The Chosen since Vaugner told us of the alliance."

"Goblins," Rowe said. "Can't say that I've ever heard of you. But there's a lot I've never heard of that I've recently encountered."

"Right," Dunstan said. "We like being mysterious. Keeps us out of trouble. But, we've certainly heard of Tryans. Wait until my people see you and your glowing skin. And you're so tall. I fear I'd probably only come up to your waist," he said with a laugh.

"But most Tryans aren't as tall as Rowe either," Liam said.

"Aye," Rowe replied with a nod.

The quiet streets were shrouded by a thick fog that seemed to come from the stones of the street, like water dripping on a hot surface, causing steam. Still, Lilae was transfixed by the odd design of the buildings. It looked like each building had hundreds of indentations with metal doors, much like the flats of Gollush, yet she was sure that each flat was smaller, perhaps only housing one or two goblins at a time.

Her suspicions were validated when she noticed that some of the metal doors were left open, revealing two cots secured to the wall, where two goblins slept; one chest and a squat table were opposite their beds.

It seemed that the goblins lived simple lives, where all they needed were beds, somewhere to store their belongings, and somewhere to eat.

Not every goblin slept at that hour. An older goblin with a long pipe stood on the steps of one of the buildings, purple smoke wafting from his nostrils as he watched them with small, beady black eyes.

He blinked, but his eyes watched them until they passed by.

Once they reached the center of the city, they stood before a tall black tower.

The Keep.

Dunstan hopped from his horse and tied it to a tether on the street. He motioned them to follow.

He was right. He was barely as tall as their waists, with heavy boots, woolen pants, and gray cloak that covered his head and revealed a tiny sword at his hip.

Something told her that despite his size, he knew how to wield that sword. The door was flush with the ground, unlike the other buildings, which had steps leading to the doors.

It was open, and they walked inside, where a tall, thin young man stood in the shadows of the entryway, his hands folded behind him, a smile on his handsome face.

Lilae stared at him and his wavy blond hair that reached the tops of his ears and just above golden brows. Green eyes met hers, and his smile widened.

"Dear me," he said. "The rumors weren't untrue."

Lilae didn't know what that meant, but she kept quiet as Delia approached him.

"Vaugner," Delia said, her face brightening.

Lilae's brow lifted as she watched Delia. There was something new in her eyes—an adoration she'd never seen her show for a man. Ever.

Vaugner opened his arms and wrapped them around Delia.

"My dear, Delia," he said, closing his eyes as they held onto each other. "It is so good to see you again."

THE KEEP WAS DARK AND EERIE, but Delia's sudden excitement intrigued Lilae more than the mystery that surrounded them.

"I am so glad you dropped that horrid disguise," Delia said to Vaugner once they broke their embrace. She rubbed his cheeks, and touched his hair. "You looked as if you'd fall apart. This form is much more becoming."

There was a tenderness to the Elder's voice that Lilae was unused to. Though Delia was like a mother to Lilae, she couldn't recall hearing such a relaxed tone directed at anyone but her.

"I know," he said with a chuckle. "I use it during my travels. I admit I prefer the anonymity of it. No one thinks twice about a decrepit man. Still, it did give that Shadow Elf, Dragnor quite a scare though. Kept him from poking around in our affairs."

"I'm glad you gave him a scare. He deserves much worse."

"Oh, don't worry," Vaugner said. "He will get exactly that." He looked Delia up and down. "You've changed forms again as well."

"Yes. The Avia'Torenan woman's form wasn't as strong as the one I use now," Delia said, running her hands through her long black hair, pulling out tangles. She beamed, and hugged him once again. "How I've missed you, Vaugner."

"You flatter me. It's only been weeks since we've seen each other." His eyes twinkled with mischief. "You'll have the children thinking there's something *romantic* going on here," he teased with a wink.

Delia cleared her throat, her face flushing. "Now, that's enough jest, Vaugner."

Vaugner nodded. "Of course, dear." He turned to Lilae and Liam and clasped his hands together. "Now, look at you two. More perfect than The Ancients even anticipated. What a pair."

Lilae glanced at Liam.

"Nice to meet you, Elder," Liam said with a bow of his head.

"We've met before, Liam. You just don't remember it," Vaugner said, but didn't elaborate before turning his gaze to Lilae. "I have a surprise for you. One that cannot wait."

When he reached his hand out to Lilae, she hesitated before accepting.

"Come, dear," Vaugner said, his green eyes nearly hypnotizing her as the friendly smile on his face widened.

Lilae placed her hand within Vaugner's, feeling a strange buzz of energy as their flesh met. The sensation was unnerving, but her body acquiesced, telling her that it was okay to trust him.

Vaugner gave a quick bow to the others, his hair falling into his eyes. He raked it back with his wiry fingers and motioned to an archway to the right of the main entrance.

"Make yourselves comfortable in the sitting room. Lilae and I will return shortly."

Vaugner then guided Lilae from the entryway and down a narrow stairway that led to a large open space set in the center of six other sets of stairs. The levels of the Keep were astounding. Chandeliers hung above the wide room that connected all of the staircases, yet above them were more balconies, and floors blocked off by stones and doorways.

Fires blazed in large copper pots that stood before the openings and archways of the different rooms that branched off from the main floor.

Once they left the Keep—the innermost structure of the castle, she found the ancient building to be more of a maze than a home for the original rulers of Torgrid. With confusing halls and corridors that seemed to go on forever, the castle wrapped around the entire back of the city.

As Lilae explored her surroundings, she realized that much of what she saw didn't make sense as some of the stairways led to nothing but stone walls or open windows with bars. It was much like a confusing maze, and she was fortunate to have Vaugner leading the way.

"Where are we going?" The air tasted stale as they reached the center floor and turned to descend down yet another staircase that led into darkness.

"Patience," Vaugner said, his voice echoing. He gave the back of her hand a pat. "Soon, all will be revealed. Just know that you will be quite pleased."

Lilae pursed her lips and trusted him. Her heart raced as she tried to imagine what surprise he had for her.

Unless it was Dragnor's severed head, she wasn't sure what else it could be that would bring her any joy.

"What do you remember of your father, Lilae?"

The question caught her off guard.

"Pirin?"

"Yes, he was your real father. I was led to believe that you knew that."

Lilae licked her lips. "Yes. He told me the day he died. He was a remarkable father, even when I was unaware that he was more than my protector and trainer. He treated me as well as he treated his other daughters."

"Did he? I am happy to hear that." He paused for a moment as they turned a corner and walked up a new staircase. "We never intended to deprive you of the love of a family, Lilae. Delia made it her mission to make it so that you didn't lack the love and care of family. You know she loves you like a daughter, right?"

Lilae nodded. Delia was the only mother she'd ever known. "I do."

"And that she didn't rescue you from the palace until times were truly dire?"

Frowning, Lilae stopped walking. She looked up at Vaugner in the dim light. “I don’t understand that. Not one bit. Why did she let Dragnor hurt me?”

Flashes of being whipped by Dragnor nearly took her breath away. She swallowed and crossed her arms over her chest.

Vaugner tugged on the high collar of his shirt and looked to the ceiling. He spoke under his breath. “So, she hasn’t told you everything.”

Lilae’s eyes narrowed. “What do you mean? What is everything?”

“Perhaps its not the right time.”

“Tell me now,” Lilae demanded. She clasped her hand over her forearm and softened her voice. “Please.”

Vaugner’s eyes lowered to hers, his face more serious than she’d seen it in the short time they’d known each other.

“You were meant to be captured as a means to infiltrate the enemy compound.” He leaned down and lowered his voice to a whisper. “Only you could break Emperor Kavien’s curse.”

Lilae’s eyes widened.

Vaugner stood to his full height, which was a few inches taller than Lilae. “And we believe you did break his curse. But it counts for nothing since Dragnor and the blasted Bellens gave him yet another curse to cover their mistakes.”

Lilae rubbed her temples. “Is that the surprise? Because I am not pleased. Not at all.”

Vaugner cracked a grin. “No, ma’am. That was merely valuable information I believe will clear your mind and distrust you felt for Delia.”

“But—”

He lifted a finger. “No. You can’t hide anything from me, Lilae. I saw it in your eyes. Forgive her. She holds your best interest above everything. When she escaped the Wexcyn’s takeover of the Underworld, she went directly to you. To protect you.”

Lilae sighed. He was right, and she hadn’t even noticed it. It had been weeks since she’d escaped with Delia, and she hadn’t made an effort to discuss the questions swimming in her mind. She nodded, and chewed her lip. She hadn’t even realized just how much trust she’d lost in Delia.

"Come now, no need to fret. You can talk to her later. There is still a surprise to present."

Lilae clutched her arm as she followed Vaugner to a door at the end of the hall.

"Here we are," he said, and opened a door with a gentle push. "Go on."

Lilae let out a breath before stepping inside.

What she saw inside sent her to her knees as her hand clasped her mouth.

Inside, the room was light with furnishings that reminded her of their home in Lowen's Edge. Such warmth filled her as her eyes stared at the two blonde girls that waited inside, smiles on their beautiful faces—faces Lilae never thought she'd see again.

"*Holy Elahe*," she breathed in shock as Risa and Jaiza rushed and tackled her with hugs and kisses.

All sounds were muted by the confusion in her head. Her stomach churned. Her heart thumped against her ribcage.

These girls—they looked like Risa and Jaiza—but her sisters were dead.

A dream.

It had to be.

Stunned, Lilae knelt there as they hugged her, crying, unsure if any of it was real. The tears came then, from the deepest depths of her soul as she poured out all of her sorrow and pain.

Dream or not.

She clutched them both and squeezed her eyes shut.

Lilae would never let them go.

"IS SHE THE ONE?" An unfamiliar voice whispered from nearby.

Lilae tensed. As she opened her eyes, they widened at the sight of two Shadow Elf women. For a moment she doubted that anything she saw was real.

"Yes, Mai," Risa said, pulling Lilae to her feet by the hands. She kissed both of her cheeks. "This is our dear sister that we told you about."

"Lilae," Jaiza said, smoothing down Lilae's unruly hair. "I can't believe you are here. We have missed you dearly."

"I missed you too," Lilae said, her eyes fixed on the Shadow Elf girls. "I thought you were dead." Her voice caught in her throat as she faced Jaiza and cupped her face in her hands, before she turned to do the same to Risa. "Dear Elahe. I am dreaming."

"No," Jaiza said. "We are here. We traveled a long way to find you."

Lilae's beaming smile faded as the elves drew closer, their white tattoos glowing in the pale light from the fire in the back of the circular stone room.

"Lilae," Risa said, pulling her forward to the elves. "This is Ayoki and Mai."

Lilae's brows lifted.

It couldn't be.

"Ayoki? From Gollush?"

The shorter Shadow Elf nodded, her eyes widening at Lilae's question. She looked from Mai and back to Lilae, yet didn't say a word.

"Ayoki is mute," Mai said. "But, how did you know who she was?" She kept close to Ayoki as her eyes narrowed at Lilae.

"Pretica told us about you two—that you were taken by Bellens," Lilae said. "But we found out the truth."

Mai nodded. "She betrayed us. Her own blood."

Vaugner stepped into the room. "Come, ladies. Let us celebrate this joyous reunion."

Lilae nodded, and as her eyes met with Ayoki's, she noticed a glint of something within them. A fear. Perhaps even a shred of grief.

Lilae knew that look and feeling all too well. Though they didn't speak, she and Ayoki shared something with that brief look. Pulled along by Risa, Lilae smiled again and headed out of the room and back through the Keep.

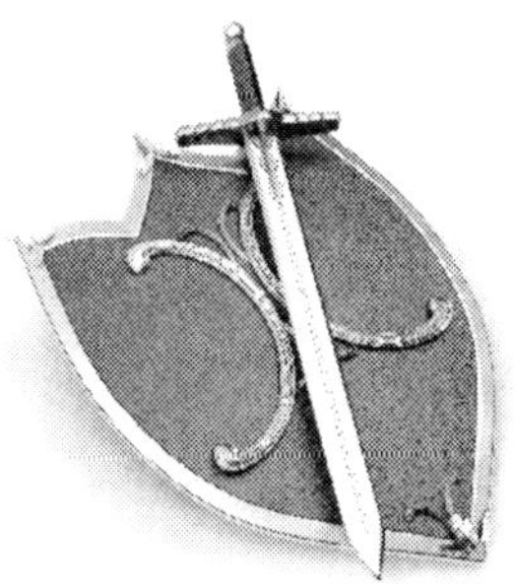

AS THE HUMAN GIRLS WERE LED to the dining hall, Vaugner turned to Ayoki and reached a hand out to her.

She looked down at his pale hand and back to his eyes, shrugging.

He took her hand into his and gave it a pat.

"Come with me," he said, leading her away from the dining hall where the Elder, humans, and the Tryan men prepared for a late meal.

Ayoki didn't feel as though she fit in. Even Mai seemed comfortable in these new surrounding that felt so foreign to Ayoki.

How could she relate to anyone that knew nothing of what it was like to not have a voice?

"Good question," Vaugner said.

Ayoki stopped walking and pulled her hand away. She raised her brows as she looked at Vaugner.

"Yes. I can read your thoughts," he said. "It isn't an uncommon ability for an Elder. Especially someone as old as me, who has learned a vast amount of skills. Please, don't be afraid."

Afraid? Ayoki folded her arms across her chest. *I know the fear in everyone else's eyes.*

"I know you do," Vaugner said, sitting down on a bench draped with a green knitted blanket in the corridor outside of the dining hall. "I know that you have suffered and have seen a great many things. Why don't you tell me about it?"

Ayoki didn't sit down. She frowned as she looked at Vaugner. *I didn't ask for this power. I never wanted it. I want my voice, and a life free of the darkness inside of me.*

He nodded. "That is understandable. All of The Chosen wish to have normal lives at times."

Do they? She couldn't imagine such a thing. Their power couldn't be as plagued by evil as hers.

"Each of you has a strength that The Ancients recognized would complement one another."

My power complements nothing. It simply destroys. It has destroyed me. She wiped tears from her eyes with the back of her hand.

Vaugner stood and came to her. He took her hands into his own. "What if I told you that you were more powerful than them all? That you are the strongest, and this is why The Ancients gave you the most difficult of abilities."

Ayoki's eyes widened. Such a thing had never occurred to her, and still, she couldn't believe it.

"What I tell you is the truth," Vaugner said. "And I have a great deal more truths to reveal to you, if you are ready to listen."

Ayoki licked her lips, looking back to the dining hall.

She nodded. *Yes. Tell me.*

Chapter 48

THE REUNION BETWEEN SISTERS was better than anything Lilae could have imagined. She'd wanted nothing she more in the world than to have her family back, and somehow that wish had been granted. Even if it was only her sisters, and not her father or her stepmother, she was grateful.

Lilae never thought she'd would see Risa and Jaiza again. Yet, there they were, seated at a long table eating and drinking with her new friends.

She was surprised that she even had the desire to drink again, after being poisoned. However, she and the others trusted Vaugner's supply, and it was the best cause for a celebration that Lilae could think of.

Lilae couldn't stop smiling. The tears of joy had finally ceased, but her heart swelled with such emotion that she was sure they'd return at any moment.

Goblin servants tended to them and made sure their glasses were always full with water or wine. Risa and Jaiza both fawned over Lilae, playing with her hair and reminiscing. They couldn't stop hugging. It was as if they were afraid to let go, lest they be ripped apart again.

"We missed you so much, Lilae," Risa said in between sips of wine. "I know I keep saying it, but I am still in awe that we are actually together again. Jaiza and I dreamed about this day."

"I didn't even know it was possible," Lilae said. "But yes, I dreamed of it as well. For a while, dreams were the only place that I felt anything more than sorrow."

She glanced at Liam, who sat beside her. He gave her knee a squeeze under the table.

Life couldn't be more perfect then at that moment. Her sisters were there. The man she loved was there.

What could go wrong?

"When we were separated in Lowen's Edge, we thought we'd never see you again. The soldiers took us and a few other women to their ships."

Jaiza nodded, her eyes red from crying. "But I saw you leave on a different ship once we docked in Avia'Torena, and I knew we would find our way to one another somehow."

Lilae eyes welled up again. Her heart was full of joy, but sadness filled her throat whenever she looked at Risa and Jaiza's many scars. Like Lilae, their scars tattooed them now. All over their arms and legs were small cuts and welts.

Their arms were branded with a seal much like Lilae's crescent seal that meant she belonged to Kavien. The twin's brands were of two stars, the seal of the Duke of Avia'Torena.

Lilae didn't ask, for she knew what they suffered. The harem girls had warned her about the Duke. He was cousin to Kavien, and she was his pet. The Duke had been denied Lilae's company. Kavien had protected her in more ways than one.

There was one thing she did want to know.

"Tell me," Lilae began. She rubbed the rim of her cup of wine with her fingertip and lowered her eyes. "I watched Pirin die that day," she said before pausing. "But what of Anic?"

She looked up at the both of them, afraid of the answer, but desperate for the truth.

She could feel Liam's eyes on her, practically reading her thoughts and anticipating her emotions. He took her hand into his, and she was grateful.

For too long she had obsessed over her guilt of letting the twins die; she had suffered from false information. Hope filled her that Anic might be out there somewhere, enslaved or forced into Kavien's army, but alive.

Jaiza looked at Risa. Her shoulders slumped and she shook her head. Her eyes had the answer and Lilae didn't want to hear more.

"Oh," Lilae said. "Thank you."

"To Anic," Risa said, raising her glass. "A brave and kind young man."

Everyone nodded and joined her.

"To Anic," they said in unison, joined glasses, and took a drink.

Silence filled the room after everyone drank from their glasses.

Lilae looked at Ayoki, who like Liam drank water. Their eyes met again, and Lilae found herself drawn in by her eyes. She wished they could speak to one another. She was The Seer, and there was so much they could share about their powers.

"So," Jaiza said, turning her attention to Delia, who sat at the opposite end of the table, across from Vaugner. "What is next, Delia?"

"How soon can we leave?" Delia asked Vaugner.

"Give me a few days to prepare everything. I want to give Ayoki something before you leave."

"Good," Delia said. "In a few days we are off to Auroria. There, we will prepare the Northern armies. Avia'Torena is ready for war; so we must also be ready."

"Great," Risa said, sighing. "It's going to take forever to travel back to Auroria."

"How far is it?" Liam asked, taking a bite from a sweet roll with white frosting.

Jaiza laughed as she and Risa shared a look. "It only took us eighteen years to travel from Auroria to Lowen's Edge. Granted, we stopped in different villages and lived and worked for a while, I think that might cut our journey in half."

"Great," Lilae grumbled.

"Honestly, I'm not looking forward to it. But, it is our birth home," Risa said.

"I can't say that I remember much of it. Snow. Lots of snow," Jaiza said. "So high that you'd get stuck inside your house some days because the snow would trap you."

Lilae remembered nothing of her birthplace. Delia had taken her from her parents the night she was born, and never looked back. Still, she'd dreamt about it often, especially after she'd met her brother, the new King of Auroria.

Still, her mother awaited. Her real mother. The thought of meeting her turned Lilae's stomach sour. She simply hoped the woman would measure up to how she imagined her to be.

Kind and loving. Not like her stepmother, Lhana.

"Yes," Vaugner said, nodding his head as he tapped his fingertips on the wooden tabletop. "It is far indeed. *But…*" his eyes lifted, a mischievous glint within them. "It will take us minutes to arrive."

Everyone turned to him.

"What?" Liam asked. "How is that possible?"

"Don't question the man, Liam," Rowe said, downing his second cup of ale. Wine wasn't his drink of choice. "I'm sure the Elder has some tricks up his sleeves."

Vaugner chuckled. "How right you are, Rowe." He nodded at Delia. "But what you have in this very room are two Elders."

"Not just any Elders," Delia said, a small smile on her lips as her eyes locked with Vaugner's from across the long table. The candles, placed in beautiful golden holders set on the table, cast an eerie glow on her pale face.

"We are both Gatekeepers," she said, her smile widening.

"And what do Gatekeepers do?" Vaugner asked them, leaning back in his chair.

Lilae's brows knitted in the center. "You take the dead to the Underworld."

"Yes," Vaugner said. "And how do we do that?"

"You open a Gate, right?" Mai asked, her dark eyes looking from Delia to Vaugner as she leaned over her half-eaten plate of grapes and cheese.

"Of a sort. There isn't a physical gate. What Gatekeepers do is take the dead to the Underworld. We Gate them."

"We can travel anywhere in the entire world of Ellowen, as long as there is another Gatekeeper to allow us to reach the next point."

"Is that like what I did when we escaped the palace?" Lilae asked, remembering the rush of vanishing with Delia and Garion and reappearing at The Barrier.

"Similar," Delia said, nodding. "What you did is part of your power, but it is limited. You can take yourself and one other, maybe two."

"But Delia and I can Gate as many as we want, as long as we know the other is coming, or where they are going," Vaugner said.

"Amazing," Liam said, his eyes widening.

"See," Rowe said. "I told you. Tricks."

Vaugner's chuckle lowered into an almost haunting laugh. "You have no idea just how *tricky* we can be," he said, his eyes casting a flicker of a glow as he lifted his gaze to Delia's.

Chapter 49

DESPITE THE FOREST COVER, it was a hot day, and Aria sweated inside her carriage. She fanned herself and shook the front of her dress to let air in.

Soon, she would be inside her Kingdom once again, and the work to ruin Sona would begin. Such thoughts turned her stomach as she remembered that she also had to save her people from the devastating plague that ravaged her home.

Yoska had flown ahead to make sure everything in the palace had kept up without her. She hoped that all was well. Yoska was loyal and had been for as long as she could remember.

She sighed deeply and glanced out the window at her right.

She sat up straight at what she saw. Elders waited outside the gates of Oren as Aria approached.

Their black forms sent chills along Aria's arms. She rubbed the gooseflesh and stared at them as they started to take a different form.

Her heart raced as one of the Elders took on the form of a woman with long gray hair, a thin body, and big blue eyes that made Aria clamp her mouth with her shaking hand.

Mother?

It couldn't be. Her mother had been dead for more than forty years. Did some of the dead become Elders?

Aria shot up from her seat and stuck her head out of the window. "Stop the carriage," she shouted, her breath quickening as she watched the beautiful woman that had raised her walk to the front of the other Elders.

Once the carriage was stopped, Aria turned the door's latch and pushed it open. The warm air hit her as she hopped down to the leaves below.

"Aria," her mother, Annisa, said with a faint smile on her face.

"Mother?" Aria asked. "Is that really you?" It couldn't be. How was this possible?

Annisa nodded. "Come to me. Let me look at you. It's been so long."

Baffled, Aria lost her words as she ran to her mother like a little girl having found their way home after being lost.

Tears stung her eyes as she choked on sobs. "It cannot be."

The moment Aria was close enough to touch her mother, she fell into her outstretched arms.

"Dear Elahe," she said, breathless as she breathed in her mother's scent. She pulled away. It wasn't the scent she remembered, but more like coal and wet dirt.

"Listen to me, Aria," Annisa said, her eyes narrowing as she held Aria out at arm's length. "I only came to tell you something—something that will soothe your troubled mind."

Aria searched her eyes. They were different, filled with wisdom and knowledge that Aria could never comprehend. "How did you become an Elder?"

Shaking her head, Annisa stroked Aria's hair. "That is unimportant. I came here to tell you that Liam is alive. The woman that tried to kill him did not succeed. He was blessed by the fairy Mother Tree."

Aria's jaw dropped. She quickly snapped her mouth closed as a surge of joy and relief filled her veins.

"That is the best news you could have ever delivered."

"That is not all. He is in great danger, as are you. You must turn and leave this place, Aria. Right now."

"You know that I cannot abandon my people. Would you have abandoned them if you were in my position?"

Annisa looked to the other Elders, who had taken on forms of various common folk.

"That's enough," one of the male Elders said.

Aria's eyes widened. She knew his face. "Drefen?"

He nodded. "This one has never heeded sound advice. I was to be her son's Elder, and she declined so she could train him herself."

"You cannot disagree that I did a good job, can you?"

Drefen, tall and thin, with shoulder-length black hair shook his head. "I cannot, but you must listen to Annisa this time. Oren is doomed."

Aria took her mother's hand. "Come with me. Surely, you could lend some assistance. Together, we can help the people of Oren. It doesn't have to end this way."

"Your optimism is refreshing," Drefen said. "But, The Charmer has other plans in store for this place, and for you above all."

Aria began to reply when the Elders vanished.

She awoke up with a start, her heart pounding. Sweat beaded on her face, arms, and between her breasts as she caught her breath and sat up on the plush carriage seat. She hurried to look out the window.

The Elders were gone.

What was all of that?

A warning?

Perplexed, Aria sat back down, disappointed that the encounter with her mother hadn't been real. She settled back against the seat's back and sighed.

"Approaching Oren, Queen Aria," the footman announced.

Aria sighed, fanning herself against the smothering heat. "Thank you. Proceed to the palace."

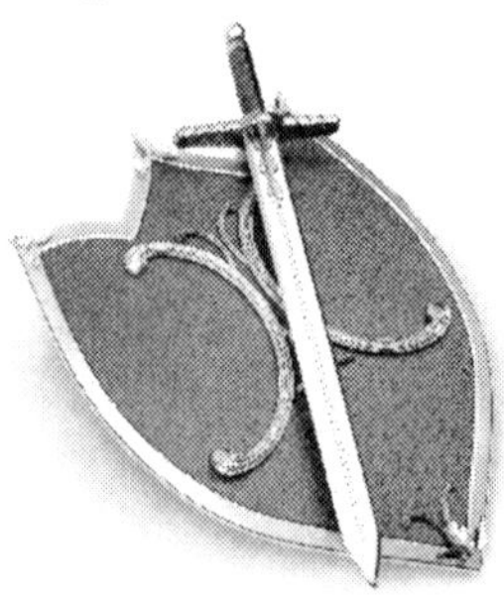

Inside, Oren was a desolate place. Once, the streets had been packed with commerce and interaction. As Queen Aria rode through the gates and down the main road that led from the forests to the palace, they surveyed the odd emptiness of it all.

Queen Aria stepped from her carriage before the main staircase of her palace.

Her eyes rose to the sky. The green aura still clung to her Kingdom, casting a hazy fog over the streets. Mist beaded on her face, like a spray from the sea that stood in the distance behind the palace.

Something was off. The guards watched her, and yet they did not bow.

"Aria! Wait," Lord Franco called, as he hurried down the white stairs. "Your trip was taken at the worst possible time. I did warn you."

Aria folded her hands before her and watched him reach the ground, his long blue robes dragging along the stone as he carried his staff along with him.

Lord Franco's bushy white brows rose as he stood before Queen Aria. There was a fear within them that made Aria's body tense. "What is it, Franco?"

He put his hand on her shoulder and led her back to the carriage. "You must leave, immediately," he whispered, handing her a bronze box. "Lady Sona has taken the palace. Hurry, before her guards see you."

Aria's cheeks reddened. She couldn't believe what she was hearing. Sona was smart. And quick…quicker than Aria had anticipated.

"Where is she?"

Franco nodded to the palace. "Inside."

"No. This cannot be. She has Charmed my people." She glanced at her palace, resisting being led back to her carriage. "Tell me what happened, Franco."

"Charm or not, they have made her Queen and believe she can end the plague." Franco tried to turn her around. "Come now, Aria. We can talk as soon as we are far from the city. She has a bounty on your head, and I refuse to watch you be beheaded."

"Of course she can end the blasted plague," Aria said. "She is responsible for it!"

"There is no way to prove such a thing," Franco said, shaking his head. "There is only one option, and you *must* leave. Now."

"No," a voice called from the top of the stairs. "Stop her!"

Aria looked up to see Sona standing there in a flowing white corseted gown.

Wearing Aria's gold circlet.

Aria seethed, her hands curling into fists. The time for being proper and cool had ended. She envisioned ripping Sona's throat out.

Before she could react, the soldiers rushed to her. She gasped at their roughness as they yanked her from the carriage by her arms.

"I am your Queen," she growled. "You pledged an oath to *me*. Not this blasted imposter." She tried to wrench free from their tight grasp, her heart pounding when they didn't budge. "Come to your senses, men. This is treason!"

Lord Franco was apprehended as well.

"Send them both to the dungeons for sentencing," Sona said with a devious grin that turned Aria's blood cold.

Chapter 50

AFTER THEIR LATE SUPPER, Lilae and Liam headed outside to the dark garden of plants and bushes absent of colorful flowers. Their blooms were of black and white, with the occasional yellow buds of a flower Lilae had seen in Avia'Torena.

Holding hands, he led her to a fountain that had statue of the Ancient, Telryd—the human god.

"We finally made it," he said. "After everything in Gollush, I was worried things would have taken a darker turn."

"Me too," Lilae said. "Dragnor hasn't tried to torment me in a few days. I just hope he's given up. Though, I doubt he ever will."

"I'm sorry you have to go through that," he said, standing before her. He titled her chin up and kissed her lips. "But, as long as I am around, nothing will ever hurt you again," he whispered against her lips.

Lilae smiled and closed her eyes, the effects of the wine warming her body from the shoulders down. She felt good, free, relaxed, and her desire for Liam was intensified. She let her hands slip into his hair as he held her by the waist.

"I know. I'll never let anyone hurt you either," she said. "Somehow, I think Telryd and the other Ancients approve of what we have."

"Why else would they let us heal one another?"

Lilae nodded. "Exactly. They must have known we'd be so close."

Liam stroked her cheek, the buzz of insects their ambient background noise.

"How do you feel about being apart tonight?" he asked.

She sighed. "Well, I haven't seen my sisters in over a year. As much as I will miss having you in my bed, I can't help *not* wanting to let them out of my sights again."

"I understand. I think you should keep them close. I've never seen you so happy."

She looked up at him, the blue of his eyes almost glowing. "I've never been so happy," she said. "With you, with having them back, with the Elders having a solid plan to put this world back together. I almost feel like there is hope—that together we can do this."

"I agree. I feel it too," he said.

Lilae's heart pattered in her chest as Liam kissed her again. She let out a moan as his tongue caressed her lips and found entry into her mouth. She closed her eyes and tasted the sweet honey from their dessert on his tongue.

Laughter came from the castle as Risa and Jaiza ran into the garden. Rowe chased them.

They stopped when they saw Lilae and Liam, covering their giggles.

"What's this?" Risa said as Lilae pulled away and wiped her mouth.

Lilae glanced at Liam, blushing.

He kissed her again. "Sleep well," he whispered and turned to Rowe. "We should turn in. Don't you think?"

Rowe looked from Lilae to Liam and nodded. "If you have something…more important to do," he said, clearing his throat. "I won't get in your way."

Liam put a hand on Rowe's shoulder, turning him around. "Bedtime," he said.

Rowe winked at Lilae. "Good night, ladies."

Lilae watched Rowe and Liam leave, avoiding the questioning looks from her sisters.

Once the men were gone, their grins widened.

"Oh, little sister. You're back to breaking hearts again, aren't you?"

Lilae rolled her eyes and headed back to the castle.

She'd never hear the end of it. They'd done the same when they'd believed something romantic going on with her and Anic. It had embarrassed Lilae so much that she'd considered breaking things off with the poor blacksmith's son.

She smiled to herself. This time she didn't care who knew.

Chapter 51

THIN SLIVERS OF SUNLIGHT spilled through the window of her room inside Torgrid Castle. All throughout the night, faint creaks and what sounded like whispers kept Lilae awake.

Loud chatter and activity urged her to finally get up and face another day. She was exhausted, having barely slept.

Lilae's head thumped with pain, and her stomach was unsettled.

Too much wine, she thought, and groaned as she sat up on her pillow.

As she crawled onto her knees to look out the window, Jaiza also woke up with a yawn.

Rise still snored under the covers they shared.

To Lilae's surprise, goblins were awake and swarming the streets with their daily tasks. Short and dressed in similar hues of blue and gray, they looked like children to Lilae.

"I hope there is something for breakfast," Jaiza said, sitting up from her space in the bed between Risa and Lilae. "I'm craving bacon." She pulled the covers over her legs and rested her back on the stone wall while Lilae continued to look out the keyhole-shaped window.

"Me too," Lilae said, her stomach grumbling. She hadn't had anything as delicious as fresh cooked bacon in ages. "That sounds good."

"Bacon?" Risa called, pulling the covers from over her head. She stretched her arms above her and turned onto her side to face Lilae and Jaiza. "Lies," she said with a yawn. "I don't smell any bacon."

Jaiza cracked a grin. "I never promised any, Risa. I just said I craved it. How about you get up and go make some?"

"No, ma'am. *You* were always better in the kitchen."

Lilae turned to them, smiling. "How about we all go down and cook for everyone?"

Jaiza nodded "Good idea, Lilae. It's the least we could do for Vaugner and for Ayoki especially."

"You said that she saved your lives," Lilae said as she pulled her nightgown over her head.

"Yes," Jaiza said, but her eyes narrowed as she walked to Lilae. She reached out and touched Lilae's tattoos. "Goodness, Lilae. What is this? What happened here?"

Lilae's smile faded. She tensed under Jaiza's touch and stepped away. Embarrassed, she quickly snatched her shirt off the bedpost and put it on. If only she could hide her tainted skin forever. But, the ink ran deep. She feared she'd never be rid of it, or the memories that came along with it.

"Dragnor did it to me. It's a curse."

Jaiza's brows furrowed as she watched Lilae get dressed. "What kind of curse?"

Shrugging, Lilae buckled her belt and knelt down to put on her shoes. "It makes me ill. That's all. Liam and I found a way to fight it."

"You did?" Risa asked. She and Jaiza shared a look. "Tell me about this method you and Liam discovered."

Lilae turned away, her cheeks growing bright red by the knowing tone in Risa's voice.

"It's nothing," she muttered. "He and I can heal each other. Now, tell me what happened with Ayoki. How did she save you?"

Risa grinned and pointed to Lilae. "Changing the subject. Don't think I didn't notice. I knew there was something going on between you two. We weren't too drunk to notice your kiss."

Jaiza waved a hand at Risa, shushing her. "Hush, Risa. It's none of your business what Lilae and Liam do to *heal* each other," she said with a grin that matched her twin.

Sighing, Lilae stood tall and crossed her arms across her chest. "Are you going to tell me what The Seer can do or not?"

Lilae hoped her cheeks weren't still red, but could still feel the heat within them.

Risa's shoulders rose to her ears. "She ripped the skin off a bunch of soldiers."

"And kept ripping them apart until they were nothing but dust. It was horrifying," Jaiza said.

"I wasn't horrified," Risa said. "I was jealous."

Jaiza rolled her eyes. "You were scared too."

"Not really." Risa shook her head, her eyes widened. "Seriously, Lilae. It was amazing. I just wish I had a power like that."

"She's lying," Jaiza said, turning back to Lilae. "I have never seen anything like it." Her brows rose. "Except that day in Lowen's Edge. When you made the sky turn red and spit fire onto everything. I can't decide which of you has the scariest power."

Lilae licked her lips, imagining the power they described. She also remembered how euphoric her power had felt the day Jaiza described in Lowen's Edge. Something had snapped within her, turning her into a being driven by destruction.

Her hands began to shiver. She clamped them together, frowning down at them when they wouldn't stop.

A gasp escaped her lips as her chest tightened, making it difficult to catch her breath. Jaiza's image before her started to blur. Her skin grew hot, and her knees weakened, sending her to the floor with a loud thud. Lilae had no control over her body.

She whimpered, her entire body locking and shutting down.

Help. Help. She wanted to speak, but the words wouldn't come out. It was as if something unseen clutched her throat.

No. Panic took over. Lilae couldn't breathe, move, or regain control of her body.

What she *could* do was feel Dragnor activating his curse.

Liam.

Jaiza touched her, her frantic voice nothing more than a dull whisper as all light faded despite Lilae's eyes being wide open.

Something crashed through the window, and yet Lilae couldn't move. Whatever towering creature had entered the room tossed Risa and Jaiza to the walls with a thud of broken bones.

"Lilae!"

Chapter 52

DAWN CAST ITS FAINT GLOW on the city, waking Torgrid's interesting breed of people. The goblins left their buildings in hordes, as if someone had rung a bell and made them leave their homes.

Curious looks lifted to Liam and Rowe, although no one spoke to them. Children smiled and waved, their little faces brightening at seeing the strange glowing men outside the castle.

Liam nodded at them and waved back, returning their kind smiles.

In just a few days, they would embark on their next journey, one that would determine the fate of Ellowen.

Such a heavy notion weighed on Liam's mind as he and Rowe sat outside of the Keep, enjoying the fresh air as they waited for the others to awaken. Memories of Lilae's laughter the night before put Liam at peace as his eyes followed the goblins down the road to the mines outside of the city.

Liam's smile faded as he watched a young mother shuffling her four children toward a large stone building separate from the tall towers that served as their homes.

If only his mother could give him a sign that she was alive. His stomach churned each time he thought of her.

Seeing Lilae smile with such vibrancy was enough to pull him from his dark thoughts of plagues and death back home. He'd give anything to see that smile every day—for the rest of his life.

Such a notion should have frightened Liam, but it didn't. It made an excitement brew inside that he had never felt.

Was it possible to feel such strong feelings for a girl he'd just met only weeks ago? Sona had destroyed his heart with her betrayal, but the moment he'd met Lilae, it was as if she was an instant remedy and renewed him.

Knowing that she was willing to return to Oren with him one day brought a smile to his lips. Liam pictured her walking through the palace gardens in a beautiful dress, her long hair styled in the Oren way; her smile directed at him made his smile widen.

"We should probably wake Lilae and her sisters," Liam said to Rowe. "Get started with preparing for our Gate."

"Maybe," Rowe said. "But, they were pretty drunk last night. I'd let them rest a bit. You know nothing of the headache a night of too much ale or wine can give a person, especially someone as small as those women."

"I suppose you're right," Liam said, glancing to the left when Ayoki stepped from the front door. She didn't look their way, but graceful, yet shy, she walked over to a stone bench and sat down with her back pressed against the wall of the keep.

She drew her legs into her chest as she watched the sky above, a perplexed expression on her face. She leaned forward, as if focusing in on something.

Ayoki was a mysterious creature, one that intrigued him. After what they'd learned about Pretica's betrayal, he also felt pity for her.

"So," Rowe said, breaking Liam from his thoughts. "Are you going to tell me what happened between you and Lilae last night?"

Liam cleared his throat, drinking the brew the castle cook had prepared for him that morning. It was potent and lifted his spirits within moments of his first sip. He drank to stall answering Rowe's question, all the while hoping his cheeks didn't blush at the memories of the night before.

"What's that?" Rowe said, breaking Liam from his thoughts.

Liam looked up, following Rowe's gaze to the clear night sky. His eyes narrowed as something flew across the sky—a flutter of fabric. Was it a dress? Or robes?

His eyes followed the movement, warnings brewing in his belly.

"It's a woman," Liam said, incredulously. His eyes widened as she flew closer, her black dress fluttering with the wind, her long black hair wiping around her body.

Her eyes fixed on him.

Ayoki stood and looked to Liam, her face paled in comparison to her usual dark complexion. Her brows were furrowed.

Liam stepped backward as the woman grew closer. A whistle filled their ears. Loud and shrill, it resonated through the entire city, making the lines of goblins stop their trek to work. They turned to look up at the gray sky.

Where had the sun gone? Darkness fell as the clouds blocked out the sun, and the air grew cold, sending goosebumps up Liam's arms and neck.

"Get Delia and the others," Liam said to Ayoki, drawing his sword as, from the dark clouds, something large fell through them.

A goddess.

Chapter 53

COLDNESS FLOODED LILAE'S BODY as she opened her eyes to a dark place. The pain of the curse had subsided, yet Lilae was disoriented when she looked around.

Jaiza and Risa.

Where were they?

Where was she?

Realization hit her full force, and she whimpered when she realized that she was no longer in the bedroom in the castle.

Dragnor?

She scrambled to her feet. Her breaths quickened as she looked at her surroundings, stumbling backward. Her eyes darted from one end of the empty rectangular room to the other. A startling chill in the air made Lilae's teeth chatter. Her breath puffed out of her mouth before her as she exhaled.

Where was Dragnor? Where were his torture tools?

She whimpered, too afraid to face him again like this.

Meet me in the real world, Lilae pleaded. *Where I can end this.*

She knew that he awaited her, ready to torture her body and torment her mind.

Instead, silence welcomed her along with an eerie feeling that she was being watched. She saw something in the corner of her eye. A shadow moved under the cloak of darkness.

Lilae forced herself to speak. “Who is there?” While she asked the question, she truly didn’t want to know. She wanted to escape this place and return to her sisters.

She clutched her arms and walked backward across the slightly damp stone floor until her back was pressed against a similarly damp wall.

“Lilae?” A familiar voice called from one of the dark corners.

Lilae tensed. All color drained from her face as her heart thumped against her ribcage.

“Kavien?”

Her hands flew to cover her mouth as tears sprouted from her eyes.

Kavien.

Out of the shadows, he stepped toward her.

Tall. Swarthy. Handsome.

Naked.

Her eyes swept up the toned muscles of his nude body to fix on his gray eyes. Such adoration and relief filled his gray-eyed gaze as he continued to approach her, unabashed by the display of his body.

“My dear, Lilae,” he whispered, his hand outstretched toward her as he walked. “This cannot be.”

Shaking, Lilae considered closing the gap between them. Still, a mild distrust kept her planted in one spot. Her body wanted to be near him. Her mind yelled at her to resist. Whatever this dream world was, she didn’t feel comfortable.

This was not the same dreamscape she shared with Liam. This place was the exact opposite.

“You’re all right,” she said, tilting her head as she took note of every detail of his face. “Dragnor said he would kill you if I didn’t return to Avia’Torena.”

Kavien’s jaw clenched. “He bluffs. He cannot touch me.”

“But, he was the one to curse you.”

Kavien looked away in silence, his eyes cold.

She couldn’t believe just how much she’d missed watching him. His features were unlike the fair-skinned men from the north of Eura. With clear dark skin and almond-shaped eyes the color of the sky before a storm, under thick dark lashes, full lips that she could still taste, he was still one of the most attractive men she'd ever seen.

Something flashed before Kavien's eyes, making him stop abruptly. Fear. His face went ashen.

"We don't have much time. Dragnor is pulling you to his consciousness, but finally, I have you. I've been trying *every single day* in hopes that I would you see again, if only for a second. I knew that if I kept trying, that I could bring you here."

Lilae took a step forward. The urge to comfort him was stronger than the warnings inside her head.

"Don't let him take me, Kavien," Lilae said, fear striking her heart at the thought of another torture-filled night.

This place—in its dark eeriness, was better than a minute with Dragnor.

"Don't touch me," Kavien said, looking behind him as if he'd heard something. "They are watching us. I don't know what will happen if we touch. But, dear Elahe, I'd give anything to touch you right now."

Lilae nodded, unsure of who *they* were, but intrigued by the notion of being in Kavien's arms again.

She licked her lips. "All right. What is this place?" She rubbed the gooseflesh on her arms beneath her shirt sleeves.

"Misery," he whispered, his shoulders slumping as he looked down at the floor.

"How do we get out of here?" Lilae asked rushing over to the stone wall to search for some sort of door. Her fingers traced the grooves, hoping to find a clue. She remembered something and paused. "I can get you out of here."

Kavien's eyes returned to her and he pushed fallen hair away from his face. Hope flashed before them as he watched her. "Blasted spirits, I have missed you more than freedom itself. Not a day has gone by that I haven't thought about your beautiful face. But, it is not going to be that simple."

"Yes," Lilae said, nodding, ignoring the warnings that churned in her belly.

Her entire abdomen was tight with anxiety, yet as she looked into his eyes—eyes that were full of love for her, she was afraid and torn.

She lowered her voice to a whisper. “What do you need?”

Kavien rubbed his face with both of his hands, and Lilae willed her eyes to stop exploring his sculpted body. She’d never seen a naked man before, and her eyes lingered a bit too long for her own comfort.

Pursing her lips, she scolded herself for such curiosity in the face of danger, but the way Kavien looked at her made her face grow red.

A screeching sound resounded through the small room, making Lilae jump. She braced herself.

Something flew across the room. A bat-like creature? A shadow…or a being of some sort. It happened too quickly to be sure.

Kavien crossed the room to grab Lilae by the arms and pushed her into the wall. His arms wrapped around her, as if shielding her.

“Leave her alone!”

Lilae’s eyes widened. She could see nothing with Kavien’s body pressed hard against hers. His scent was familiar. She’d smelled his masculine aroma for months, every night as he slept in the bed beside her box and the times they’d slept in the same bed.

The time they kissed.

Her breath came out labored as he held her midair against the wall.

The screeching grew to a deafening roar, and Lilae closed her eyes, willing it to stop.

“Go away! She is not yours. You want me. Not her.”

The noise faded.

Silence filled the room but Kavien seemingly waited for the horrific cries to return.

“What were those things?” Lilae’s eyes searched the room for whatever had flown out of the darkness.

“The Horrors,” he said, holding her in place.

Lilae looked at him, her brows furrowed.

“The voices I hear. They are responsible for them. Except, now, they are more real than I ever realized.”

“Are they gone?”

"I think so," he said, releasing her. He set her on her feet, but didn't move away. His eyes searched her face as he stroked her cheeks. "We *can* touch."

Lilae's lips pursed as she looked up at him, his cold fingers still managing to warm her.

In her dreams with Liam, they'd never been able to touch. Each time they attempted, they'd be met with a bright light that shot them back to the present.

What made this different? His hands moved to her shoulders, and slowly, he rested his forehead against the top of her head. Lilae chewed her bottom lip as his breath warmed her face.

"I can't believe I brought you here," he said into her hair, breathing her in.

Lilae's eyes fluttered closed. "Neither can I." The cold of the room started to seep into her skin, chilling her bones. "I fear something is going horribly wrong in the real world. We have to get out of here."

"I know," he said. His hands slid into her hair, and he drew in a deep breath. "But, you're not going to like the journey."

Chapter 54

THE FLYING WOMAN SOARED through the sky like an eagle, graceful, powerful. A bright light lit her trail as she descended from above the clouds like a falling star.

Liam, Rowe, and Ayoki stood there, watching as the woman in white landed before them.

Liam had never seen something like this woman.

Not outside of the ancient texts, and he could not believe his eyes.

It is not possible.

Medium-height, with long lavender hair and brown skin, she had blue eyes that reminded Liam of the brightest Orenian sky. She was strikingly beautiful, but what he knew about her was more frightening than having Wexcyn stride into the city.

Her gaze locked with his as she glided across the stone pathway to him.

"Prince Liam Marx," she said, not a hint of a smile on her stern face. Her skin was flawless, free from any lines or emotion. "You know who I am. Don't you?"

Liam flinched when he heard the screams of women far into the distance. He looked over his shoulder at the castle.

They were screaming Lilae's name.

"Pay attention, and you will all be allowed to live," she said.

Liam swallowed, panic filling his eyes as his breathing quickened. He turned his gaze back to the frightening woman before them and nodded.

The goblins ran back to their homes to hide, quiet and efficient as if they'd done this before. There were no screams of terror, just action.

"You are Litha," Liam said, his blood running cold. The legends and stories of her notorious reign were unsettling.

Lips pursed, Litha nodded. "Good job. I've been watching you. And, I am impressed." She motioned to Rowe and Ayoki, and to Delia and Vaugner as they left the castle to join them—their faces ashen as they beheld the goddess before them.

Mai stayed inside, peeking around the open door, her fingers clutching the wooden frame.

"Most mortals know nothing of the gods of the other worlds. But you, smart boy, have taken it upon yourself to feast on knowledge. I *love* that."

Liam didn't know what to do. His heart pounded in his chest as he fought to keep the utter terror from filling his eyes.

He knew what this woman—no, she wasn't a woman. Not an ordinary woman. Litha was the Goddess of Law, and he knew what she was capable of.

"What do you want with us?" Vaugner asked; his eyes narrowed as he looked Litha up and down. "You have no business here. Ellowen belongs to the Ancients."

Litha did smile then, a smile that didn't disarm any of them, it only struck fear into the deepest depths of their hearts.

"I execute the sacred Law of *all* the worlds, *Elder*. Ellowen, The Abyss, Aden, Varon, etc. etc. Break a Law and you belong to me."

Liam's eyes widened as a giant in glowing white armor landed before them, holding Lilae's limp body in his arms.

At least eleven feet tall, the giant man's eyes held a white light that scanned Liam and the others from above.

Lilae.

Why was she unconscious?

"What have you done?" Liam shouted the question before he could stop himself.

He didn't care about anything but protecting Lilae at that moment. He drew his sword, the glow intensifying to an enchantment that made the tense air sizzle all around him. Teeth gritted, his glare met the dark stare of the man that held Lilae.

"Let her go."

The Goddess of Law clasped her hands out before her. "Listen, Liam. You will put your sword away and lower your tone. We don't need four dead bodies strewn about this lovely city, do we? Your Elders didn't bring you here to bury you. My sheriff here has already greatly injured the two human girls," Litha said. "Someone should tend to them."

Delia held her hand out. "Please," she pleaded. "Let the girl go. She has broken no sacred Laws."

Litha shook her head. "No. *She* hasn't. But I need her. Just for a while. And I will return her. You have my word."

"Take me with you," Liam said, lowering his sword. Anything to stay by Lilae's side. He'd give up his life for her if it were necessary.

Litha's eyes brightened. "Of course, you can come along. I am pleased. I didn't even have to barter with you."

She summoned a small blue orb and let it hover before them like a glowing ball.

Liam glanced back at Delia.

She looked from Litha to the sheriff that held Lilae, and Liam could tell that she was holding her breath as her eyes beheld the orb.

"Where are you taking them?" Delia asked, wariness in her eyes as she held Liam's gaze.

The warnings—they shouted at him from inside. Liam was torn. He had to save Lilae. He'd already lost enough. There was no way that he was going to let the Goddess of Law take her away from him.

Litha shot Delia a glare. "It is none of your concern. I strive to keep the balance in all of the worlds."

"Liam," Delia said, the color in her cheeks draining. "Fight with everything you have."

Liam froze. He sucked in a breath as Delia reach into her cloak and pulled out a long, red bone. With a few indistinguishable words, she tossed it before her.

He tightened his grip on the hilt of his sword and his eyes followed the bone as it flew through the air. It spun and sparked, and landed as a man.

A skeleton man.

Garion stood to his full, towering height as a black substance trailed along his red bones, fusing to them until he looked like a shining statue. To Liam, it looked like the skeleton was dressed in armor.

"Garion," Delia said through clenched teeth. "Grow and save Lilae."

"That was incredibly unwise," Litha snarled and tossed the blue orb into the sky.

The morning sky went purple, and the veins in Litha's face became pronounced as she roared.

"You could have let this meeting go on peacefully. Instead, you bring your *pathetic* reanimated man. Alas, you prefer death and destruction. I will play along."

A loud whistle emanated from her full lips, and with it, she summoned bat-like creatures the size of humans from the sky.

Hundreds of them.

"KILL THEM ALL!"

Vaugner sighed as the creatures let out loud roars, their waxy black wings outstretching the span of their wiry black arms, before running toward Liam and the others.

"And I thought today was going to be a good day," Vaugner said, his eyes going black. "Here goes."

Vaugner raised his arms toward the sky as though he lifted something very heavy. The tension in his face and neck convinced Liam that he did indeed lift something, yet his eyes couldn't make it out.

The sounds of running from inside the castle came to Liam, vexing him as he sliced through the first two creatures that reached him. Black blood spurted into the air, splashing Liam's face.

Liam stumbled backward as glanced back toward the strange sounds and beheld the most horrific scene he'd ever witnessed.

Skeletons—dead men and women ran from the catacombs of castle like a stampede, pushing Mia from her hiding spot. She screamed and crawled away from their ranks to hide beneath one of the benches.

Litha's face turned bright red as she watched the ground shake and rumble as more skeleton men shot from the beneath them, their bones all fused with the same black substance that covered Garion's.

Vaugner shot Litha a look. "Best to leave now," he warned her with a wink, and his body morphed from that of a man, to a black mass that shot through the city, targeting Litha's companions.

Delia followed suit, shifting from her human form to her Elder form, nothing more than black smoke that dispersed like a storm cloud.

Liam feared that Litha was not here to keep order as she'd claimed.

Litha's smile faded as she watched the Elder's fly through the city, tearing through the army of beasts as if they were pieces of parchment tossed into a fire.

If only there weren't so many, Liam might have believed they actually had a chance against the Goddess of Law.

Garion grew just as Delia had commanded. His legs widened and stretched upward, all the while his arms and body morphed to match the dimensions of his new height.

The sheriff faced the giant skeleton, and like two nightmarish beings, they squared off against one another.

Garion slammed his fist into the side of the sheriff's face, causing him to drop Lilae's body, sending her flying to the ground.

Liam panicked. "No!"

"Don't hurt the girl," Litha shouted, her voice booming through the city, making Liam wince. "We need her."

The sheriff reached for Lilae, but Garion caught her instead, using his armored foot to kick the giant in the chest. A loud yell came from the sheriff as he fell to the ground with a crash of stone beneath him.

He slid into one of the buildings, stones falling all around him, exposing goblins inside their homes. The goblins screamed and ran toward the back where they were safe from the battle outside.

Liam started to run for Lilae, when Litha shot black light from the palms of her hands. He gasped and swung his sword full circle, squeezing his eyes shut as the light from his body multiplied outward, to create a barrier between him and her power.

"Mai! Ayoki! Rowe!" he called to them, making sure they were close enough to be protected by his Shield.

The Shadow Elves ran to him, as did Rowe, and Liam completed the air shield to encircle them all with a sharp ring of steel.

Relief flooded him as the Shield stood between them and her dark power. He wiped sweat from his forehead, and the black light shot through the Shield, effortlessly, whistling like a bird in the wind.

Liam swallowed. His Shield dissipated and left them all vulnerable to her power.

Litha cackled then. Her shoulders shook. "Funny. Very funny," she said. "Now, about those dead bodies I mentioned earlier."

Throat dry, Liam looked back at his friends, and told them the only thing he could think of.

"Run."

Chapter 55

"DO NOT RUN NOW," Litha said, her voice seeming to invade their minds. "We were just starting to have *fun*."

Delia appeared beside Liam. "I will get Lilae. Get the others inside the castle," she lowered her voice, her eyes darting to Litha's dark spawn. "We will Gate as soon as everyone is inside."

The whistle of Litha's power shook the ground, and Delia lifted her staff, the light intensifying as she concentrated her Elder powers on them. Every creature in direct view of her staff froze midair, as if something held them in place.

They didn't move, or fall, and Liam couldn't wrap his mind around how that was even possible. As he watched the skeleton army Vaugner had summoned fight against the other creatures, he realized there was so much he would never understand.

He nodded. "We will see you inside."

Delia spun and shifted back into her true form.

Liam watched her head toward Lilae.

Creatures flew around the square, and Liam did his best to fight them off. He grunted as the talons pierced his shoulders and pulled him back. The pain shocked him, yet he didn't have time to think about it.

Liam raised his sword to the sky, calling forth the lightning that begged to be unleashed. The thunder that proceeded his lightning roared over the chaos below as electric threads shot down and onto the creature that gripped Liam.

The smell of burnt flesh filled Liam's nose as he rode the lightning down to the ground, his sword ready for whatever was next.

Rowe ushered Ayoki toward the castle, grabbing any creature that was in his way and tearing them in half with his bare hands.

Litha's black rope of power sizzled through the air like an arrow set ablaze. It chased Rowe and Ayoki.

"Hurry," Liam shouted, his sword impaling another creature into the ground.

He used his foot to wedge his sword from its body and glanced over his shoulder to see Mai scramble from her hiding spot and led the way toward the front doors of the castle's keep.

Liam saw the lights heading straight for the others and called out. "Watch out," he yelled, running toward them.

Rowe cried out in pain.

Like a punch to the gut, Liam was left breathless. He skidded to a stop, his eyes widened in utter shock as Litha's fire wrapped around Rowe and yanked him to the ground, burning through his clothes and skin.

Liam's face turned red. "No!"

Litha appeared before Liam, her nostrils flared. "Should have listened to me," she whispered, and pulled the black lights along like a rope, Rowe's body being flung into the dark sky as if he were weightless.

"Let him go," Liam pleaded, his voice breaking as he watched his best friend in the entire world suffer. "I will do whatever you ask."

"Too late," Litha hissed and sent Rowe higher into the sky, the cords of power wrapping and tightening around his body, melting through his skin until they reached bone.

Rowe's cries turned Liam's blood cold. He ran his sword into Litha's body, desperate to stop her.

Teeth bared, he ran her through, and yet she only smiled as her body floated through the sword and Liam until she rematerialized behind him.

Liam's eyes rose to Rowe, knowing that he couldn't survive this kind of threat. Tears burned his eyes as memories of their time in the Order filled him. Rowe had saved his life more than once and had been the most loyal friend he could have ever dreamed of.

"Please," Liam whispered, the tears streaming down his face.

If Rowe died, Liam knew that he would be forever changed. He balled up his fist and closed his eyes, his heart pounding in his chest as his worst fears were being realized.

"Please," he repeated.

Chapter 56

KAVIEN HELD ONTO LILAE as he waved his hands along the stone walls of his cursed prison. "If we can find a way to unlock this door, I can escape and send you back to the present."

Lilae breathed in, her eyes examining the dark gray stone. She nodded, glancing at Kavien as she tapped her lips. "If you think it's truly possible."

"I do," Kavien said with a nod. "The mind is a powerful thing. It can beat the curse that seeps through my body." He lowered his eyes, his brows furrowing. "I won't have to waste another minute waiting for Sona to cure me."

"Sona?" Lilae asked, stepping away from Kavien.

Kavien pursed his lips as he looked down at Lilae. "You know who I served, Lilae."

Lilae continued to back away from Kavien. "I do. I also know that she tried to kill The Storm." She pushed hair out of her eyes, as she narrowed them at Kavien's face.

"Tried?" Kavien asked. "You're saying that she didn't succeed?"

Appalled, Lilae wrenched free from Kavien's grasp around her shoulder. "Right. I am saying that," she said. "He is alive."

Kavien sighed.

Lilae's cheeks reddened. "Did you bring me here to help free you so you can come after those that I love? Do you plan to kill me?"

Kavien's eyes widened as he shot a look at her. "What nonsense, Lilae. Why would I ever try to kill you?"

"We are enemies," Lilae said into the darkness that grew the farther she backed away from Kavien. "We've always been enemies."

She suddenly felt very foolish. How could she expect Kavien to do anything but what Wexcyn ordered him to do? If she helped him, he would only turn around and wage war on her and her friends.

"You are not my enemy. I told you that I wanted to escape the entire war with you. Why can't you understand that?"

Lilae tensed at his voice as it rose from soft to terse frustration. Memories of his quick temper returned.

"You said love, Lilae," Kavien said, his brows rising. His eyes turned cold as he stared at her.

Pain began to seep back into Lilae's flesh, creeping onto her like an itch she couldn't scratch because it went so deep. She looked down at her hands, watching them flicker between transparent to solid.

She didn't look him in the eyes. "Yes," she said. "I love him." Speaking the words aloud gave them even more weight, enough to erase any doubts Lilae had about her true feelings.

"Who?"

Lilae embraced the pain. She needed to ride it back to her present self, away from this prison.

Away from Kavien.

"The Storm," she whispered as her eyes met Kavien's. Startled by the disappointment in his eyes, she shook her head at him, mouthing the words 'I'm sorry,' and faded away.

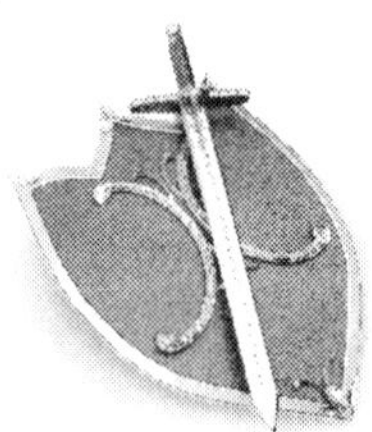

A BRIGHT LIGHT BLINDED LIAM.

The pain of losing his greatest friend left him numb as he shielded his eyes, backing away from whatever new terror Litha to join the battle.

He fought to keep his eyes open to face it, and found himself gasping as Rowe's body was carried down to the ground by someone Liam never thought he would see again.

He fell to his knees, his face wet with tears.

Nani appeared inside the light, her wings glittering in the sunlight that now shone through the bright blue sky, Litha's darkness dissipating.

Nani knelt over Rowe, and held his face in her hands. His Tryan glow brightened as did her body as she healed him with her fairy power.

Rowe reached up and pulled her down into a hug that made Nani smile. When she stood, she ignored Litha and flew over to Lilae and Delia.

Liam watched Litha as her eyes followed Nani. His heart soared at seeing Lilae stir under Nani's power.

The fairy god simply had to touch Lilae to awaken her. Lilae gasped for air, as if she'd been drowning. When she realized Nani had saved her, she also hugged her. Nani helped Lilae to her feet, her eyes locking with Litha's as she did so.

"Go to them," Nani said.

Lilae, nodding, ran straight to Liam with a mixture of joy and relief on her face.

Lilae crashed into Liam, wrapping her arms around his neck and kissing him before everyone.

Litha laughed, clapping her hands, and Lilae let go to turn to her.

"Who is she?" Lilae asked him, finally surveying the battle scene all around them.

Liam frowned at Litha, wondering what could possibly be so funny.

"Hello there, little god," Litha said as her shoulders shook with laughter. "I am very pleased to meet you."

Nani didn't return the smile. In her radiant glow, she approached Litha. "Leave," she said, holding a weakened Rowe in her arms. "Now."

Litha smoothed her dress and scanned the destruction around her. "Of course," she said. "It seems one of the most important Laws has been broken. Now, I have work to do."

Delia appeared beside Liam, helping him to his feet. "No, Litha," she said. "Don't do it. You don't know what this will do to our world."

Litha shrugged. "I do not care. I only execute the rules, and your fairy *Ancient* has broken the most important one by interfering. The rules strictly state that none of the Ancients shall enter the realm of the mortals in times of war. And what do we have here? *An Ancient*."

"You planned this," Delia said, pointing to Litha's face.

"I did no such thing," Litha said. "Why should I care who wins this petty war?"

Liam began to follow what was happening, and held Lilae in his arms.

"I think you do care," Delia said. "Somehow, you have a stake in who wins the war, and I have a feeling I know which Ancient that is."

"Oh," Litha said, feigning innocence. "Interesting theory."

Litha summoned the orb once again and with a blast of light, she, her sheriff, and the remaining creatures vanished.

Lilae clutched Liam, wrapping her arms around his neck.

"I saw what they've planned," she said.

Liam's brows furrowed as he looked into her green eyes. "What is it?"

"Wexcyn," Lilae said, breathing in a deep breath. "Litha is going to free him."

Chapter 57

ARIA LICKED HER DRY LIPS. Days without food or water had left her weak. She pulled her knees into her chest as she pressed her back against the cold, damp wall of the Orenian palace dungeons.

The wails of the other prisoners were her nightly lullaby, not that she could tell day from night anymore. The tiny cell was absent of any windows. Not even the door had a window or bars.

Complete and utter darkness smothered Aria like a blanket.

And the mice were her only company. How they had entered the room was a mystery, for not even Yoska could make his way to her.

She opened her eyes to the pitch before her and groaned as her stomach grumbled. She doubted that anyone would bring her food or water besides the cup of cold oat porridge that the guard set onto her floor once a night.

She flinched once the door to her cell was opened, letting in a small ray of light that still hurt her eyes.

"Time to face the executioner," one of the men who waited outside said as two guards entered the cell.

"Dear Ancients," Aria prayed. "This can't be the end. You cannot let this happen."

There was no reply, and Aria refused to break her composure as the two guards grabbed her by her arms.

Though her face was free of emotion, her insides were a storm of rage, sorrow, and fear. She never imagined dying in such a way. Cyden's teaching were coming in handy now as she kept calm in the face of death.

She just wished she'd heeded his warnings and that of her mother. As they walked her from the dungeons to the doors that led outside, Aria turned off her ability to hear the thoughts of those around her. She couldn't stomach the horrid thoughts her people had about her. With her power, Sona had turned everyone against her.

In mere days.

Aria shuddered to think of what the woman could do with more time.

At least I tried, Aria thought as she faced the audience of her people who had come to watch her beheading.

Completely withdrawn from the situation, Aria focused on the stone walls of her palace. The large blocks were perfectly stacked and were still shiny, even though the sea air had buffed it with its salty air for centuries. She counted those stones—anything to keep her mind off the sharp ax the executioner held.

Aria couldn't look at her people, yet she did find one in particular she would meet head on. Her eyes met those of Sona's as she stood on the balcony in a painted white chair, her hands folded on the railing before her.

"Wait," Sona yelled from above.

"Yes, Queen Sonalese," Captain Strongbow called.

"Don't forget to cut off her hair first," Sona said.

Aria's eye twitched. The corner of her mouth turned up into a snarl.

"You will regret this, Sona," Aria said, directly into Sona's mind.

Aria watched Sona's lips curl into a grin.

She was held by her arms as one of them pulled out a sharp knife. She squeezed her eyes shut as he began sawing away at her long beautiful hair. He held the black mass out before her eyes, and when she opened them, a whimper escaped her lips. She'd never cut her hair in all of her forty years. Having such an intimate part of her taken away hit her harder than she'd anticipated.

They left her hair uneven and short like a boy's.

"Perfect," Sona sneered.

Aria's lips parted as they pulled her back to the chopping block. The blood of previous criminals stained the wooden platform. Murderers, rapists, and those that committed the darkest and most evil of crimes had proceeded her. At least Aria had sought the truth and knew exactly who deserved such punishment. It was a bitter thought to know that she was the first innocent victim of this form of punishment.

Her heart pumped wildly within her chest as she was pushed down to her knees.

"Aria," Yoska's voice called from the distance.

She looked up to see him fly toward the palace, relief and sadness filling her. *Don't come any closer, Yoska.*

No, he thought. *I cannot allow this to happen to you. I will not.*

You don't have a choice. They will catch you and kill you too if you reveal yourself.

Aria hated to send him away, but she was relieved to see him one last time. To see someone who loved her before she died was truly a gift.

Thank you for coming to me one last time.

No, he thought, his voice wavering.

Aria held her breath as Yoska flew straight to her, landing on the wooden platform. "Yoska. Leave. Quickly!"

Sona shot to her feet and pointed to Yoska. "Grab the eagle. I have some questions for him."

"No. Leave him alone," Aria pleaded, breaking her composure.

The guards reached for Yoska, and he turned to her, his dark eyes meeting her tear-filled gaze.

Aria's voice caught in her throat as Yoska closed his eyes…and transformed right before everyone.

There was a collective gasp from the crowd as they watched Yoska's eagle body spin and morph into a creature that hadn't been seen by Tryans in hundreds of years.

Yoska, Aria thought, her chest heaving as she fought to catch her breath and make sense of what just happened.

His body stretched tall and his body became lean. There was a shimmer across his stark, nude white skin that made him look unnatural in their realm. He glanced at Aria and then to the men that had tied her to the stake.

You're a Silver Elf?

All anyone could hear was the sound of the wind as Yoska turned to her and nodded.

I am.

Yoska's eyes were no longer black, but a silver that reflected the light.

Surprise filled his eyes as he looked at his hands.

They shook and Aria raised a brow, wondering if he even knew what had just happened.

His chest heaved as he touched his short, silver hair.

"My curse is broken," Yoska whispered in awe.

A whisper rose from the people of Oren, until shouting filled the entire square.

"KILL THE ELF," Sona shouted, her eyes wild with bewilderment and what was, perhaps, fear. She kept shouting the same thing as if she knew something Aria hadn't quite figured out. "Kill him! Kill him! Kill him!"

Soldiers started to rush the platform, and Yoska lifted his hand.

In a flash, the enchanted elven sword that had hung in her vaults for centuries met the palm of his hand. He wrapped his hand around the hilt, and within seconds, he was clothed in shining black armor.

Steel.

Aria swallowed, stunned by what she beheld.

Her mind raced as she tried to comprehend what she'd just witnessed, and her eyes widened at the realization.

Yoska is The Steel.

His eyes glowed, and with speed she'd never seen, he made three swift slashes that sliced through three soldiers. The blood splashed onto the faces of those closest and dripped down Aria's cheeks toward her lips.

Yoska sliced through the ropes that bound her. "Aria," he said, finally looking at her with his silver eyes.

Goosebumps knitted her exposed arms. She finally saw the true Yoska.

"Come," he grabbed her by the forearm and lifted her from the stake, the sword in his other hand.

He clutched her tight to his chest, looked deep into her eyes, and together… they vanished.

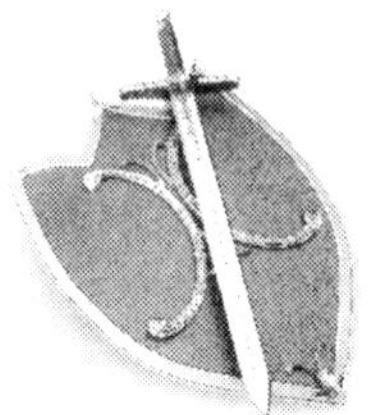

BRIGHT LIGHT WELCOMED Kavien as he opened his eyes. Numb and disoriented, he squinted against the light that nearly burned his eyes.

Where was he? The smell…smelled like home.

Move, he thought, and focusing on his arms first, his body obeyed.

Power filled his body as he shot up from the bed that had been more of tomb, and he froze the instant he saw the man in the room with him.

Kavien fell to his knees, utterly stunned by what he saw. The bright light that emanated from his body was what Kavien had seen when he was awakened.

Lilae, he thought, despair taking over the brief moment of joy he'd felt.

His face went stern, complacent, as his eyes lifted to the man that stood in his quarters, shrouded in light, skin the color of polished bronze, dark hair pulled into a ponytail. He bowed his head, tired of fighting what he knew his destiny to be.

What else could he do? Lilae had betrayed him yet again.

"Welcome to Eura," Kavien said, coldness filling his heart. His jaw tightened as he looked up at the man before him. "Father."

EPILOGUE

LIAM HELD LILAE IN his arms, Rowe at one side, Nani at the other. The twins and the Shadow Elves waited behind.

Grand Master Neru met them in the Goblin City, ready for the quest ahead. By his side was his greatest pupil, Kenichi.

The young Shadow Elf man held Ayoki's hand, a smile on both of their faces.

No one had to die.

This time.

Liam closed his eyes and kissed Lilae's forehead. He would hold on tight to the ones he loved and never let go.

"Are you ready?" Delia asked, her hand firm on the stem of her staff.

Lilae and Liam nodded.

"We are ready," Liam said, rubbing Lilae's forearms.

They shared a look—one that gave him no doubts of her feelings for him. After the havoc Litha had set upon the Goblin City, everyone knew that everything was different.

What was coming to Ellowen would bring dark times, suffering, and death.

It also brought together a group that Liam was confident would face that threat admirably.

"Let's go then, shall we?" Delia said, nodding to Vaugner who stood across from them in the center of the city.

He outstretched his staff, as did Delia, and together they created a portal that would transport Liam and his small army to the mysterious North of Eura.

Auroria.

"Step into the light," Delia said. "I will be behind you and will close the Gate."

Nodding, Liam stepped forward, Lilae's hand within his.

Together, they said goodbye to the Goblin City, ready…for whatever Wexcyn sent their way.

He was powerful, a god, a master manipulator.

Liam was certain Wexcyn was pleased with himself. He'd used Litha to force them to break one of the sacred Laws, and would now be free to walk Ellowen once again.

Liam looked ahead, the world blurring as he and Lilae were sucked away.

Wexcyn's brilliance was astounding—but, *somehow* he forgot that while he could now walk Ellowen—the other Ancients could as well.

War was on the rise, and this time the odds were stacked in Lilae and Liam's favor.

THE END

Thanks for reading! If you enjoyed this book, please consider leaving a review.

Dawn of the Forgotten: Book Three of the Eura Chronicles will be released January 2017.

Discover *Goddess of War*, a Eura Chronicles spin-off novella here.

* * *

Don't Forget to Subscribe to K.N. Lee's Newsletter to Receive Freebies, Exclusive Content, Cover Reveals, Giveaways, Sales, and More!

(link to newsletter here)

Exclusive First Look:

DAWN
of the
FORGOTTEN

SONA FLEW ON HER WYVERN above the smoke and fire of Willowmere, a small kingdom in Alfheim. Her eyes searched for any movement other than the writhing and frantic jerking of burning Silver Elves.

She smiled at the chaos.

The once beautiful village was devastated by flames.

"Steady now, Tollie," she said to the wyvern as it glided just out of reach of the flames.

She would help as much as she could to secure the destruction of Alfheim. The Shadow Elves were doing a pretty good job already, leaving her only smaller cities and villages to ruin. Despite their best attempts, there were already scores of Silver Elves and Tryans who had been warned.

It was time to head to Avia'Torena.

Her grin faded. As much as she had enjoyed taunting him, she didn't look forward to meeting Kavien's wrath.

Her glare shot to Silver Elf soldiers that seemed to come out of nowhere.

Tall, silver haired elves swarmed from the caverns of the Cascadian mountains. They were all in light armor with shining weapons.

Finally, Sona thought. *A real fight.*

They spotted her and archers began shooting sparkling arrows through the darkness toward her. She led Tollie to the ground and hopped from the wyvern's back.

Many of the soldiers had gone to the valleys to fight the Shadow Elves, leaving their homes unprotected. She figured this small troupe had been informed of her attack and had hurried back.

Sona slid her swords from their harness strapped to her back and gave them a simultaneous swing through the air. They glowed green with her Tryan Enchant and she stood before her wyvern, waiting.

Tolie camouflaged itself with the ground and stealthily slipped away unseen. Wyverns were amazing rides, but they were annoyingly afraid of outright battle. They would carry their master through fights, but would hide at the first chance they got.

The soldiers gathered together.

Organized.

Unafraid.

Interesting, Sona thought.

She walked toward the huddled group of soldiers as their shields went up. In unison they used their Agility to attack her from all positions. She stood their transfixed for a moment. She'd never seen Silver Elves in *real* battle. They moved similarly to the Shadow Elves, but there was such grace. Her mouth hung open for a moment as they seemed to move above the ground.

Then, they attacked.

Everything became extremely fast. The sparkling swords and maces went after her.

She dodged them, sliding through the mud and slashing through their legs with her enchanted swords. It sizzled through their armor and many were taken aback. It had been centuries since Tryans and Silver Elves had fought each other. Soon they realized the key to fighting her fairly.

Agility wasn't key.

Vanish was.

Sona gasped as her sword was thrust into a Silver Elf. He had become translucent, her sword hitting nothing but air. She stared at her sword

Her shoulders slumped.

Vanish wasn't fair.

Neither was she.

Sona reached inside her pocket. She ran a finger along the smooth metal. Each race had a talisman, created during the first war of the races to protect them.

It was unfortunate the Tryan talisman was in the hands of a little boy.

She'd find him, and she'd take it…just as she'd stolen the Silver Elves' talisman.

Sona couldn't wait to activate it.

Her eyes flickered up.

Now was a good time as any.

EXCLUSIVE EXCERPT

GODDESS *Of* WAR

PROLOGUE

"THEY WILL BOTH have to die," Litha said.

Nausea filled Kellian's gut as he looked down at his twin children. They practiced their swordsmanship in the clearing behind their manor in the countryside of Latari.

Parthi directed them in the proper technique of the East, making their strikes fluid, smooth, and precise.

Kellian's heart was broken. He had a devastating choice to make. His children were chosen to join countless others in the selection of the next ruler of all the gods of Aden, Latari, and Gilborn.

"I don't agree with this decision," Kellian said to the Goddess of Law as she watched his children with that cool gaze of hers.

She glanced over her shoulder, her long lavender hair flowing down her back and to her heels.

"You always were a rebel. This time, the Council has made their demands clear. Do you not have faith?"

Kellian turned his gaze from his former wife to his current wife, the mother of his beloved children. He wasn't strong enough to make the decision.

Allana's sparkling gray eyes met his. Tears clouded them. She shook her head.

"Don't look at me. You know how I feel about all of this," Allana said. She shot a glare at Litha. "I'd rather keep my children here in their home and forget all aspirations toward ruling this world."

"Then it is a good thing your opinion doesn't count for anything," Litha said to her, her cool blue eyes going from Allana to Kellian. "Now is not the time to have doubts, Kellian.

You've had ten years to think this over. Pick one now, lest the Council punishes you for such blatant stalling."

Kellian's shoulders slumped. "I cannot send them to their death."

He avoided the gaze of his darling daughter, Preeti and his son, Vineet as they finished their lesson and looked up at them. How would he tell them what was about to happen?

Allana stepped to Litha, the tears trailing down her cheeks. "How can you be so cold about this? If you had children, you would send them to their death without a second thought, you heartless witch."

A ghost of a smile crept onto Litha's lips. "You're right. I would send them without a second thought."

"Right," Allana said. "Because you are a heartless witch."

"Because I have faith."

"Lord Kellian," Greyon, Kellian's advisor said. He stepped in from the inner corridor of their two-story home, carrying his staff along with him. With a long black beard, olive-colored skin, and hair that reached his lower back, Greyon looked as though he could have been Kellian's father. "There is a way around the Council's ruling."

Litha grimaced at him, shoving him aside.

"No. We do not need your advice. The Council was clear on this, and as the Goddess of Law, I deem it unlawful to shirk their demands." Litha stood nearly as tall as Greyon, with her white shall pulled tight across her shoulders.

"Right." Greyon stepped back; his head lowered in submission. "My apologies, Goddess."

Allana walked out through the archway to her children.

Kellian shook his head at Greyon. "Sometimes I curse the Council and their *holy* rulings," he said before following his wife.

Litha stayed behind, her mouth pursed at hearing Kellian's words.

Kellian nodded for Parthi to leave the children. The master trainer bowed before leaving through one of the gates to the barracks where Kellian's army trained and resided.

Kellian watched Allana bend to her knees before the young girl and boy. They were identical twins, with their mother's bronze skin, long black hair, and gray eyes. It seemed that the only trait they'd inherited from Kellian was their height and athletic build. At sixteen, they were already the height of most adult gods in the empire.

Allana looked at the two closely, her gray eyes full of sorrow.

Kellian looked away with a deep sigh.

The satisfaction on Litha's face as he glanced at her brought his rage to a boil. She didn't do this for their world. She did it because she wanted him to suffer. What could be worse than losing his beloved children? The chance of one of them being chosen to rule was thin. Even if one were chosen, the other would be lost forever.

Either way, one of his children would die.

Litha gripped the balcony railing. "You are lucky that we have two children. Your chances are at least greater than most of the gods."

Kellian couldn't speak. He knew that if he did, he'd say something that would increase Litha's hate for him. She was a Greater God, one with power far greater than Kellian's as a Lesser God. Still, he imagined himself crushing her throat in his fist.

Greyon put a hand on Kellian's shoulder. "Do not worry. I will take care of Preeti and Vineet's arrangements."

"Fine," Kellian said with finality. It was as if his children had not just been condemned to execution at the Cliffs of Ranoun with hundreds of other sacrifices.

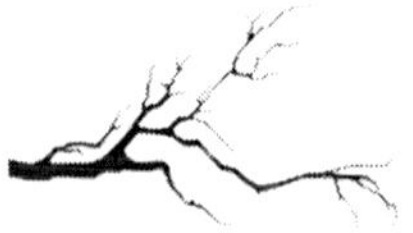

Kellan stood beside Allana as they watched the grand procession. Dawn had barely filled the sky with sunlight as Preeti and Vineet marched out to the Cliffs of Ranoun with all of the other sacrifices. They wore their best garments, shiny and rich in red color. Indeed, everyone in attendance wore their most lavish clothing.

It was time for a reckoning.

He knew how terrible the sacrifices were. The Cliffs of Ranoun would either claim them or send their bodies hundreds of feet into the sharp rocks at the bottom. After that, only the powerful waves from the Ranoun Ocean could cleanse their bodies from the rocks.

This is how the gods chose their rulers. Not through war, or through ancestry.

Sacrifice was the only way.

Kellian could only hope that the gods would find both of his innocent children worthy. He couldn't stand the thought of watching them die.

Litha sat back in her chair, her legs draped over the side as she drank a goblet of wine. Her smooth brown skin seemed to glow beneath their red sun. All eyes went to her when she stood.

Litha's eyes met Kellian's a smirk deepening the dimples in her cheeks.

"Let the ceremony begin."

Preeti and Vineet followed the others. The heat of the red sun beamed down on Vineet's light bronze skin, making sweat glisten on his forehead, soaking through his garments. Even his feet battled the heat as he walked along the burning hot dirt toward the cliffs.

His eyes darted from person to person. Fear bubbled in his stomach as he watched the reactions of the people around him. Some had tears streaming down their faces, others screamed as they were pulled along like prisoners. The ones that interested him the most were those that had stern faces full of purpose and determination and those with serene smiles.

Their smiles made his skin crawl. Even he could tell that nothing good was about to happen. From what he knew of this event, he would not survive. Tears streamed down his face as he realized that he would never see his family again.

Why were they chosen for this? Neither of them wanted to rule. They simply wanted to live out their lives like normal gods.

He held Preeti's hand, giving it a squeeze when she showed hesitation.

"Come, sister. We have to go."

Preeti bit her bottom lip but nodded.

Vineet knew her thoughts and feelings. He wanted to cry as well.

What did it matter if anyone saw them cry?

On this day…he and his sister would die. They all would.

No amount of pampering or pep talks the week leading up to now could hide that fact or ease his fears.

"Go with dignity."

"Do not show your fear."

"This is a beautiful thing."

"It's an honor," they said.

"The Cliffs are all knowing."

"Perhaps you could ascend from the sea and rule our world. You never know…"

Vineet did know. Either way, one of them would die. He glanced back over his shoulder, hoping to catch a glimpse of his mother and father. There they were in the distance, watching.

He paused, staring back at them. His heart was broken. He would never see them again.

The sudden quiet all caught Vineet and Preeti's attention. When they looked around, they saw that the procession had stopped.

It was time.

Vineet took a deep breath. He tried to be strong, and yet he could feel his hands shaking. The Clerics ushered everyone forward. Like fools, they would toss themselves off the cliffs and into the sea. From such a height it wasn't possible to survive such a fall.

Could it be me? Vineet asked himself the question that was on the minds of everyone there.

His feet moved slowly as his eyes bore into the back of the teenage boy before him. An elderly woman stepped in between Vineet and Preeti, taking their hands into hers.

Vineet glanced at her, forcing a brave smile. He had no idea how he was staying so calm. He did it for Preeti. Others seemed to lose their mind the closer they got to the edge. They flailed and screamed, all while the Clerics told them to be brave and to not ruin this beautiful day.

High Cleric, Orthon stood on a pedestal and spoke to the crowds. With arms outstretched he smiled. "Ignore the cries of anguish and agony, brothers and sisters. This is a beautiful day. I can feel it. One of us will be chosen on this day. We should rejoice." An arm draped in white gowns stretched toward the cliff. "Smile at your destiny."

Vineet wished that Orthon would toss himself off the cliff with a smile. He closed his eyes and took a breath.

"I'm afraid," Preeti said in her soft voice.

"Everything is as it should be," the elderly woman said. "Do not worry yourself."

Vineet pursed his lips. Knowing that Preeti was the brave one and still felt fear turned his stomach. Why couldn't he protect her?

What was the point of training with her in weaponry? Or history and language skills? There was so much Vineet wanted to do with life.

Everything they'd experienced and learned was all for nothing now. Every second that passed by brought him closer to death, and it frightened him to no end.

As they reached their spot at the edge of the cliff his lower lip trembled. The sea below was beautiful. Green mixed with purple and blue. One could almost forget that it was full of Teranic, and not water. One fingertip in that pool and you'd lose an entire arm to its wicked magic. Like fire, it ate everything. The waves crashed on the slick black rocks below as bodies fell or were tossed against their will.

Vineet's heart pumped with fear as he watched those bodies enter the water never to be seen again.

The screams and sounds of waves below made his throat clench back a yelp of his own.

He swallowed the lump in his throat, looking over at Preeti.

His beautiful sister. She didn't deserve this.

Vineet considered grabbing her and flying away to somewhere safe, somewhere he could protect her, but the older woman wrapped her arm around Vineet and Preeti's shoulders.

"We go together, all of us?"

Preeti burst into tears.

Vineet nodded, unable to speak or barely see through his own tears.

"I'm sorry, Preeti," he whispered.

The woman kissed them both on the forehead, tenderly.

"Bless you, children," she said, and before Preeti and Vineet could lose their nerve, they jumped with the old woman.

Cold air blew into their faces, like a gust of wintry wind laced with sharp knives. Vineet's mouth opened, fighting back the wind that affronted his face, sending chills through his body.

Was this was what death felt like?

He found the cold air odd since it was such a sweltering hot day under the red sun. The air sucked his screams away, filling him with an odd sensation of drowning before he even hit the water.

They fell slowly, slow enough that the descent made it possible to look from side to side.

The old woman was no longer there.

He panicked. *What's happening?*

Someone grabbed him from behind.

"I've got you," a familiar voice said.

Vineet couldn't speak or scream even if he wanted to, but he knew that voice. It was the old woman, and he was no longer falling. His face paled as he realized that she held him still in mid-air, halfway between the cliff and the sea.

Preeti stood across from him, on nothing but the clear air. Her gray eyes were wide in a look of wonder and confusion that matched his own.

The old woman's face didn't look so wrinkled anymore. Her hair looked less gray and more silver, braided long to her feet. She smiled at him as her skin went from pale to smooth ash. Silver eyes gazed into his.

"How long I have waited."

Vineet felt odd standing on nothing at all. He was sure this was a dream or perhaps he was already dead because he'd never seen anyone stand on the air like this.

But Preeti was there as well. Were they *both* dead?

Waited for what? He wished his mouth would work. He had so many questions.

Her smile widened.

"To choose *two* gods worthy of ruling this world."

Chapter 1

THE SCREAMS OF the dying would have been better than the silence of that morning. Kellian was used to battle. He'd fought for the army of their world's gods for centuries.

War was his profession. As a general in the Aden army, Kellian thought he had seen it all.

Fighting demons and shadows from other worlds had hardened him, yet seeing his home in ruins was something he was not prepared for.

The air was thick with the stench of blood. Vultures feasted on fresh corpses, squawking as he passed them by as if he'd snatch their meals from under their beaks.

In heavy boots, he walked along the blood-covered pathway. Eyes wide with panic, he ignored the dead soldiers and kept his gaze fixed on the entrance to the manor.

As he ran through the golden doors, nothing mattered at that moment but making sure his beloved family had not passed on to the world of the dead.

When he reached the living chambers, the door was already broken down, and the stench of death filled his nostrils despite the frost that seeped in from broken windows.

Frost? In this weather?

Preeti. His daughter. She must have used her power on whoever did this.

Kellian froze at the archway when he saw his wife's body nailed to the wall. Snow covered everything in the room.

His eyes lowered to his blood-covered boots. The image of her bruised corpse would never leave his memory. The body of her personal bodyguard lay beside the door to the secret exit with a gaping hole in his chest.

Who dared to harm his family?

Did they know what kind of revenge he would exact upon them?

The manor was surrounded by a wall with sentries and archers equipped with the best weapons made by the Dreamweavers. No one could enter his home without proper authority.

Whoever did this must have been known by his guards?

Litha.

Kellian balled up his fists. Heartbroken and filled with rage, Kellian crossed the room to pull his wife from the wall. He yanked the thick nails out one by one and clutch her to his chest.

He'd sent his children to the sacrifice. They had emerged from the Cliffs of Ranoun without a scratch. Why were they being punished?

He now realized how deep the betrayal went. Litha called him away to meet with the Council so that she could do this.

Kellian searched the room for any signs of his children.

"Preeti?" His voice carried along a chilling wind that swept into the room and out the broken window. "Vineet?"

There was no reply. His heart raced as he searched the entire manor, checking every room and calling their names.

Neither were anywhere to be found.

Unable to look upon his wife's body, he covered her with the evergreen bedsheet.

He opened the door that led to the secret passageway. Once he stepped through, he paused.

He heard something. A faint shout.

Kellian stepped forward and strained to hear. The howling of the wind seemed to follow him, and he knew that Litha was still there somewhere.

A muffled cry of what sounded to be a young girl came to him.

His eyes widened. He dared to hope.

"Desi?

"Master!"

She's still in the chest.

Kellian ran down the dark hallway. Once he reached the end of the hall where it forked in two directions, he pushed another secret hatch in the stone wall right before him. This is where he kept his valuables. No one, not even his staff knew about it.

Another door was revealed.

Pulling the door open, he looked down into a hole in the ground that was four feet deep and three feet wide. Inside the hole was a beautiful golden chest adorned with intricate black symbols engraved by the holy clerics of Latari.

Kellian pulled the chest from the ground and set it on the stone floor.

"Master?"

He stared at the chest, relief flooding his body. There was still hope.

He knelt to the chest and inserted the key. One turn of the lock and a sharp clicking sound resonated in his ears. The lid opened on its own.

"Master Kellian," Desi called as she stretched her small arms, and flew out of the chest. She rubbed her gold-colored eyes with a yawn.

Her face looked up at him with and joy.

"You're late, Master," she said as she hovered before his face, the size of his hand, with white wings.

He watched as gold tendrils of light raced up and down her skin and through her green hair, making her body light up the entire hallway.

"Tell me what happened."

Desi's smiling face turned sour.

"Everyone was killed. They didn't have a chance. The Goddess of Law had the Red Beast with her."

Litha left nothing to chance.

"Where are the twins?"

"The Goddess of Law took them."

Rage started to rise within Kellian. He wanted to smash a hole in the wall but restrained himself. He needed to get his children back before Litha discovered what they could do.

He should have known that he would never truly find peace. Even as a god, there were always those that sought to ruin him.

Not with Litha still living and breathing. The woman would not be stopped until she got what she wanted. The only problem was that she wanted something he couldn't give.

Kellian listened to the howling of the wind, his rage building with each mention of Litha. "Where did she take them?"

"Oh, Kellian," a familiar voice said from behind him.

Kellian clenched his jaw as he turned to face the woman with the long lavender hair, brown skin, and white tattoos.

Litha, the Goddess of Law.

Desi pointed to Litha, her thin black eyes narrowed. "Can I kill her, Master?"

Kellian shook his head. "No, Desi. I will."

Litha lowered her eyes as she circled him, her hands folded behind her back. "Did you think I would let you use your children to ruin me?"

"You killed her."

Litha nodded. Her face was without emotion. "I did. I told you I would."

"I loved her."

"Yes. I know," she whispered. "I've only just begun to destroy everything you love."

"Why did you have to kill everyone? They were innocent."

A small laugh made him glance up at her. It was easy to remember why he once loved her. She was beautiful beyond words. Long lavender hair flowed down to her naked ankles. He swallowed as his eyes went up the length of her shimmering gown.

"They were in my way," Litha said. The bitterness in her voice made every word more and more powerful.

Kellian shook his head. "You've really lost all of the qualities I once loved in you."

"Perhaps," Litha said, her eyes darkening.

"My children were chosen to rule. I had no part in the decision."

"I no longer care," Litha said. "I will not be ruled by children. Not in this life or the next."

"Please, Master," Desi whispered. "Let me kill her. I can do it!"

"Shh," he said, waving her away.

"You deserve a slow death."

The glow of her blue eyes hurt his, but he didn't back down.

"No, Kellian," Litha said, pulling an orb from behind her back.

A smirk came to Litha's face, and Desi started buzzing around Kellian's head, blocking his view.

"Run, Master," Desi shrieked, tugging on Kellian's collar with her tiny hands.

Litha released the glowing orb, letting it hover before Kellian's face. Within it, he saw nothing but black.

"You do."

CHAPTER 2

FROM INSIDE A cage, the world seemed bleak.

Especially for the children of a god that had been sent to his eternal slumber. Even if their father was one of the lesser gods, the twins were meant to rule them all.

They had been chosen through an act of sacrifice. None of that mattered now.

Their beautiful manor was the scene of a massacre. Mother and father were dead.

Now the Vault was their home, with all of its dark and dismal glory.

They couldn't even grieve the loss of their parents in peace.

Preeti could barely lift her head from resting on her brother, Vineet's lap when Pavvi entered the dungeons.

Dressed in leather armor made in Pollos by the Dreamweavers, he was too skinny to even be considered for any occupation in the army other than a prison guard.

With wild red hair and freckles scattered all over his cheekbones, Pavvi reminded Preeti of a ragdoll she used to have as a child.

Vineet smoothed Preeti's hair. He leaned down to whisper in her ear. "It's time."

Pavvi pressed his smug face to the bars as he looked down at them.

"Supper time!"

Preeti winced as he poured their soup onto the already damp stone floor. As she watched the thin liquid splash and trail though the floor's creases, her stomach grumbled. Neither of the twins had eaten in days. Pavvi only fed them their meals once a week, and that cycle had gone on for months.

"Just leave us alone, Pavvi," Preeti said, her bright gray eyes glaring at him.

"Why? You're so fun to watch suffer. Come now. Just lick it off the floor. I won't tell anyone the infamous Latari twins eat just like dogs."

Preeti's face heated. If only she could get her hands on her swords. She imagined grabbing his lips with her fist and slicing them off with her sharpened blade.

Closing her eyes, she imagined his cries of agony.

One day…maybe today.

She'd never killed anyone and had never wanted to until she and Vineet were charged with treason and imprisoned by the Goddess of Law.

How could she convince anyone that they were frauds when everyone in attendance saw them get sacrificed, and come back from the Cliffs of Ranoun alive?

Preeti coughed, the back of her throat dry. She and Vineet would have to conserve their energy if they wanted to escape.

"Bastard," Preeti said under her breath.

Pavvi kicked the bars with his thick boot. "What was that?"

Preeti sighed. It took everything in her to stand, even more, to hobble over to the bars of her cell. She wrapped her hands around the bars, standing right before him.

Pavvi jumped back, fear in his eyes.

"Get back!"

"Why do you have to be so hateful? What have we ever done to you?"

He grabbed a long, silver pole and stabbed her through the bars with it.

Hope filled her body even faster than the intense heat that entered her belly.

Despite the pain from harnessed lightning, Preeti grabbed the sharp end of it and ripped it away from Pavvi's grasp.

A triumphant grin came to her face as she flipped the pole to point its end at Pavvi.

It worked.

His face turned ashen as he looked down at the sharp end, sparks of lightning racing up and down the steel.

"Good job, Pavvi," Preeti said. "You can be so predictable."

Vineet came to his feet. He stood as tall as Preeti, which was about a half foot taller than most humans. They shared the same straight black hair, large gray eyes, and matching intricate black tattoos on their light bronze-colored flesh.

Vineet was built much more muscular, but Preeti had a slim, athletic build that made her a formidable opponent even to men. Nonetheless, Pavvi looked ready to soil his pants at the sight of them not looking half as downtrodden as he'd been led to believe.

They were gods after all.

Vineet stood beside Preeti, his eyes piercing into Pavvi as he reached a hand out to Preeti. "Go on. Hurry."

Preeti glared at Pavvi once more. For weeks he had wasted their daily rations of food, pestered them, and poked them with the lightning stick any chance he got.

Revenge was not something father condoned, but it was so hard to not retaliate now that they had the chance.

Preeti's lips curled into a snarl.

"Stay still, or I will send you shooting to the moon, you pathetic piece of filth."

Pavvi nodded, his eyes wide, body tense.

Preeti placed her hand in her brother's, and together they took the lightning into their bodies. The shock nearly blew Preeti to the floor, but Vineet grabbed her, holding her steady.

"Good girl," he said. "Now get us out of her!"

Preeti could barely hear his voice over the shouts inside her own head. Pavvi took her hesitation as a chance to escape. One step toward the door and Vineet opened his left hand, sending black lightning into their tormentor's body.

Like a hand, the black lightning wrapped around Pavvi's neck and yanked him back.

Eyes black, Vineet grinned as he closed his fist.

Pavvi let out a raspy gasp as his body flew into the ceiling, and back to the ground in a crunch of bones.

"Hurry, Preeti. Don't second guess yourself now."

Preeti clenched her teeth, the vibrations of her bones shaking her to her core. She fought with the lightning and the pain, Vineet's hands keeping her from breaking down completely.

A female voice shouted at them from the other side of the wall.

Go!

Go!

Go!

Preeti opened her eyes with a screech, and with a release of all of that power, the prison walls crumbled to dust that lingered in the air like soot from the volcanoes back home in Latari.

They had seconds to Leap. Preeti didn't waste any of them.

"Ready," she shouted over the calls from the guards as they ran to capture them.

Vineet nodded. Face set with purpose, he wrapped his arms around Preeti, and together their bodies were catapulted into the sky.

Every sense was heightened as Preeti held onto her brother, praying that they would survive this night.

A glowing orb caught them mid-air, holding them in its warmth.

Desi, their pet fairy, smiled at them with her green hair floating in the air.

"Good job," Desi cheered. Her power lifted them higher and higher into the sky. "You did it!"

She pointed to the stars. "Hold on now."

Hope was theirs once more as they soared like a shooting star from Aden, the land of the gods, to the one place where they could hide from their captor.

The Abyss; also known as the human world.

EXCLUSIVE EXCERPT FROM

SPELL SLINGER

FEAR THREATENED TO CRIPPLE YARA as she passed the servants harvesting the grapes of Torrington Orchard.

It was a cool autumn morning, and yet Yara felt sweat bead on her forehead and in the crease between her bosom.

"Good morning, my lady," one of the workers said, bowing her bonnet-covered head.

She feigned a smile, and yet her heart pounded inside her chest as she hid the blood that stained her bodice by letting her long white hair hang over her narrow shoulders.

Be brave, Yara thought as she wrung her shaking hands.

"Hero," she spoke to the wind. "Please get me out of here. I'm serious this time."

Yara broke into a run toward the stables, no longer caring who she vexed by her sudden action. She didn't have much time. The body would surely be found at any moment.

The sun warmed her cold cheeks as she looked to the sky.

Come on, Hero. Hurry.

She grabbed her long navy skirts into her fists as her feet pounded the stone path that led to the front gate. Soldiers stood guard on either end of the locked gate, their swords secure at the waist.

A squawking sound came from the distance and Yara snatched off her wedding band, tossing it into the bushes that lined the road.

Her heart thumped in her chest as one of the soldiers glanced her way. He narrowed his eyes at her. "Where are you going?"

She ignored him, keeping her attention fixed on that gate. They'd hang her if she ever got caught, but she had to risk it.

A royal decree was announced**.**

Magic is abolished.

All Spell Slingers are to be executed.

Those with magic must go to the capital of Allarya for evaluation.

Those who resist will be executed.

There was no way she could stand by and let her father be executed. Life as a concubine was over for Yara. It was time to stop running from her destiny.

To be a Spell Slinger.

A grin came to her face, despite the tears that trailed down her cheeks as a tall young man dressed in all black appeared outside of the gate, his pale skin almost translucent as he held a hand out toward her.

Black hair that covered his dark eyes. Clean shaven, and baby-faced, Hero was her greatest friend, one that would risk his life to save hers.

She chewed her lip, quickening her pace as she prayed that they would both survive this.

"Ay," the guard shouted, drawing his sword. "Stop right now, miss. We don't want to have to hurt you."

Yara ignored them. She needed every bit of concentration to do what she'd been planning for the past few days. She would have served her time in this horrid place for all eternity if they'd have left her family alone.

The king wanted to abolish magic, and no one could stop him.

Except Yara.

She gritted her teeth and with a burst of energy shot outside of her body, a blue aura encircling her as her soul *unfused*.

Hero cracked a grin, his eyes narrowing behind strands of black hair. "Good girl," he whispered, a black mist shooting from his hand and reaching for her like a raging wind.

The soldiers stumbled backward, having never seen such a display of raw power.

As if encased in ice, Yara's entire body went cold as her soul left it behind. Her body was indeed frozen in place as her consciousness rode her soul out of the magic-bonded gate.

No human, shifter, or sorcerer could exit that gate.

But, a Meta could.

Born half sorceress, and half Meta, Yara could do many things that the world had never even heard of.

As Hero pulled her soul to his open palm, she felt safe and warm, having shed her human form.

Once through the gate, he tucked her soul into his body and shifted into a crow.

Soon, Torrington Estate would be far behind them, and Yara would need to create herself a brand new body.

YARA NEVER EXPECTED TO BE sold off to the county sheriff as his tenth concubine. At twenty-one, she was broken mentally and emotionally, and now without a father.

Too late.

This was her entire reason for exposing herself and running away from Torrington Manor. Having heard that King Loric was targeting Spell Slingers, she'd had no choice but to at least try to save her father.

Tears welled in her eyes as she looked at her father's body, hanging from the fir tree in front of her family's mountain cabin.

At least they didn't burn him.

She glanced at Hero as he waited up in a tree. His crow form was a blessing when outlawed in seven counties.

Yara was thankful for such a loyal friend. He'd rescued her and kept her safe while she summoned the energy to recreate her old body.

"If you'd have come back just yesterday, you might have caught him before the execution," a familiar voice called from beside her a few feet away.

Yara wiped my face dry with her sleeve and turned to see Pae standing there, her arms folded across her green dress.

"I told you our time's running up. I suspect magic will be no more within a few years," she said, her white hair lifting with the crisp fall breeze.

Though she was fifteen years older than Yara, they could have been twins.

Silver eyes that matched Yara's looked her up and down.

Though Yara was fully dressed in leather pants tucked into her boots, and a black shirt with a hood that covered her bright hair, she felt naked under her gaze.

Always had.

"If you hadn't of sold me, I could have protected you both."

"I did what I had to—to protect the family from you." Pae looked cross, her eyes narrowed, her hair lifting with a passing breeze. "Where is your husband?"

"Dead," Yara quipped. "And a concubine is not considered a wife, Pae. So, he wasn't my husband."

Pae tilted her head. Her face paled. "Did you kill him?"

"I did what I had to."

"Dear spirits."

"He deserved it."

"What is wrong with you, Yara? You can't kill a man for beating you now and again. Especially if he owns you."

"Of course, you think so," Yara said. "You beat me plenty whilst I was growing up. And why? Father never raised a hand to *you*."

"That's different," Pae said. "I'm your mum. And pain is the only way children learn."

Frowning, she turned back to her father. Someone had stolen his shoes.

"Why is he still hanging? I'm grabbing an ax and cutting him down."

"You do that, and they will use that ax to chop off you head." Pae sighed, her body becoming more and more translucent with each minute.

Yara stared at her wondering if she ever loved her father. Growing up, they never showed affection for each other. It was as if they were no more than business partners, come together to raise one shy girl with too much power to be allowed around others.

"You'd best be on your way out of Kempsey. They're determined to abolish magic. That means Spell Slingers all over are being strung up all over."

"I'll leave after I bury him."

Pae sighed. "Stubborn girl. Give me a minute, and I'll help."

"Don't you need to get out of the sun?"

"I'm fine. I can last a while longer," Pae said, her voice growing distant as if she'd be carried away by the wind.

Being a Meta, Pae was a creature of the night. Sometimes Yara thought she'd just used her father for his power, to remain a solid being in the human world—instead of a woman that resembled a ghost more than an actual person.

They buried Bronson behind the cabin, and Pae even sang a little song from her world for him.

"Bye, Pae," Yara said, slinging her pack over her shoulders and heading for the paved road that led to the main highway.

"Yara, wait! Where do you think you're going?"

"The capital."

"Allarya? Why?"

Yara glanced back at her, fire in her silver eyes. "To kill King Loric. Either come along or leave me be."

Pae's eyes widened. "Have you gone mad?"

"No," Yara said, turning to look ahead.

Allarya was far from their little rural village, but she owed her father revenge. She owed their entire kingdom a chance at a better life.

"I'm not mad, mother. I've just gained some courage," she whispered.

CHAPTER 3

THE DUSTY ROAD AHEAD WAS a constant reminder of the life Yara was leaving behind. It was also a beacon of hope.

Yara twisted her long white hair into a bun at the top of her head and yawned. She hadn't slept in what felt like days. Using so much energy to recreate her body had taken more out of her than she would have liked. She just hoped that there would be no trouble on the road. This new body was weak, and would need a few days to be able to defend itself.

Knowing that Hero was close by gave her a small measure of relief. Sharing a body was such an intimate experience, and she would forever be bound to Hero because of it. They could summon one another whenever they pleased.

Dark clouds started to roll by. A storm was brewing, and she knew that it brewed for her.

Watching. Searching. Ready to strike her dead.

If she could stop King Loric along with his laws and reign of terror, she would be free to live her own life for once. As long as she didn't get herself killed.

Death frightened her more than anything.

Tears streamed down her face as she remembered her father's last hug. It had been longer than usual, and full of love that she knew he had for her. Neither could have known that it would be the last one that they would share.

Pae had never hugged Yara in that way, and it was because of her that she'd been sent to a form of slavery most young women in Allarya knew all too well.

One day, they'd have a choice of who they married. Another reason King Lori needed to be stopped.

The screeching of a crow stopped Yara in her tracks.

Hero.

She wiped her tears with the back of her hand and sniffled.

"Are you all right, Yara?" He asked her as he landed on the road, and returned to his human form.

"No," she said. "I'm really not. I miss him, Hero."

His brows furrowed as he walked beside her. "I know. He was the kindest man I've ever met. Except Red."

Yara tensed at the mention of Red, the gamekeeper of Westerbrook Manor.

"Look, Yara. I wasn't going to tell you, but I thought you should know. It might even cheer you up…if even for a little bit."

He raked his slick black hair out of his face, revealing green eyes that matched the sky on the brightest summer day. His face was narrow and pointed at the chin, but nice to look at.

There was a time when she thought she had feelings for Hero but realized that it was just her loneliness and their strong bond.

Yara squinted at him. "Tell me."

"Asher's joining the royal army. He leaves tomorrow. I thought you'd want to say goodbye to one more person. Seeing as we might not ever come back and all…" he said, his voice trailing.

"Dear spirits," Yara said, looking down the road. She scratched her chin, torn.

Westerbrook Manor wasn't far. She might be able to stop by and see Asher. Truth was, she wasn't sure if she was strong enough to say goodbye to him—despite their memories together being the only thing that helped her make it through the day.

"Thank you," she said and chewed her lip.

She had to see him. One last time.

About the Author

K.N. Lee is an award-winning author who resides in Charlotte, North Carolina. When she is not writing twisted tales, fantasy novels, and dark poetry, she does a great deal of traveling and promotes other authors. Wannabe rockstar, foreign language enthusiast, and anime geek, K.N. Lee also enjoys helping others reach their writing and publishing goals. She is a winner of the Elevate Lifestyle Top 30 Under 30 "Future Leaders of Charlotte" award for her success as a writer, business owner, and for community service.

Author, K.N. Lee loves hearing from fans and readers. Connect with her!

knlee.com

Street team: facebook.com/groups/143998252628952 4/

Newsletter: eepurl.com/3L1gn
Blog: WriteLikeAWizard.com
Fan page: Facebook.com/knycolelee
Twitter: twitter.com/knycole_lee
The Chronicles of Koa Series Page: facebook.com/thechroniclesofkoa

Titles by K.N. Lee

The Chronicles of Koa Series:

Netherworld
Dark Prophet
Lyrinian Blade

The Eura Chronicles:

Rise of the Flame
Night of the Storm
Dawn of the Forgotten (Coming Soon)
The Darkest Day (Coming Soon)

THE GRAND ELITE CASTER TRILOGY:

Silenced
Summoned (Coming Soon)
Awakened (Coming Soon)

THE FALLEN GODS TRILOGY:

Goddess of War
God of Peace (Coming Soon)
Love & Law (Coming Soon)

STANDALONE NOVELLAS:

The Scarlett Legacy
Liquid Lust
Spell Slinger

MORE GREAT READS FROM K.N. LEE

Netherworld (Urban Paranormal Fantasy) ***Demons, ghouls, vampires, and Syths?*** The Netherworld Division are an organization of angels and humans who are there to keep the escaped creatures from The Netherworld in check in this action-packed paranormal thriller.

Introducing Koa Ryeo-won, a half-blood vampire with an enchanted sword, a membership to the most elite vampire castle in Europe, and the gift of flight. If only she could manage to reclaim the lost memories of her years in The Netherworld, she might finally be able to move forward.

The Scarlett Legacy (Young Adult Fantasy) ***Wizards. Shifters. Sexy mobsters with magic.***

Evie Scarlett is a young wizard who yearns from an escape from her family's bitter rivalry with another crime family. But this time she may be the only one who can save them.

Goddess of War (Young Adult Fantasy) ***Unsuspecting humans. Fallen gods in disguise. A battle for the entire universe.***

After escaping the Vault, a prison for gods, twin siblings Preeti and Vineet make a desperate journey to the human world where they must impersonate the race they are meant to rule and protect.

Silenced (New Adult – Paranormal Romance) **Silence kept her alive. Magic will set her free.**

Willa Avery created the serum that changed the world as humans, witches, and vampires knew it.

Liquid Lust (New Adult Romance) **Sohana needed a fresh start.**
Arthur--a British billionaire has an enticing offer.
Neither expected their arrangement to spark something more.
Spell Slinger **(Fantasy Romance/Steampunk)**
Lady by day.
Evil fighting vigilante by night.

Yara Ortuso always knew she'd follow in her father's footsteps as a Spell Slinger--until her mother sold her off as a concubine to a lord, after a forbidden romance
Discover more books and learn more about K.N. Lee on knlee.com.